力得文化
Leader Culture

Follow
23 堂心理學英語課
成就你的
職場巨星之路

練家姍 ◎ 著

由 求職面試、職場定位、瞭解老闆 與 同事 ... 等
引領你進入心理學世界讓你 人見人愛、立於不敗

面試【提點+回應】+ 老闆的【溝通術和應對策略】
☆ 面試官【OS】+ **5**大【類型】
☆ 老闆四大【管理模式】+【應對策略】+**6**個【DOs and DON'Ts】

> **Maria**是具潛力的候選人,面試官也對其專業感到滿意,但卻...(請參閱 **1-2**)
> **Sarah**於同事離職後就忙的焦頭爛額,期許與老闆溝通,但卻...(請參閱**2-4**)

工作滿意度和工作倦怠 +同事相處
☆ **7**個找工作技巧 + **7**個提升工作滿意度的小撇步
☆ **8**大令人討厭的同事類型+ **5**種好競爭的同事特質

> **Annie**找到夢想工作,對工作也很滿意,但卻被指派...(請參閱 **3-1**)
> **Joe**連續為本月最佳員工,本以為能升職為銷售經理,但公司卻...(請參閱 **4-4**)

了解員工+正向態度
☆ **5**大員工類別+ **7**種心理學理論+ **6**大管理員工的方法
☆ **5**個負面工作態度的【行為】+【原因】

> **Darren**在家具店工作,很喜歡這份工作,但後來卻發現...(請參閱**5-3**)
> 找到夢想工作後,學經歷俱佳的**Delia**更深信能獲得升遷機會,但公司卻選了...(請參閱**6-4**)

Preface 作者序

忙盲茫！在職場中團團轉的人們，是不是感覺自己快被淹沒了？到底要怎麼做，才能好好的面對工作？

英文與工作，的確是許多人目前生活的重心（或困境）。感謝貴公司做了這樣的規劃，將學習英語及職場情境合而為一，作為本書的出版契機，讓讀者能夠在學習英文的同時，也能獲得職場心理學的相關知識或技巧。唯個人能力畢竟有限，無法完整包含職場心理學中無盡的喜怒哀樂與箇中奧妙！不過，希望讀者可以藉由本書，了解到面對職場最好的方式一正向態度。無論是對主管、對同事、對自己、及對工作本身，唯有保持正向的態度，才能泰然處之，讓困境迎刃而解。這也是本書要傳達最大的重點！

Contents 目次

Chapter *1*

The Psychology of
Job Interviews

面試心理學

1-1

The Job Interview
How to Do Your Best!
面試－如何做到最好！

情 境對話 I

🔸 The day before Paul's job interview

Paul is worried about his interview tomorrow. "I am so dead! I have a job interview tomorrow, but I am not ready yet! What am I going to wear? Where is the company located? What does the company do? ...I am so nervous! I hope the interview goes really well. I don't want to waste my time for the interview if they will not offer me a job!"

🔸 Paul 面試的前一天

Paul 正擔心著他明天的面試。「我完蛋了啦！明天要面試，但我還沒準備好！我該穿什麼？公司在哪裡？公司是做什麼的？我好緊張喔！希望面試可以順利。如果他們根本不會錄用我，我可不想浪費時間去面試！」

The day of the interview

Paul is almost late for his job interview, but he is still looking for his tie. He is also wondering how to get to the company.

Five minutes after the scheduled time, he is running and stopping at the office doorway out of breath. He finally gets into the interview room and apologizes for being late. He shakes hands with the interviewer with sweaty palms.

面試當天

Paul 快遲到了，但他還在找他的領帶。他也在想要怎麼去公司比較好。

已經過了原訂面試時間五分鐘了，他才氣喘吁吁地跑進公司。他終於進到面試辦公室，並為他的遲到道歉。他用著出汗的手向面試官握手。

The interviewer

"Can you introduce yourself?"
「可以介紹一下自己嗎？」

Paul

"Um... OK...Um... I am Paul. I am now 24 years old. I graduated from Department of Marketing, XX University this year...Um..."
「嗯…好…我叫 Paul，現在 24 歲，今年畢業於 XX 大學的行銷系，嗯…」

The interviewer

"OK. Can you let us see your Degree Certificate and Transcript?"

「好。可以讓我們看一下你的畢業證書和成績單正本嗎？」

Paul

"Oh, right. Um... I think I forgot to bring the documents...I am sorry."

「喔，好。…啊！我忘了帶了！抱歉！」

情 境對話 II

The day before Arron's job interview

Arron has a job interview tomorrow, too. He is making final preparations for the big day. He has done research of the company, so he has some ideas about what the company does, and what the job role he applies for would be. He has also prepared answers for possible interview questions.

Arron 面試的前一天

Arron 明天也有面試。他現在正在為這個重要的日子做最後的準備。他已經閱讀了一些與這家公司相關的資料，所以對這家公司以及他應徵的職務已經有所了解。他也針對常見的面試問題進行準備。

The day of the interview

Arron wakes up early, gets everything ready and makes sure he arrives at the company earlier. He stays calm, and talks to himself: "I am the best candidate for this position! I will definitely do the best in the interview! I can make it!"

He shakes hands with the interviewer firmly. He keeps smiling, looks at the eyes of the interviewer all the time. During the interview, he answers every question with confidence, even those tough ones. He shows excitement and enthusiasm because he is really interested in this company and position. At the end of the interview, he shakes hands with the interviewer again and says, "Thank you very much, Mr. Wang. I really appreciate that I could have a chance to be here. I really enjoy talking to you in the last one hour." He knows that he has done his best. Even if he will not get the offer, he knows it is not the end of the world.

面試當天

Arron 很早就起床準備就緒了，也要確保會提早一些到公司。他保持冷靜，並告訴自己：「我是最棒的候選人！在面試中我一定會表現得很棒！我可以做到！」

他有精神地與面試官握手。他保持笑容，並隨時注視著面試官。在面試過程中，他回答問題時都表現出自信，即使面對較為困難的問題時依然如此。他表現出興奮與熱忱，因為他對這家公司與這份職務相當感興趣。在面試的最後，他再次向面試官握手致意：
「王先生，真的非常感謝您給予我面試的機會，能榮幸能與您有一
小時的對話。」他知道自己表現得很棒。即使到最後他沒能錄取，
他也知道這不會是世界末日。

達 人剖析

░ Your preparation 你可以做的準備

▲ **Be prepared!** 一定要準備！

This single think can change your interview and make
you become a competitive candidate!

1. Prepare what you are going to wear. Dress
   professionally!
2. Prepare your transport and make sure you are on
   time.
3. Do some research and have some knowledge of the
   company.
4. Prepare possible interview questions and answers.

　　這個簡單的想法就可以改變你的面試，也可以讓你成為更
有競爭力的候選人！

1. 準備你要穿的衣服。要穿得專業！
2. 準備你的交通工具，務必要準時。
3. 做一些功課去認識這家公司。

求職面試心理

了解你的老闆

找到對的工作｜職場定位

你與同事

帶人要帶心

升遷與｜工作態度

4. 準備一些可能會問的問題與答案。

▲ **Preparing your mind, too! 準備好你的心！**

1. **Mental imagery 心像法**

The psychological research suggests that people who imagined the interview went well could increase chances of getting the job offer (Knudstrup, Segrest and Hurley, 2003). You can visualize yourself performing really well in the interview. You can even see yourself being offered the position. This allows your memory to associate positive feelings toward the job interview scenario.

　　心理學研究（Knudstrup, Segrest and Hurley, 2003）發現，想像自己的面試會順利進行，將會更提高自己的錄取率。你想像著看到自己在面試中表現得很好，並獲得錄取。這樣的方式可以讓你對面試場景有正向的記憶與正向的感受。

2. **Positive self-talk 正向的自我對話**

Talking to yourself positively is also a famous psychological strategy to increase your confidence. According to (Knudstrup, Segrest and Hurley, 2003), possible verbal self-guidance could increase self-efficacy and confidence. Before the job interview starts, try to talk to yourself like the followings:

"I can enter the room with confidence."

"I can shake hands firmly."

"The interviewers want to know about me; they will listen closely and ask me some interesting questions."

"This is going to be enjoyable."

"I can do the best job in the interview room."

　　正向的自我對話也是很知名的心理策略，目的是增加自信。在一項研究中發現（Knudstrup, Segrest and Hurley, 2003），正向的、言語上的自我引導可以增加自我效能與自信。在面試之前，試著跟自己說：

　　「我可以有自信地走進辦公室！」

　　「我可以有精神地握手！」

　　「面試官會想要了解我；他們會仔細地聽我說話，並問我一些好問題。」

　　「面試過程將會很享受。」

　　「在那辦公室裡我會做得最棒！」

職 場小故事 I

At the beginning of a job interview, Roger is a bit nervous. He is really concentrating on what the interviewer is saying and asking to him. He is trying not to make any mistake, and really trying to make a good impression. However, he is too concentrate to put a smile on his face. When the interviewer is trying to say something funny, Roger does not respond at all. He is still focusing on how to answer the next question right. It

求職面試心理

了解你的老闆

找到對的工作｜職場定位

你與同事

帶人要帶心

工作態度｜升遷與

is perfectly normal. However, Roger misses the chance to build rapport with his interviewer.

在面試一開始，Roger 有一點緊張。他非常專注於面試官說了什麼及問了什麼。他試著不犯任何錯誤，且努力營造好的印象。然而，他太專心了，以致於沒有什麼笑容。當面試官說些輕鬆好笑的事，Roger 也沒有反應。他一直專心地想著要怎麼回答下一個問題。這樣的狀況極為正常。但是，Roger 錯過了與面試官建立好關係的機會。

職 場小故事 II

Lillian feels nervous easily. Whenever she feels stressful, she does not have good coping strategies. Before the interview, she always worries that she may screw up. At the beginning of the interview, she even forgets to shake hands with the interviewer. While she is talking to the interviewer, she is too nervous to concentrate. Although she is trying to pull herself together, the situation is getting worse. Her eyes are looking down and her body is shaking. She cannot think straight, nor talk to the interviewer calmly. After the interview, she feels upset about herself because she cannot speak anything right.

Lillian 是個容易緊張的人。每當她有壓力時，她總是處理得不好。在面試前，她一直擔心自己會搞砸。在面試一開始時，她也忘了先向面試官握手。當她與面試官說話時，也因為太緊張而無法專心。雖然她試圖振作，但情況卻越來越糟。她的眼睛一直看下面，她的身體也在發抖。她無法思考，也沒有辦法冷靜地與面試官說話。面試後，她對自己感到生氣，因為她什麼話都表達得不對。

達 人提點

🎯 Gain more points in the interview 為自己的面試加分

In addition to your professional abilities, you should also get some practice in your soft skills. Moreover, do not let your nerves affect your performance. The following strategies can help you gain more points in your job interview!

除了你專業上具有的能力外，你也需要培養一些軟性能力。此外，不可以讓緊張破壞了你的表現。試試下列方法，讓你的面試更加分。

A. Building rapport 建立正向關係

Rapport is a positive emotional connection between people (Buskist and Saville, 2001). It can be viewed as the developing of trust, understanding, respect, and liking between two persons. It can be extremely useful in an interview situation. This connection may determine who could get the job offer in the end. The interviewer is more likely to appoint someone they personally like!

正向關係是人與人之間情感上的連結（Buskist and Saville,

2001）。這樣的關係是基於兩個人之間的信任感、了解、尊重與喜歡。在面試情境中，建立正向關係將會很有幫助。這樣的情感連結甚至會影響到誰被錄用但誰不會被錄用。面試官當然會錄取一個他個人比較喜歡的人！

Psychologist Tregoning (2013) provides five tips to build rapport with the interview:

心理學家 Tregoning (2013) 提供了與面試官建立正向關係的五個技巧：

1. Smile and maintain eye-contact 保持微笑及注視

Body language is essential when communicating with others. Your voice, speed of your introduction or even your hand gestures can be a powerful influencer on whether you get a job. In addition, maintaining eye contact and smile conveys the message that you are interested in the other people.

肢體語言是與他人溝通時很重要的部分。你的聲音、說話速度、甚至手勢等都會深深影響著你是否會被錄用。此外，保持眼神注視與微笑，可以讓對方知道你是對他們感興趣的。

2. First impression 第一印象

We all know first impression is far more important. If someone is approaching with his head down or with the

求職面試心理

了解你的老闆

找到對的工作 職場定位

你與同事

帶人要帶心

升遷與工作態度

hands in the pockets, we may think that he is withdrawn from the social interactions.

我們都知道第一印象相當重要。若有一個人低著頭、手插口袋朝我們走來，我們可能會覺得他對這樣的社交場合感到退縮。

3. Mirroring 模仿

Occasional mirroring of the interviewer's posture, energy levels and tone of voice for some moments will unconsciously make the interviewer feel that you are fully engaged with him/her! But don't do it the wrong way.

有時模仿面試者的姿勢、精力狀態及語調等會讓面試官無意識地覺得你有充分參與。但請勿用錯方式！

4. Remember the interviewer's name 記得面試官的名字

Learn the name of your interviewers and address them personally by name. You will be immediately endearing by doing so.

記得面試官的名字，並找時機說出他的名字。這麼做會讓你立刻受到面試官的喜愛。

5. Listen well 仔細聆聽

If we feel nervous during the interview, we may find ourselves not fully concentrate on what the interviewer has to say. What you can do is trying repeating back some of the key things the interviewer says to show that you have understood and given them the impression you approve them. This is also called *Reflective Listening*, which can show others that you really understand their point, and make you look and sound interested and intelligent.

　　當我們在面試中感到緊張時，我們可能沒辦法專注於面試官所說的話。你可以重複面試官的重點，讓面試官覺得你了解並同意他們所說的話。這也稱為傾聽，可以讓他人看到你全然了解他們的重點，也讓他人看到你對他們感興趣，也藉此表現出你的聰明才智。

Managing your stress 壓力管理

Job interview causes a lot of stress for most of us. When you are under stress, you are more likely to misread the messages of the interviewers, or send inappropriate body signals during the interview. Sometimes stress can be helpful, but if stress becomes constant and overwhelming, it can damage your performance by disrupting your thinking and talking.

面試對大部分的我們而言都充滿壓力。當你處在壓力下，你可能會錯誤解讀面試官的訊息，或送出錯誤的肢體信號。有時壓力是有幫助的，但若壓力持續存在且大到讓你無法承受，就可能會打斷你的思緒與說話，減損你的表現。

How to deal with stress during the interview? You cannot change your interviewer, but you can change yourself. You can adapt to a stressful interview and regain your sense of control by changing your expectations and attitude.

　　要如何處面試時的壓力？你無法改變你的面試官，但你可以改變你自己。你可以改變你的期待與態度，以適應面試中的壓力，並重新掌控自己。

達 人提點

1. View your interview from a positive perspective.
換個角度面對你的面試
EX:
Great! This is my 10th interview, which gives me more practice, and I can meet new people and have further ideas about what the company does.

例如：
　　太好了！這是我的第十次面試，表示我有更多練習的機會。而且我也可以認識更多人，並多了解這一家公司在做些什麼。

2. Do not worry about the result too much.
不要太擔心結果

Ask yourself how seriously the interview result will affect you in the long run.

問問自己，面試的結果對你而言會有什麼長期的影響？

EX:

If the answer from the company is NO, will I still be upset 6 months later?

例如：

如果我被公司拒絕，我六個月後還會如此生氣嗎？

3. Avoid to demand yourself perfection.
不要對自己要求完美

Set reasonable standards for yourself
為自己設定合理的標準

EX:

Do you feel unhappy if your best friend does not perform perfectly in her job interview? Maybe not. So please do not do it to yourself. Tell yourself "It's OK, I am good enough."

例如：

　　若你最好的朋友在面試中沒有表現得很完美，你會不高興嗎？可能不會吧！所以也不要這樣對你自己。告訴自己：「沒關係，我已經夠好了。」

4. Focus on the positive. 專注在正向的部分

Take a moment to reflect on all the positive qualities and advantages you have.

花幾秒鐘檢視自己的正向特質與優勢。

EX:

Although I cannot answer every question perfectly, I have good professional skills and knowledge. I also have the excellent ability of problem solving.

例如：

　　雖然我無法完美回答問題，我仍有很棒的專業技能與知識。我也有很棒的問題解決能力。

5. Use your imagination. 用你的想像力

Your might have some strategies to reduce stress. However, you cannot really listen to music, eat some chocolate, or take a walk in the middle of your interview. The best way is using your imagination to help you feel more relaxed.

你可能已經有一些減壓了方法。但是你沒辦法在面試中去聽聽音樂、吃巧克力或去散散步。最好的方法運用你的想像力來幫助你放鬆。

EX:

Picture someplace in your mind that is peaceful; imagine a beautiful baby is smiling happily at you, etc.

例如：

在腦海中想像一個會讓你感到平靜的地方；或想像一個可愛的寶寶正在對著你開心的笑著。

Vocabulary 字彙

- ★ Preparation 準備
- ★ Candidate 候選人
- ★ Visualize 視覺化
- ★ Self-guidance 自我引導
- ★ Confidence 信心
- ★ First impression 第一印象
- ★ Body language 肢體語言
- ★ Reflective listening 傾聽
- ★ Perfection 完美

- ★ Competitive 競爭的
- ★ Mental imagery 心像法
- ★ Scenario 場景
- ★ Self-efficacy 自我效能
- ★ Concentrate 專心
- ★ Rapport 建立正向關係
- ★ Mirroring 鏡像、模仿
- ★ Manage stress 壓力管理
- ★ Advantage 優勢

1-2

Interviewers' Questions and Their Secrets

面試官的問題跟他們的秘密

情 境對話

Imagine that you were a hiring manager. You were having a job interview with a candidate who just left his last job. Would you feel happy about the candidate spending most of the time thinking, or even being silent rather than talking about his/herself or answering the questions? Or would you feel comfortable if the candidate was over excited and chatty that he or she shared everything to you, good or bad, that you were not even interested about? Would you think it was helpful that the candidate seriously criticized his or her former employer or colleagues? Would you hire a candidate who showed too many flaws in their answers?

　　想像你是個人力資源經理。你正在面試，而候選人剛離開上一個工作。若此人在面試中花很多時間思考甚至時常沉默，而非談論他們自己或回答問題，你覺得這樣好嗎？若此人過度興奮，不論好的壞的事情都與你分享，你卻對這些都不感興趣，你會覺得舒服嗎？若此人一直批評他／她的前老闆或前同事，你會覺得有幫助嗎？你會錄用一個在回答中不斷表現出缺點的人嗎？

I bet the answers for questions presented above are NO! If you hope the interview goes on smoothly, it is suggested that you prepare some frequently asked interview questions beforehand. Think about how to respond effectively to these questions in order to show your advantages rather than disadvantages. The followings are some frequently asked questions and possible answers, some of these answers are inappropriate (as answered by Candidate A), but some of the answers are more promising (as answered by Candidate B). Additionally, the psychological rationale is provided, which tell you the reasons for better answers.

　　我猜上述問題的答案都是否定的！如果你希望面試順利，建議你要事前針對常問問題多作準備。想想要怎麼有效的回答以展現你的優點而非缺點。接下來提供幾個面試常見問題及可能的答案。有些答案是不適當的（候選人 A 的答案），有些答案則較為適切（候選人 B 的答案）。此外，也提供心理學上的原理，說明適切答案背後的理由。

Q1

Tell me about your last work.
說說你的前一份工作

Candidate A

"My last boss was horrible. He treated us like we were his slaves!"

「我前一個老闆很可惡！他都把我們視為奴隸！」

Candidate B

"Although I had some disagreements with my previous boss, I still respect his leadership. I have learned many valuable experiences from my last job."

「雖然我與前老闆有些意見上的不合，但我仍然尊重他的領導。我從前一個工作中學到許多寶貴的經驗。」

Don't be a troublemaker 不要成為麻煩製造者

The interviewers might act like you can tell them everything; however, this is a terrible mistake. Do not criticize your former employers or colleagues. The interviewers may consider you as a troublemaker. They may wonder whether you are hard to get along with, or you will do the same thing to the new employer.

面試官可能讓你以為你可以知無不言，但這是個天大的錯誤！千萬不要批評你的前老闆或前同事，不然面試官會認為你是個麻煩製造者。他們會擔心你是否很難相處，或你是不是會對新老闆做出同樣的事。

Q2 How did you deal with difficult situations in the past?
過去在遭遇困境時，你是如何面對？

 Candidate A

"When I was 15, my parents were divorced. I felt so angry! That summer, I locked myself in my room every day. My school performance was getting worse, and I was helpless."

「當我 15 歲時，我的父母離婚了。我好生氣！那個夏天，我每天把自己鎖在房間裡。我的學業表現越來越差，我覺得好無助。」

Candidate B

"When I was in my late teens, I was seriously sick. I stayed in the hospital for 8 months. I could not go to school. I was frustrated about the situation for the first couple months. One day, I talked to myself that I am going to live a better and meaningful life, since life is too short to be wasted."

「在我青少年時，我生了很嚴重的病。有八個月的時間都待在醫院裡而不能去上學。前兩個月我覺得好挫折，直到有一天，我告訴自己將來一定要活得更精彩、更有意義，因為生命實在太短暫了，不容浪費。」

In control 掌控局面

You have to show the interviewer that you controlled the difficult situations, rather than letting them knock you down. So they can trust you that you have the abilities to cope with difficulties and control every situation while you work for them.

你必須告訴面試官你可以控制困境，而不是被困境打敗。這樣你與他們工作時，他們才能相信你有面對困境的能力，並掌控每個狀況。

Q3 What is your greatest weakness? 你最大的缺點是什麼？

Candidate A
"I can't really think of any weaknesses."
「我想不到耶。」

Candidate B
"I am working very hard to stand in front of people and make good presentation. Although it is not that easy for me, I am getting better.

「我很努力地訓練自己可以站在眾人前面演說。雖然這對我而言不容易，但我已經進步很多。」

Self-reflection 自我反省

Candidate A lacks of the ability to self-reflect. The interviewer wants to see how do you face challenges? Can you be self-critical? They want to see you have self-reflection, insight, and courage.

候選人 A 缺少了自我反省的能力。面試官想要看看你是如何面對挑戰？你是否可以自我批判？他們希望看到你有自我反省、省悟及勇氣。

Q4 What is your desired salary for this position?
你的希望待遇如何？

(Candidate A and Candidate B have a similar background, and are applying for the same position.)

（候選人 A 與候選人 B 有著相似的背景，且申請同樣的職務。）

Candidate A
"I would respect the salary system of your company."

「我會尊重公司的薪資制度。」

"Based on by qualification and past working experiences, I believe NT55,000 is fair for me."

「依據我的資格與過去的工作經驗,我相信 NT55000 是我認為合理的薪資。」

In the end, the respective salaries for Candidate A and Candidate B are NT 30,000 and NT 42,000! But why?

Anchoring 錨定效應

Asking for a higher salary instead of negotiating down to the desired range. Although it's a risky move, but the interviewer might increase the offer by more than 10%.

先提出較高的薪資,然後再協商到合理的範圍。雖然這麼做是步險棋,但面試官可能可以給你比原本預定多 10% 的薪資。

Anchoring is a cognitive bias that influences the way people assess probabilities. This was first theorized by Tversky and Kahneman (1974). It describes that people tend to rely too heavily on the first piece of information offered (the "anchor") to make subsequent judgements. Once the anchor is set, other decisions are made only by adjusting away from that anchor. Imagine a 15-year-old son needs NT 1000 for the school trip. He asks his Dad to give him NT 2000 (the "anchor"). His Dad refuses the number, but then more likely to give him NT 1500!

錨定效應是一種認知上的偏差，會影響人們的判斷。這個理論是在 1974 年由 Tversky 與 Kahneman 所提出。人們通常會過度依賴最原始的資訊（即稱為「錨」），然後依此進行後續的判斷。一旦錨定位妥當，其他的決策就僅會以錨作為判斷的依據。試想 15 歲的兒子需要 NT 1000 參加學校旅遊。他向爸爸要了 NT 2000，爸爸拒絕了，但是很有可能給兒子 NT 1500！

Q5 Where do you see yourself in five years?
五年後你會成為怎麼樣的人？

Candidate A

"I would like to be the manager or director of the Department in five years!"

「我想要成為部門的經理或主管。」

Candidate B

"I will be ambitious and hardworking to develop my skills and knowledge in five years. I am extremely interested in this position, so I am willing to invest my 5 years time learning all aspects of the job, and to see myself progressing and be an expert in this field."

「在這五年中，我會積極努力的發展專業技能與知識。我對這個職務非常感興趣，所以我很願意花無年的時間學習與這份工作所有相關的事務，然後讓自己成為這個領域的專家。」

🏮 Show your enthusiasm 展現你的熱忱

When answering this question, do not overestimate your abilities. Additionally, do not be arrogant and assume you have got the job. You have to be realistic, and show the interviewers that you are an enthusiastic candidate, but with the right attitude.

當回答這個問題時，不要高估自己的能力。此外，不要太過傲慢並假設你已經被錄用了。你要更為務實，向面試官表現出你的熱忱，但要用對的態度。

職 場小故事

Maria is a hardworking university student. She plans everything for the future. However, just before she graduated from the university, she broke up with her boyfriend. It caused her a lot of pain. She was too sad to do anything for the whole year. Most of her university friends have found jobs during this year, but she just stayed at home crying. One day, she looked at the mirror wondering there must be something wrong with her, so she started to get some professional help. With the professional assistance, she is getting better.

Maria 是一個很認真的大學生。她已經預先計劃未來。然而，在畢業前夕，她與男朋友分手了。這帶給她極大的痛苦。一整年來，她都因為過於傷心而無法做任何事。她大部分大學同學都陸續找到工作了，但所做的只有待在家中哭泣。有一天，她看著鏡中的自己，覺得自己這個樣子不對勁，所以她開始尋求專業協助。有著專業人士的幫忙，她感到好多了。

Meanwhile, she is hunting for a job. She did pretty well during the university. She also had some experiences of part-time jobs in the relevant field. She thinks herself as a strong candidate. She spends a lot of time preparing for the big day. During the interview, the interviewers feel satisfied about her professional backgrounds. However, they are interested in the reason why she is not employed currently. She does not know how to answer this. On the one hand, she does not want to cheat. On the other hand, she does not want them to find out that she was knocked down. In the end, she gets a rejection letter.

同時，她開始找工作。在大學期間她表現得非常好。她也有相關的兼職工作經驗。她認為自己是個很有競爭力的候選人。她花了很多時間為面試做準備。在面試時，面試官對她的專業背景很滿意。然而，面試官也好奇為什麼她目前沒有工作。她不知道要如何回答。一方面，她不想要欺騙；但另一方面，她不希望面試官發現她被擊垮。最後，她被拒絕了。

Do you know the secrets behind the interviewers? The followings are the reality in the minds of the interviewers.

你知道面試官背後的祕密嗎？以下是面試官心中真正的想法。

They prefer someone who is currently employed!
他們比較喜歡目前就業中的候選人

The hiring managers often would rather hire someone who currently has a job. It's a cruel truth because those who are not employed are more eager for a job! If you have been unemployed for a long time, they may wonder what is wrong with you. So write something down like volunteer work, continued education, etc. to mask a gap on your CV.

人事經理通常較會錄用目前在職的人。這是個殘酷的事實，因為待業的人更需要一份工作！如果你有好長一段時間沒有工作，他們可能會想你出了什麼問題。所以寫下一些事情來填補履歷上的空白，如志願工作，繼續教育等。

They are looking for a reason NOT to hire you!
他們在找「不」錄用你的理由

They often look for reasons to exclude you rather include you. Lower school grades, poor formatted CV, etc. are often risky elements to get you in the NO category.

他們通常會找拒絕你的理由，而非錄用你的理由。學校成績不佳、履歷格式不夠好等，通常是讓你被拒絕的危險因子。

If you tell them your previous salary, they may use it to against you!
如果說出你之前的薪資，他們可能會用此來應付你

If you say an exact number, you may not have too much range to negotiate your salary. You could say your previous company preferred you keep it confidential. Or, you may say you are looking for an increase, about X %.

如果你説出具體的數字，你的薪資可能沒有太多協商的空間。你可以説前一個公司希望你保密。或是説你期待薪資可以增加 X%。

They spend less than 30 seconds on each CV!
他們花不到 30 秒的時間審視每份履歷

These hiring managers have to go through hundreds of CV; thus, they really have no time to read through each one in details. So, take a look of your CV. If it is not easy for highlights, it is not going to get you call back. Make your CV clear, concise, and tailored specifically to the job you want.

人事經理每次要看上百份履歷，他們真的沒有時間好好地仔細閱讀每分履歷。所以，檢視一下你的履歷。如果你的履歷無法讓人一目了然，你就不會被叫去面試。讓你的履歷清楚扼要，並針對所申請的工作調整履歷內容。

求職面試心理

了解你的老闆

職場定位 找到對的工作

你與同事

帶人要帶心

工作態度與升遷

The followings are some interview questions which are not so straightforward. These questions are asked for secretly assessing some of your personality or abilities.

有一些面試問題並不直接清楚。這些問題是為了檢視你的一些人格特質或能力。

Access culture fit 檢視文化適應程度

Culture fit is just as important as the candidate's skills, abilities, and experience for the position. So the interviewers might ask some questions to reveal other aspects of cultural fit, such as:

文化適應與候選人所具備的技術、能力與經驗同樣種種。所以面試官可能藉由一些問題來看看你的文化適應程度,像是:

If you could be doing anything, what would you do?
What are your top three values?

如果你可以做任何事,你會做什麼?
你最重視的三個價值是什麼?

Access personality 檢視人格特質

The interviewer needs to get some ideas about the candidate's personality to make decisions about hiring fit.

面試官需要了解候選人的人格特質,以做為是否錄用的參考。

Tell me about your favorite book or movie?
Tell me about your role model?

告訴我你最喜歡的書或電影？

告訴我你的偶像是誰？

Access business acumen and continuous learning
檢視商業敏銳度與上進心

Business acumen and commitment to the continuous learning are important in this competitive world. They do not want to hire someone who just stays at home watching TV after a work day.

在這個競爭激烈的世界，具有商業敏銳度與願意持續地學習是非常重要的。他們不想雇用一個下班後只是待在家裡看電視的人。

What do you read when you have time?
Have you noticed any blind spots in our business and how would you improve them?

你有空時都看什麼書？

你覺得我們這個領域有什麼缺失？你會如何改進它們？

V ocabulary 字彙

★ Acumen 敏銳度 　　　★ Rationale 原理

求職面試心理

了解你的老闆

找到對的工作 職場定位

你 與 同 事

帶 人 要 帶 心

升遷與 工作態度

1-3

Different Personas of the Job Interviewers
面試官的人格特質

情 境對話

Ryan has just graduated from the University. He has been job-hunting for a while. He has sent quite a few applications, and five of the companies give him the opportunities to interview. The followings are parts of each interview.

Ryan 剛從大學畢業。他找工作已經一陣子了。他寄了不少申請信，其中五家公司請他去面試。以下是他在五家公司面試的部分內容。

面 試官剖析 Scenario A

Interviewer A is standing in the doorway, looking at Ryan with smile.

面試官 A 站在門口，並對 Ryan 微笑著。

Interviewer A

"Good morning, Ryan. It's a lovely day, isn't it? We are really glad that you can come here for this interview. Are you ready? Shall we get started? Now, could you please introduce yourself?"

「早安，Ryan。天氣很好對吧？我們很高興你能來面試。你準備好了嗎？我們可以開始了嗎？現在，請你介紹一下你自己。」

Ryan

"I am Ryan. I am 26 years old. I graduated from XX University. Um..."

「我是 Ryan，現在 26 歲。我從 XX 學校畢業，嗯…」

Interviewer A

"Maybe you can tell me more about your major, your professional skills and knowledge, or something like that."

「也許你可以說說你主修什麼，或是你有哪些專業技能與知識。」

Ryan

"Oh, yes. My major was Public Health. I really care about the environment and human health, that was why I chose to study in this field. During the four years in the University, I have learned natural sciences, social sciences, and medical sciences.

「喔，對。我主修公共衛生。我對環境與人類健康非常關心，所以我選擇了這個系。在大學的四年中，我學習

求職面試心理

了解你的老闆

找到對的工作｜職場定位

你與同事

帶人要帶心

升工作態度遷與

了自然科學、社會科學與醫學等課程。」

Interviewer A
"It sounds great! So which subjects were you particularly interested in?"
「聽起來很棒。那你最感興趣的科目是什麼？」

Ryan
"I had an excellent performance at the statistics and health policy."
「我的統計與健康政策兩科表現得最好。」

Interviewer A
"Good. Now, tell me if you attended any association or club in the University?"
「很好。現在跟我們說說你有參加那些社團？」

面 試官剖析 Scenario B

Interviewer B is 10 minutes late for this interview. He starts to ask questions as soon as he arrives the room.

面試官 B 遲到了 10 分鐘。當他一踏進辦公室，就馬上開始問問題。

Interviewer B
"It's Ryan, aren't you? It's a little bit late, so we have to start right away. Now introduce yourself."
「是 Ryan 對吧？有點晚了，我們直接開始。先介紹你自己。」

Ryan

"I graduated from XX University. My major was Public Health. I have some knowledge about natural sciences, social sciences, and medical sciences."

「我畢業於 XX 大學。我主修公共衛生，有學到一些自然科學、社會科學與醫學等相關知識。」

Interviewer B

"Public Health? Then why do you want to be here? Don't you know we are trading company! Do you have any relevant experience?"

「公共衛生？那你為什麼來這裡？你難道不知道我們是貿易公司嗎？你有貿易相關工作經驗嗎？」

Ryan

"Oh, yes. I stayed in one trading company for a part-time job for one summer."

「喔，有，有一個暑假我在一家貿易公司打工。」

Interviewer B

"It means nothing! Do you have any knowledge about import-export trading?"

「那不代表什麼！你有進出口貿易的知識嗎？」

Ryan

"Um…I did learn something in that trading company, but..."

「嗯…我在那家公司的確學到一些，但是…」

求職面試心理

了解你的老闆

找到對的工作 職場定位

你與同事

帶人要帶心

升工作態度與

Interviewer C is coming in the interview room with a piece of paper with all the questions on it. After he sits down, he stares at the piece of paper most of the time.

面試官 C 手中拿著一疊要問的問題進入辦公室。當他坐定後,他大部分都盯著手上的紙。

Interviewer C
"Um...Ryan, please tell me which University did you graduate from?"
「呃,Ryan,請告訴我你是哪所大學畢業的?」

Ryan
"Ok, I graduated from XX University with my major of Public Health."
「好,我畢業於 XX 大學,主修公共衛生。」

Interviewer C
"Now tell me what kind of person you are."
「接下來,告訴我你是怎麼樣的人?」

Ryan
"I am a hard working, enthusiastic, and easy-going person. I care about the environment and people around. So I sometimes volunteer to work in the community and the hospitals."
「我是個認真、熱忱且隨和的人。我關心環境與人類,所以我有在社區及醫院中從事一些志願工作。」

Interviewer C

"Now please explain why you want to work with us?"

「你為什麼想要來這裡工作？」

Ryan

"As I said earlier, I care about the environment. I have learned that this company puts a lot of efforts saving the rainforest and the animals. I really admire what you do."

「正如同我剛剛說的，我關心環境議題。我知道貴公司花很多心力在拯救雨林與動物。我非常欽佩貴公司的這些行動。」

Interviewer C

"Ok, that's all I want to know. Thank you for being here."

「好，我問完了，謝謝你過來。」

面 試官剖析 Scenario D

Interviewer D is talking over the phone about what happened last evening while Ryan is standing in front of him. Five minutes later, Interviewer D is finally ready for the interview.

當 Ryan 走進辦公室時，面試官 D 正在講電話，聊著昨晚發生的事。五分鐘後，面試官 D 終於準備好要面試了。

Interviewer D

"Hi, Ryan. I have read your CV. You said you graduated from the XX University. Oh, that's great! My sister graduated from there, too. I once visited her and your University. The City is lovely, and I really like buildings of your University. And you said your major was Public Health."

「嗨，Ryan，我看了你的履歷。你説你畢業於 XX 大學。歐，太好了，我姊姊也從那裏畢業。我曾經去那裏看她，那個城市很棒，且我也很喜歡你們學校的建築物。還有，你説你主修公共衛生。」

Ryan

"Yes, I did. I..."

「對，我…」

Interviewer D

"I have a friend who also studied Public Health. She now works for the government. You also attended the Film Club in the University. You know what? I do like watching movies. So what is your favorite movie?"

「我也有一個朋友是念公共衛生，她現在在政府部門工作。你還有參加電影社啊？你知道嗎？我也很喜歡看電影。你最喜歡的電影是什麼？」

Ryan

"My favorite movie is Sense and Sensibility, directed by An Lee. I..."

「我最喜歡的電影是李安導演的理性與感性…」

Interviewer D

"I know it's a lovely movie."

「我知道那部，很棒的電影。」

面 試官剖析 Scenario E

Ryan is walking in the interview room. There are three interviewers sitting there and waiting for him.

Ryan 走進辦公室。有三位面試官正在等著他。

Interviewer X
"Good morning, Ryan. Please sit down."
「早安 Ryan，請坐。」

Interviewer Y
"You may start introducing yourself as long as you are ready."
「當你準備好後，可以開始介紹自己。」

Ryan
"Good morning. It's my pleasure to be here. My name is Ryan, I graduated from the Department of Public Health, University of XX. In this Department, I have learned natural sciences, social sciences, and medical sciences."
「早安。我很榮幸可以來這裡。我叫 Ryan，畢業於 XX 大學公共衛生系。我有修過自然科學、社會科學與醫學等科目。」

Interviewer Y
"Public Health? It's a little bit far from what our company does, isn't it?"
「公共衛生？這跟我們公司的領域差的有點遠不是嗎？」

Interviewer Z

"What is your expertise?"

「你的專長是什麼？」

Ryan

"I am particular interested in numbers, so I had an excellent performance at the statistics."

「我對數字特別感興趣，所以我很擅長統計。」

Interviewer Y

"Statistics! We do need someone who is the expert of statistics, don't you think so, Mr. Z?"

「統計！我們的確需要統計人才，不是嗎，Z 先生？」

Interviewer Z

"We do. Our Department starts to develop monthly statistical reports."

「我們的確需要。我們的部門開始要建立月報表。」

Interviewer X

"Tell us more about your skills and abilities?"

「告訴我們更多你會的技巧與能力。」

達 人提點

Are you familiar with one or more job interview scenarios described above? If you were Ryan, how would you feel and what would you do to deal with these different situations?

你對以上的面試場景是否熟悉？如果你是 Ryan，你會有甚麼感覺？你會如何處理這些狀況？

These five examples represent different characteristics of the interviewers. Kate Warren, who is the Director of one Global Recruitment Services, has identified 5 classic personas of the job interviewers. She also provided some ideas of how to deal with different interviewers.

這五個面試例子分別代表了不同特質的面試官。Kate Warren 是全球招募服務公司的執行長，她將面試官特質分為五大類，並建議人們如何面對不同特質的面試官。

1. The nice person 好好先生小姐

This kind of interviewers ask easy questions. They smile, nod and give lots of verbal and physical cues for you to be on the right track.

這類個面試官問一些輕鬆的問題。他們會微笑、點頭並給予許多口頭上與肢體上的提示，好讓你正確回答。

Benefit:

You may feel less stress and think you have done a great job during the interview.

好處：

你較不會感到壓力，並覺得自己在面試中表現得還不錯。

Challenge:

They are afraid or uncomfortable to ask you tough

questions, but they need to know more about you in order to decide if you are the right person for this position.

挑戰：

他們不太會問一些尖銳的問題，但他們又需要進一步了解以你以決定你是否是最合適這個職位的人。

Strategy:

You can talk more if they do not ask tough questions. You could say something like "You may wondering how I have learned these skills. Let me explain to you..."

策略：

即便面試官沒有問你尖銳的問題，你可以自己多說一點。你可以這麼說：「你可能在想我是如何學校這些技術，讓我解釋一下。」

2. The inquisitor 審問者

This kind of interviewers have prepared many challenging questions for you. One of the purposes of these questions is to determine your problem solving and analytical skill. They also want to judge whether you can perform calmly while you are under stress.

這類的面試官準備了許多具挑戰性的問題，目的是為了檢驗你問題解決與分析能力。他們想要判斷你在壓力下是否可以冷靜。

Benefit:

You have many opportunities to show the interviewers different aspects of your abilities, if you can answers these questions with confidence.

好處：

如果你能有自信的回答這些問題，你有許多機會表現自己不同層面的能力。

Challenge:

Asking tough questions may cause you a lot of stress. They are more likely to tripping you up.

挑戰：

這些尖銳的問題可能會帶給你很大的壓力。他們就是想要看到你自亂陣腳。

Strategy:

Stay calm. You should answer the questions as best as you can. When you answer the question, you can start with "That is an interesting question..."

策略：

保持冷靜。盡可能好好地回答問題。你可以說：「這是一

求職面試心理

了解你的老闆

找到對的工作／職場定位

你與同事

帶人要帶心

工作態度與升遷

個很好的問題」，做為回答問題的開始。

3. The nervous nelly 緊張不安者

The interviewers with this type of persona hate to interview. Actually, they do not like to interact with other people. They may have social anxiety.

這類的面試官很不喜歡面試別人。事實上，他們不喜歡與他人互動；他們可能有社交恐懼。

Benefit:

You will not confront too many difficult questions.

好處：

你不需要面對許多尖銳性的問題。

Challenge:

They do not feel comfortable to stay in the same room with the strangers. They could not concentrate on the interview process.

挑戰：

他們對與陌生人共處一室感到不自在，所以他們無法專注在面試過程。

Strategy:

You could ask them some friendly questions about

求職面試心理

了解你的老闆

找職到場對定的位工作

你與同事

帶人要帶心

升工作態度遷與

themselves, like how did they get started? What do they enjoy about the job?

策略：

你可以試著問他們一些輕鬆友善的問題，像是你是如何開始這份工作？什麼原因讓你喜歡這份工作？

4. The Chatty Cathy 喋喋不休者

This type of interviewers are nice too, and are more interested in talking about themselves and things they are interested in, but you!

這類型的面試官也很友善，但他們更喜歡説自己的事或自己感興趣的事，而不是你！

Benefit:

You may feel warm and welcome in the interview environment, which could release you some stress.

好處：

在這個面試環境中，你可能感受到溫暖與受到歡迎，這會讓你少些壓力。

Challenge:

They spend all the time talking, and you will have no chance to talk about yourself!

挑戰：

他們花所有的時間在説話，而沒有機會讓你説話。

Strategy:

You can take cues from their conversation and help bring it back to you and why you are suitable for this position. Additionally, after giving an example of your previous successful experience, you can follow up by asking the interviewer: "How did you deal with the similar situation?"

策略：

你可以在對話中找到一些空隙，藉機將主題轉回到你身上，以及為什麼你適合這份工作。此外，當你説了過去某一個成功的經驗時，你可以接著問面試官：「你是怎麼處理類似狀況？」

5. The panel interview 小組面試

A panel interview is especially tricky. There may be any combination of the interviewer types together in the same room. So it is complicated to deal with different interviewers at the same time.

小組面試特別麻煩。可能會有各種不同特質的面試官共處一室。所以如何同時面對不同的面試官便有些複雜。

Benefit:

It might be a good chance for you to shine in the multiple lights. Moreover, you can learn a good clue of the workplace culture as well as red flags of the workplace by observing how the colleagues interact with each other.

好處：

這可能是讓以大放異彩的機會。此外，你可以藉由觀察他們彼此間的相處與對話來洞悉該公司的文化與地雷。

Challenge:

You might try to please one interviewer but annoy others. Furthermore, they have internal conversations right in front you, so you have little chance to talk about yourself.

挑戰：

你可能會因為討好了一位面試官，卻惹毛了其他人。此外，他們彼此內部對話，你少有機會談論自己。

Strategy:

It is critical to tell who the real decision maker is. You have to impress the key person without ignoring others.

挑戰：

你必須辨識出誰是真正的決策者。你要讓這位決策者留下深刻印下，但同時不要忽視其他面試官。

求職面試心理

了解你的老闆

找到對的工作　職場定位

你與同事

帶人要帶心

升工作態度遷與

Vocabulary 字彙

- ★ Personas 人物、角色
- ★ Challenge 挑戰
- ★ Inquisitor 審問者
- ★ Confront 面對
- ★ Panel interview 小組面試
- ★ Multiple 多元的
- ★ Decision maker 決策者

- ★ Benefit 好處
- ★ Strategy 策略
- ★ Nervous Nelly 緊張不安者
- ★ Chatty Cathy 喋喋不休者
- ★ Combination 組合
- ★ Red flag 地雷

MEMO

Chapter 2

Understand Your Boss

了解你的老闆

2-1

Your Boss's Management
老闆的管理

情 境對話 I

Tom is the Public Relations manager of the famous Technology Company. Tom has just been promoted to this position for a couple of months. So he is really ambitious and wants to get things done perfectly. His company will release new product three months later, and Tom's team is responsible for the marketing campaign this time. This Monday morning, in the routine team meeting, Tom is assigning work related to this marketing campaign.

Tom 是知名科技公司的公關部經理。他已升職有幾個月了,所以他非常有野心,且希望事情可以圓滿達成。他的公司三個月後要推出新產品,Tom 的團隊負責這次的行銷活動。週一早晨例行團隊會議,Tom 正在針對關於行銷活動進行工作分配。

Tom "As you know, our team is responsible for the marketing campaign of the new product. My target is the sales will increase by more than 50% of the last season. Now I need you all to listen carefully. Ed, you are in charge of the exhibition and media. Sue, you are doing the communication to the clients. Steven, you have to deal with the Internet marketing."

「正如你們所知，我們團隊負責這次新產品的行銷活動。我的目標是超越上一季銷售量的 50%。現在我要你們仔細聽好。Ed，你負責展售與媒體。Sue，你負責與客戶溝通。Steven，你來處理網路行銷。」

Ed
"But, Tom, I am not familiar with the media part. Maybe Sue is more suitable for this..."

「但是 Tom，我對媒體部分不熟悉，也許 Sue 比較適合這一塊…」

Tom
"I don't care. You figure out by yourself."

「我不管，你自己想辦法。」

Steven
"Our company has never tried the Internet marketing. Are you really sure we are going to this new trial?"

「我們公司從來沒有做過網路行銷。你確定要嘗試？」

Tom
"That's your problem. You have to find out everything about the Internet marketing ASAP."

「那是你的問題。反正你盡快找出網路行銷的相關事

求職面試心理

了解你的老闆

找到對的工作　職場定位

你與同事

帶人要帶心

工作態度　升遷與

項。」

Steven "But the Internet marketing is not suitable for our new product."

「但是網路行銷並不適合我們的新產品。」

Tom "If you don't want to do it, then don't! I will find someone else to replace you."

「如果你不想做，就別做了！我會找別人代替你。」

Steven "What I am saying is, we have to think about the attribute of our new product, as well as our possible customers, then..."

「我想說的是，我覺得我們應該先思考一下新產品的屬性，以及可能的客群…」

Tom "I am in charge now, just do what I say!"

「反正我主導，照我說的去做！」

情 境對話 II

The next day

The following morning, there is a proposal of the Internet marketing written by Steven on Tom's desk for the new product, but after reading it, Tom is so unhappy about it that he calls Steven to his office loudly.

第二天

第二天早晨在 Tom 的桌上放了一份由 Steven 撰寫的新產品網路行銷企劃書。但 Tom 看了過後很不滿意所以他大聲地叫 Steven 進來。

Tom

"What's this about? I told you to start the Internet marketing, but everything you wrote here is rubbish! I don't need to know the history of the Internet marketing, and I don't want to know the difficulty of doing it. Just tell me how to do it!"

「這是什麼東西？我叫你開始進行網路行銷，但你寫的都是垃圾！我不需要知道網路行銷的歷史，我不需要知道我行銷的困難度，告訴我怎麼做就好了！」

Steven

"The reason why I wrote the limits of the Internet marketing in this proposal is because I want to tell you we might encounter some problems later, so..."

「我會把網路行銷的缺點寫在企劃書裡面是因為我想要告訴你我們可能會面臨到的困難，所以…」

Tom

"That's nonsense! If you never start, how do you know whether there is problem? Just do it!

「胡說！如果沒有開始，哪來的困難？去做就對了！」

求職面試心理

了解你的老闆

找到職場對的定工位作

你與同事

帶人要帶心

升工作態度遷與

Management styles 管理模式

Every boss has his or her own management style to manage their employees. Some of them are detail-oriented, who focus on how to get things done and prefer to organize things beforehand; some of them are big-picture thinkers, who think about the big goal and the bright future. The bosses with former management style may lack of a big picture and the right direction of the company; the latter ones may not have the excellent ability of execution.

　　每位老闆有其管理員工的模式。有些老闆是細節導向，著重如何將事情完成，且傾向事前規劃；有些老闆則是願景導向，思考著大方向與美好的未來。細節導向的管理方式可能缺少藍圖與正確的方向；願景導向的管理方式則可能缺少完美的執行能力。

Monica Wofford (the author of the popular book *Make Difficult People Disappear*) has categorized four management styles. So you can observe your boss and find out which management style your boss is more likely to be, and then try to meet their specific needs.

　　Monica Wofford（暢銷書籍《讓難搞的人消失》一書作者）提出四種管理模式。你可以藉此觀察你的老闆，找出最接近的管理模式，然後試著迎合老闆的需求。

1. Commander

The boss with this style is result-oriented and wants to get stuff done. What the commander really care is whether you finish your job, rather than how you do things or why you can't accomplish the goal. Additionally, the commander does not like talking or hearing about interpersonal or personal issues; these are your problems, not his or hers.

1. 命令者

命令者老闆是結果導向，希望事情可以完成。命令者最在乎的是完成工作，而非如何完成、或為什麼不能達成目標。此外，命令者不喜歡談論人際間或個人的問題；這些是你的問題，不是他/她的。

Your Strategy:

The commander is interested in achieving performance, so you should put more efforts on getting good results. Then present the results specifically by using numbers, statistical tables, charts, or diagrams.

你的策略：

命令者最在乎達成目標，所以你要花更大努力去獲得好的成果。然後將成果藉由數字或統計圖表具體呈現。

求職面試心理

了解你的老闆

找到對的工作 ｜ 職場定位

你與同事

帶人要帶心

升工作態度與遷

2. Organizer

This type of boss who is process-oriented and want to get things done right. The organizer focuses on making good and thorough plans in advance.

2. 組織者

這類型的老闆是過程導向，且希望事情做的對。組織者著重事前完美與完整的規劃。

Your Strategy:

Provide detailed plan and schedule beforehand, and discuss with your boss. Then follow the plan to complete the work.

你的策略：

事前提供完整的規劃與流程，並與老闆討論。然後照著計劃完成工作。

3. Relater

The boss with this management style is people-focused and wants to get along with others. However, the relater may feel uncomfortable to command the employees to get their job done.

3. 關係者

此類管理模式的老闆是人際取向，想要與人相處融洽。然而，關係者可能會對以命令員工方式來讓他們完成工作感到不舒服。

Your Strategy:

Talk to your boss more often, share with him/her your daily life, your feelings or your happiness. Moreover, your relater boss will appreciate if you can do your job well and spontaneously.

你的策略：

常與老闆聊天，跟他們分享你的生活、你的感受與你開心的事情。此外，關係者老闆會因為你圓滿地與主動地完成工作而心存感謝。

4. Entertainer

Entertainer is confident and charismatic. He or she is always the center of attention. The entertainer wants to be appreciated.

4. 娛樂者

娛樂者充滿自信與魅力。他／她總是焦點的中心；娛樂者希望受人欣賞。

Strategy:

You can let your boss know that you appreciate your boss's sense of humor, and value his or her professional abilities.

求職面試心理

了解你的老闆

找到對的工作 職場定位

你與同事

帶人要帶心

升工作態度遷與

你可以讓老闆知道你欣賞老闆的幽默感，及他/她在專業上的能力。

It is interesting to know that the commander and the entertainer use animated facial expressions, and talk with their hands; the organizer and the relater listen more intently, and take time to process and think through problems. These differences also provide some hints for you to get to know your boss better.

有趣的是，命令者與娛樂者通常會有豐富的臉部表情，且手部語言豐富；組織者與關係者則較常傾聽，且花時間思考問題。這些不同之處也讓你有更多的線索去認識你的老闆。

職 場小故事

Jody is a local branch manager of the famous retail chain. She has been working in this company for 15 years since she graduated from the colleague. She is a positive, friendly, and warm person, so she gets along really well with her boss and colleagues. Because of these good characteristics, she has been promoted as the branch manager two years ago.

Jody 是一家連鎖店分店經理。她自專科畢業後就在這家公司工作已經 15 年了。她是個正向、友善且溫暖的人，所以她與老闆及同事都相處得非常好。由於這些好的特質，她在兩年前被提升為分店經理。

During the past 15 years, Jody also got married and has two lovely girls, who are 10- and 5-years old now respectively. During the first couple years since Jody's first kid was born, she had a hard time to balance work and family. Luckily, her company provided sufficient benefits and support, and gave her a lot of flexibility, so she could take care of most family matters.

在過去 15 年間，Jody 也結了婚，並有兩個可愛的女兒，分別為 10 歲和 5 歲。在她第一個小孩出生後的前幾年，她也難以平衡工作與家庭。所幸，她公司提供許多福利與支持，並給她很大的彈性，所以她可以照顧好大部分的家庭事務。

Now, Jody is the manager. She deeply appreciates the importance of providing support to her staff while they need it. Whenever her employees need her, she will be there. She also encourages female employees to look for their career as well as their happiness. She always tells her workers: "Family is the most important thing in the world. No other things can or should substitute your family."

現在，Jody 已經是個經理了。她深知給予員工所需的支持是相當重要的。當員工需要她，她都會在他們身邊。她也鼓勵女性員工除了追求工作，也該追求幸福。她總是告訴員工：「世界上沒有什麼事比家庭更重要，也沒有任何東西可以取代家庭。」

求職面試心理

了解你的老闆

找到職場的定位對的工作

你與同事

帶人要帶心

升工作態度遷與

One of Jody's worker, Rachel, who is taking a maternity leave for one year. Unfortunately, Rachel and her partner broke up, she now is a single mom with a new born baby. Rachel needs to go back to work for living. However, she can only afford part-time nanny to take care of her baby, which means she can only work part-time currently. The HR tells her that it is difficult for her to work part-time because her position is on a full-time basis. If she really has to work as part-time, she cannot be hired as a permanent employee, which means she may not get all of the company welfare. This is a dilemma for Rachel. On the one hand, she does not want to give up her current job because she has a baby to raise, and she and her baby will need health insurance which is included in the company welfare for permanent employees; on the other hand, the reality is she cannot work full-time right now, at least for the next two years. Jody knows about Rachel's struggle. She talks to the HR on behalf of Rachael. She highlights that every employee is the most valuable property of the company. If the workers have any problem, the company should try the best to provide support, rather than push them away. She suggests that the company should treat Rachael as a special case, and work together with Rachel to go through the tough time.

Jody 的員工，Rachel 目前請了一年的育嬰假。不幸的是，Rachel 跟她的伴侶分手了，她現在是個有新生兒的單親媽媽。Rachel 需要回去工作賺錢養家，但她只能負擔兼職保母的薪水來照顧寶寶，這也表示她只能做兼職工作。HR 告訴 Rachel 她難以轉換為兼職工作，因為她

求職面試心理

了解你的老闆

找到對的工作　職場定位

你與同事

帶人要帶心

升工作態度遷與

的職務設定是全職工作。如果她要做兼職，她就不能被視為正職員工，這也代表著無法享受所有的公司福利。Rachel 陷入兩難。一方面她不想放棄目前的工作，因為她需要錢養小孩，且她與小孩都需要健康保險，這是正職人員享有的公司福利；另一方面，現實上她就是無法全職工作，至少未來兩年是如此。Jody 知道了 Rachel 的困擾。她代表 Rachel 向 HR 說明。她強調每位員工是公司最珍貴的資產。如果員工有任何問題，公司應該盡力支持，而非把員工推開。她建議公司應該將 Rachel 的狀況視為特殊案例，並與 Rachel 一起走過這段艱困的時間。

達 人提點

✊ Good bosses and their personality traits
好老闆的人格特質

Good leadership can create a better working environment, and motivate the employees to have a better performance. If you are lucky to have a good boss, you should stay for a long term. The Office Vibe (officevibe.com, a company dedicates to improve company culture) has done a survey related to the qualities of great bosses, and highlights 12 personality traits as followings.

好的領導方式可以創造好的工作環境，並激勵員工有更好的表現。如果你很幸運碰上了好老闆，你應該長久待著。Office Vibe (officevice.com 的成立的宗旨是為了促進公司文化)進行了好老闆特質調查，調查結果顯示有 12 項主要特質：

1. Think positively 正向思考

They think positively, and consider every situation as a learning opportunity. They appreciate every step. They know every small step can more toward the big one.

他們正向思考,並將各種狀況都視為學習的機會。他們了解每一小步都是邁向更大一步的過程。

2. Be honest 誠實

They know themselves that they cannot know everything, so they encourage employees to contribute ideas. They also tell their staff the truth, whether it's good or bad.

他們知道自己不是全能,所以他們鼓勵員工提供想法。他們也會告訴員工實情,不論好的或壞的。

3. Delegate 授權

They are familiar with workers' skills, and assign tasks according to his or her abilities.

他們熟悉每位員工的技能,並依據員工的能力指派工作。

4. Communicate 溝通

They explain things well and help staff to know exactly what they have to do and by when.

他們會清楚解說事情，以幫助員工正確了解該做什麼與何時完成。

5. Inspire 激勵

They encourage and stimulate the employees, and help them to achieve the goal better.

他們鼓勵與刺激員工，幫助他們達到更好的目標。

6. Align the team 結盟

They respect and trust their staff. This positive atmosphere in the workplace helps the employees to work more efficiently.

他們尊重並信任員工。公司裡的正向氛圍幫助員工更有效率。

7. Balanced 平衡

They know there are many other things which are also important in their life, such as family matters or personal interests. So they allow flexibility to their staff.

他們知道生命中還有許多其他事情也很重要，像是家庭或個人興趣。所以他們給予員工彈性。

求職面試心理

了解你的老闆

找到職場定對的工作位

你與同事

帶人要帶心

升工作態度遷與

8. Give credit 記功嘉獎

They appreciate the efforts of the employees, and make sure the employees get the respect they deserve.

他們看到了員工的努力，並確保員工有獲得應有的尊重。

9. Encourage growth 鼓勵成長

They encourage staff to top-up themselves in every aspect.

他們鼓勵員工在各方面充實自己。

10. Praise 讚美

They provide the immediate feedback to help the employees to learn that they have done well.

他們給予立即的回饋，讓員工知道自己做得好的地方。

11. Mentor 指導

They are willing to coach their staff on how to do certain jobs, rather than think the staff should learn themselves.

他們願意教導員工如何做好某件工作，而非認為員工們應該自己學會。

12. Fair 公平

They treat every staff equally, so the workers feel appreciated.

他們對待每位員工都是公平的，所以員工們會感到受到賞識。

ocabulary 字彙

* ★ Marketing campaign 行銷活動
* ★ Management style 管理模式
* ★ Detail-oriented 細節導向
* ★ Big-picture 願景、藍圖
* ★ Execution 執行力
* ★ Commander 命令者
* ★ Result-oriented 結果導向
* ★ Chart/diagram 圖表
* ★ Organizer 組織者
* ★ Process-oriented 過程導向
* ★ Relater 關係者
* ★ People-focused 人際取向
* ★ Spontaneously 主動地
* ★ Entertainer 娛樂者
* ★ Charismatic 充滿魅力的
* ★ Facial expression 臉部表情
* ★ Dilemma 兩難
* ★ Delegate 授權
* ★ Align 結盟
* ★ Flexibility 彈性
* ★ Give credit 記功嘉獎
* ★ Mentor 良師益友

求職面試心理

了解你的老闆

找到對的工作　職場定位

你與同事

帶人要帶心

升遷與工作態度

2-2

The Art of Conversation
說話藝術

情 境對話

Imagine you were a parent of a teenage son. One day, you were using your laptop after dinner. However, you just couldn't get in to the website and signed in. So you asked your son for help. He just came to you and said, "How can you be so stupid? It's far too easy! Even a three old kid can do that! Next time, don't ask me these simple things, it's undermining my intelligence, and I don't have time for this!" And he reluctantly pressed few keys in your laptop, and it had been done. You still had no idea how he did that, and you felt upset about his attitude.

　　想像你有個青少年兒子。一天晚餐後,你在使用筆電。但你怎麼樣都進不去一個網站並登入,所以你請兒子幫忙。他走過來並說:「你怎麼這麼笨?這也太簡單了吧!連三歲小孩都會!下次不要再問我這些簡單的事了,這污辱我的智商耶!我沒有這麼多時間!」然後他很不情願地在筆電上敲幾個鍵,就弄好了。你仍然不知道他怎麼辦到的,而且你

求職面試心理

了解你的老闆

找到對的工作
職場定位

你與同事

帶人要帶心

升工作態度與遷

對他的態度感到生氣。

So, a boss will also feel uncomfortable if you talk to your boss with impolite sentences or bad attitude. You are your boss's employee, s/he does not pay you to talk to him/her like that. You have to treat him/her as a boss.

所以，老闆也會因為你用無禮的字句或態度跟他／她說話而感到不舒服。你是老闆的員工，他/她並不是付錢請你來這樣對他／她說話。你應該視他／她為老闆對待他/她。

達 人剖析 I

Things that you shouldn't say to your boss
不該對老闆說的話

Talking to your boss smartly and effectively is extremely important in the workplace. You don't want to annoy your boss, of course. Here are some sentences which may get on your boss's nerves. Bernard Marr, the bestselling business author, teaches you how to avoid these sentences and then try to express yourself in a better way.

聰明地且有效地與老闆說話是非常重要的。你並不想惹惱老闆。這裡提供一些可能會令老闆惱怒的句子。Bernard Marr，數本商業暢銷書籍的作者，教你如何避免這些句子，並以更好的方式表達自己。

1. **X *"Are you sure you want to do that...?"***
你確定你要這樣做？

S/He is the boss, but you are not. Remember don't teach your boss how to do his or her job. If you really have to remind your boss something that s/he may have overlooked or forgotten, you could say:

他／她是老闆，但你不是！記得不需要教你的老闆如何做他／她的工作。如果你真的需要提醒老闆他／她錯估狀況或忘記事項，你可以這麼說：

O *"In my opinion, I think we could do XXX, because by doing so it is closer to the direction you said last time."*

我個人認為，我們可以做 XXX，因為這麼做比較接近你上次提到的方向。

2. **X *"I didn't want to bother you in case the problem worked itself out..."***
我並不想要麻煩你，也許問題可以自己解決。

While you are saying so, there is a high chance that something has gone horribly wrong. Try saying something like:

當你這麼說時，有很高的可能是某件事已經嚴重出錯了。試著這麼說：

O *"I think this project is not going well as we expected; however, I am doing XXX to correct it."*

我覺得這個案子並沒有進行的如預期般順利；然而，我正在做 XXX 來修正它。

3. **X** *"If you don't do this, I'm going to quit!"*
如果你不這麼做，我就辭職！

Are you sure you really want to quit the job? If not, don't use it as an ultimatum. You could try other sentence like:

你確定你真的想辭職？如果不是，不要把這當作是最後通牒。

O *"I am afraid I have to disagree with you. This is against my values, and I will feel really uncomfortable if I do so."*

我想我可能要持反對意見。但這麼做會違反我的原則，對此我會感到不舒服。

4. **X** *"People in my generation…"*
在我這個年代的人…

Of course, your boss knows you are younger than s/he is, but s/he doesn't want to be reminded of the age. If you want to suggest a change that will benefit the company, you could say:

你的老闆當然知道你比他／她年輕，但他/她並不需要你來提醒年紀。如果你想要建議做些改變以圖利公司，你可以說：

O *"Maybe we could try the Internet marketing this time to attract more young people."*

也許我們這次可以試著網路行銷來吸引更多年輕族群。

5. X *"That can't be done."*
這不可能做得到。

Your boss pays you to solve the problems, so s/he doesn't want to hear that it can't be done. When your boss gives you an assignment, you could focus on what you can do, like:

你的老闆付錢請你來解決問題，所以他/她並不想聽到你做不到。當老闆交辦任務給你，你可以想想你可以做什麼，像是：

O *"I will think through what you just said, and see*

what I can contribute."

我會想想你剛剛説的，然後看看我可以做些什麼。

6. *X "I need a raise."*

我要加薪。

You do deserve a raise if you have specific contributions. Instead of saying you "need" one, you could start by outlining your value to this company.

你如果有具體貢獻，你當然值得加薪。與其説"需要加薪"，不如具體説出你對公司的價值：

O "The project I've just finished made 30% extra profit for the company. This is far more than we expected. I will appreciate if the company could approve my hardworking and contribution to the company by increasing the salary."

我剛完成的案子幫公司多賺進了 30%的利潤，這比我們預期的目標還高出許多。所以公司也許能幫我加薪，來肯定我的努力與對公司的貢獻。

求職面試心理

了解你的老闆

找到對的工作 職場定位

你與同事

帶人要帶心

升遷與工作態度

Things Boss Never Say To the Employees
老闆不該對員工說的話

The bosses also have to learn how to talk to their employees in a more constructive way. Saying things with a different standard and tone, addressing the issue and finding out the solutions are far more effective to get things done. Name calling will only damage your relationship with your employees. One of the famous websites in relation to the workplace, Entrepreneur, suggests several sentences which the bosses should never say to their employees. Moreover, the better ways to communicate with the workers are also advised.

老闆也應該學習怎麼以更有建設性的方式與員工談話。用不同的方式與語氣，並著重在問題與尋求解決方法上才會更快地把事情處理好。謾罵只會傷害老闆與員工之間的關係。知名職場相關網站 Entrepreneur (www.Entrepreneur.com)，提出了一些老闆不應對員工說的話。也接著建議較好的溝通方式。

1. **X "I am the boss."**
   我是老闆！

   If you are saying in a different standard to them, you can expect they will respect you.

如果你換個方式說，員工會更尊敬你。

O "I am glad to have an employee like you. So could you please…"

我很高興有你這樣的員工。可不可以請你…

2. *X "You are lucky to have a job."*
你能有工作已經很幸運了！

Being professional and confront the issue. Negativity is never the solution.

要專業、直接談論問題。否定性的討論絕對不會是解決的方式。

O "According to the monthly report, your performance is not as good as we expected. I think you could do with more training."

根據我們這個月的報告，你的表現不如預期。我覺得你需要接受多一點訓練。

3. *X "IF you don't like it, I will find someone who does!"*
如果你不喜歡，我會找別人做！

A good boss will motivate their employee. If you still say

求職面試心理

了解你的老闆

找到對的工作 職場定位

你與同事

帶人要帶心

升工作態度遷與

so, the employee will only do the minimum.

好老闆會激勵員工。如果你這麼說，員工只會做到最低要求。

O *"Could you please do some research on this project first, and then we could discuss how to divide the assignment into several parts?"*

能不能請你針對這個案子先進行了解，然後我們來討論如何將任務分工？

4. X *"Why are you the only one who has a problem with?"*
為什麼只有你有問題？

Maybe he or she just has a bad day. Don't assume s/he is having an issue.

也許他／她只是有個不順的一天。不要假設員工有甚麼問題。

O *"Are you Ok? You don't look good today."*

你還好嗎？你今天看起來不太好。

5. X *"I don't have time for this."*
我沒時間處理這個！

You are the boss, it is your responsibility to make time!

你是老闆，你的責任就是找出時間。

O *"I am quite busy this moment. Can you come back later in the afternoon?"*

我現在很忙。可不可以下午再過來找我？

6. **X *"You have no idea what stress is."***
   你無法想像我的壓力有多大。

You think your stress is greater, but it's not.

你認為壓力比較大，但事實上並不一定如此。

O *"We have several different tasks this month, so we have to work together to complete these tasks."*

這個月我們有許多不同的任務，所以我們應該一起合作完成。

V ocabulary 字彙

★ Ultimatum 最後通牒　　★ Name calling 謾罵
★ Internet marketing 網路行銷　★ Negativity 否定性

求職面試心理

了解你的老闆

找到對的工作　職場定位

你與同事

帶人要帶心

升工作態度與遷與

2-3

Mind Games Between Boss and Employees

老闆與員工的心理戰

情 境對話

Derrick is the manager of Jack. Jack was told by the secretary of his manager, Derrick, about his new job duty. The company was promoting the policy of ensuring a safe, clean, and energy-efficient working environment. Each department or sector needed to have a promoter to help implement the policy. The promoter had to draw up a plan of raising safety awareness, maintaining a good level of hygiene in the office, and making efficient use of energy. Derrick wanted Jack to take up this role.

　　Derrick 是 Jack 的經理。Jack 被 Derrick 的秘書告知他新的工作任務。公司剛推出新的政策，要求安全、潔淨與節能的工作環境。每個部門需要一位推行員來執行這樣政策。該推行員需要提出提高安全意識、維持辦公室環境衛生與提高能源使用效率的計畫。Derrick 希望 Jack 可以接下這個工作。

Jack felt a bit reluctant about the new assignment. He asked the secretary why Derrick wanted him for this position. He told the secretary that there are a few colleagues far more suitable for this position. He pointed to a strong guy and described how he was always keen on the tutorials on using fire extinguishers. He also pointed to another female colleague and addressed the fact that she washed her hands a lot and had a clean desk. The secretary innocently said to Jack that she was merely a messenger and if he had any doubts, he should talk to Derrick in person.

　　Jack 對新的工作感到不情願。他問秘書，為什麼 Derrick 指派由他接下這份工作。他告訴秘書他想到有幾位同事比他更適合擔任這個職務。他指出其中一位男同事，並說明這位同事總是熱心教人使用滅火器。他也指出另一位女同事常會洗手，也將桌子收拾得很乾淨。秘書無辜地說他只負責傳達訊息，如果有任何疑慮，應該去找 Derrick 本人說。

Jack decided to pay Derrick a visit at his office. Derrick was there.

　　Jack 決定去找 Derrick，Derrick 也有在辦公室。

Jack Hi Derrick.
「嗨，Derrick。」

Derrick

Hi Jack. What's up?

「嗨，Jack，甚麼事？」

Jack

I am not so sure about the new role you just assigned to me.

「我對你新指派的工作不是很確定。」

Derrick

Really? What is problem then? The company needs such a promoter for each sector, including ours. Someone in our team has got to do it, right?

「真的嗎？有甚麼問題？公司要求每個部門都有推行員，當然包括我們。我們部門中總要有人做吧！」

Jack

Yeah, I know. But why me? There are several people who are better than me for this.

「是得，我知道，但為什麼是我？有很多其他人選都比我好。」

Derrick

Why can't it be you? It's a task assigned by your manager. If you think you are not good at it, then just learn to be good at it.

「為什麼不能是你？這是你的經理交辦的，如果你覺得自己不夠好，就試著讓自己變好。」

Jack

Well, it seems OK if you put it this way. However, I don't think that's the right way to do this.

「你這麼說也對。但是，我覺得這麼做事不對的。」

Derrick

Oh yeah...? How should I do it then?

「是嗎？那我該怎麼做？」

Jack

Well, since it's such an important policy of our company, I think we should pick somebody that is a best fit for this role.

「既然這是公司重要的政策，我覺得應該要選一個更適合這個職務的人選。」

Jack

"I think this... I think that..." Jack continued to address his point to Derrick. He even recommended a few candidates, whom he thought would be the right people for this task. Derrick felt a bit annoyed. He started to lose his patience.

「我想應該這樣…或是那樣…」Jack 繼續向 Derrick 強調他的論點，他甚至推薦了幾位他認為更適合這個任務的人選。Derrick 開始覺得有點煩了，也失去耐心。

Derrick

See, that is your problem. You graduated from one of the top universities. You assume that you have the privilege to pick only the tasks you like or you are good at.

「你看，這就是你的問題。你從頂尖大學畢業，你就以為你有特權選擇你想做或你擅長做的事。」

Jack

...

「…」

Derrick

And you know what? It gets to me that you think you're smarter than everyone in this office, including me. Now, if you want to stay in my team, you better get back to your desk and start your plan on implementing the new policy!

「還有你知道嗎？你以為你是全辦公室中最聰明的人，也比我聰明。現在，如果你還想待在這個團隊，你最好回去開始寫你新政策的計畫書！」

達 人剖析

👣 How to say NO to your boss 如何對老闆說不

Sometimes you really don't want to respond your boss's unexpected or unreasonable requests. You certainly have your reason, but how can you convince your boss that you are unable to help him/her? Let the CareerCast.com teaches you the better ways to say no to your boss, if you really cannot complete his or her request.

有時你真的不想回應老闆突然或不合理的要求。你當然有你的理由，但你如何說服老闆你無法幫他。讓 CareerCast.com 教你，當你真的無法完成老闆的要求時如何說不。

1. Evaluate your reason 評估你的理由

You have to evaluate your reasons for not wanting to do as your boss's request. Is it just because you don't like doing? Or does the request violate your personal right or belief system? If there is no other reason that you just don't want to follow the request, you have to think about your responsibilities of this position.

你要評估你不想做老闆要求的理由。是因為純粹不想做？或這樣的要求違背了你的權益或信念？如果沒有甚麼好理由，你應該思考一下你的職責所在。

2. Say it earlier 早點說

If you are unable to complete the request, don't wait until the last minute to tell your boss. Give your boss an early notice so s/he could have alternative options to get the job be done.

如果你無法達成要求，不要等到最後一分鐘才告知老闆。早點告訴老闆，這樣他/她才可以尋求替代方案來完成工作。

3. Be rational 要理性

Even his or her demand has upset you, do not talk to your boss until you fully calm down and are in control of your emotions.

即使他／她的要求令你生氣，在你尚未冷靜且能控制你的情緒之前，不要跟老闆討論。

求職面試心理

了解你的老闆

找到職場定對位的工作

你與同事

帶人要帶心

升工作態度遷與

4. **Be honest** 誠實

If you make an excuse which is not real, your boss will find out eventually. Your boss will then lose trust in you which will also harm your career.

如果你編了一個假的理由，老闆始終會發現。你的老闆就會對你失去信任，這會對你的職涯造成傷害。

5. **Choose your words** 選擇你用的字眼

Do not start your conversation with "NO". You should start with a statement telling your boss that you always put the company's best interests as priority. Then explain the reasons why you cannot fulfill the request this time.

不要在對話的一開始就說『不』。你可以先告訴老闆你都把公司利益擺在第一。然後解釋你這次不能達成老闆要求的原因。

6. **Offer options** 提供選擇

Offering alternatives is the greatest way to convince your boss that this request will still be completed even if you have to refuse it.

提供其他可能的方式是說服老闆最好的方式，讓他/她知道，即使你拒絕了，她／他的要求仍能被完成。

求職面試心理

了解你的老闆

找到對的工作 職場定位

你與同事

帶人要帶心

升遷與工作態度

達 人提點

What is your boss really thinking about?

老闆到底在想甚麼？

Have you ever wondered what your boss is actually thinking? How does your boss interpret your actions? Is s/he annoyed with me because something I said? Here are some scenarios to show you what your boss is thinking, and how you can try to talk or act in different ways.

你是否曾經想過到底老闆是怎麼想的？老闆對你的舉動作何解釋？他／她會因為我說了甚麼而生氣嗎？下面有些情境呈現出老闆在想些甚麼，及如何試著以不同的方式回應。

EX:

You are trying to propose an amazing idea in the meeting. However, your boss just ignores your proposal.

What's in your boss's head:

It is not your proposal doesn't interest me. It is just I am miles away and thinking of other matters. So do not take it personally.

You can try:

Write an email and explain your proposal to your boss after the meeting, so your boss could take his or her time to read it and think about it.

EX:

你正試著在會議中提出很棒的想法，但你的老闆並未理睬。

老闆想甚麼：

並不是你的提案不好。是因為我剛剛分心在想別的事。不要變為是你的問題。

你可以試著：

在會議後寫一封電子郵件解釋你的提案，讓老闆有時間閱讀與思考。

EX:

You don't speak up in a meeting. You hope the boss will not notice your existence.

What's in your boss's head:

He or she pays you to be his or her employee and solve the problem for him/her, not to be an exhibition of the company.

You can try:

Provide some intelligent comments during the meeting. If you are too shy to speak in front of other people, you could write an email and say: "I have been thinking about the project we talked about in the meeting. How about..."

EX:

你在會議中沒有發言，你希望老闆不會注意到你的存在。

老闆想甚麼：

老闆付錢是請員工來解決問題，不是當公司的展示品。

你可以試著：

在會議中提出一些聰明的見解。如果你太害羞不敢在大家面前發言，你可以寫封電子郵件:「我對剛剛會議中討論的案子思考了一下，我覺得…」

EX:
You are facing some problems in your work. Actually, you have tried to deal with the problems for couple weeks, but it seems doesn't work out.

What's in your boss's head:
I really don't like surprise, especially bad news! Let me know as soon as possible when you know something is going wrong.

You can try:
Let your boss know as soon as possible if you confront any problem, and also let him/her know that you are working it out by trying the alternative.

求職面試心理

了解你的老闆

找到對的工作 職場定位

你與同事

帶人要帶心

升工作態度遷與

EX:

你工作上遇到了一些問題。事實上你已經試著處理這個問題兩週了，但尚未解決。

老闆想甚麼：

我真的不喜歡驚喜，尤其是壞消息！當事情出錯時就要盡快告訴我。

你可以試著：

當你遇到問題時，盡快讓老闆知道，且告訴他／她你正嘗試著別的方法。

EX:

It is the fifth time this month that you are late for the work. So your boss rejects your request to take a day off for the concert. Actually, you had taken three days off for a holiday last month. Your boss now drops by your desk and checks how things are going constantly.

What's in your boss's head:

Don't give me a reason to monitor your every move. I really don't like to micromanage every staff. And I can give your some flexibility as long as you can perform well in your job.

You can try:

Be a scout and have a good performance for a period in order to regain your boss's trust.

EX:

這是本月第五次你遲交案子了，所以你的老闆拒絕了你休假一天去聽音樂會的要求。事實上，你上周才特休了三天去度假。你的老闆現在也常走到你的桌邊並檢視你的進度。

老闆想甚麼：

不要讓我有理由去監督你的一舉一動。我真的不想事事都要管。我可以允許一些彈性，只要你表現得夠好。

你可以試著：

當童子軍好好的表現一段時間，重新贏得老闆的信任。

EX:

You are talking to the coworker in non-work-related conversations.

What's in your boss's head:

Having a good relationship between the employees is good. However, if you talk about non-related topics too often, you may be labeled as a distraction to others.

You can try:

If you really want to share your personal things with your coworker, do it during the breaks or lunch time.

EX:

你正在跟同事聊著非工作相關的事情。

求職面試心理

了解你的老闆

找到對的工作｜職場定位

你與同事

帶人要帶心

升工作態度遷與

老闆想甚麼：

　　同事間關係良好是件好事。但是如果你太常閒聊，你可能會讓別人分心。

你可以試著：

　　如果你真的想跟同事分享私事，在休息時或午休時做比較好。

EX:

You are complaining to the HR that you are really stressful because you have been assigned too many tasks.

What's in your boss's head:

You should fight for yourself and take care of yourself. If you feel you are overloaded, you should talk to me. Do not expect me to know your situation and do everything for you.

You can try:

Try to talk to your boss politely and specifically. Let your boss know you are doing X, Y, and Z this moment, and ask your boss if s/he can prioritize your tasks.

EX:

　　你向 HR 抱怨你壓力太大，因為你被交辦太多工作。

老闆想甚麼：

　　你應該為自己發聲，照顧自己。如果你覺得負荷過重，可以來跟我説。不要期待我會了解你的狀況且幫你處理每件事。

你可以試著：

試著有禮且具體得跟老闆討論。讓老闆知道你手邊正在處理 X、Y、Z 三件事，並請老闆列出交辦工作的優先順序。

EX:

You just gave critical feedback of your boss's work during the meeting.

What's in your boss's head:

Are you undermining my intelligence? How can you criticize me?

You can try:

Do it in private either to his/her face or through an email, rather than in public and behind his/her back.

EX:

你剛在會議中對老闆提出批判。

老闆想甚麼：

你汙辱我的智商嗎？你怎麼可以批評我？

你可以試著：

私下對老闆説，可以當面説，也可藉由電子郵件告訴老闆，但不要在公開場合或是背後説。

求職面試心理

了解你的老闆

找到對的工作｜職場定位

你與同事

帶人要帶心

升工作態度遷與

EX:

Your team did not perform well to achieve the goal this season, and your boss is upsetting about this result.

What's in your boss's head:

You just don't get it that you are part of the problem! You spend most of your time on FB or connect with people on line, rather than do your job!

You can try:

Propose a specific plan about how you and your team will achieve to the goal next time, and put more efforts on it. Stop surfing the Internet or using community websites in the workplace if that is not part of your job.

EX:

你的團隊這季表現得不好，未達目標。老闆對此很不滿意。

老闆想甚麼：

你就是不明白，其實你也是問題之一耶！你花很多時間看臉書或線上聊天，而不是在工作！

你可以試著：

提出你與團隊下次要如何達到目標的具體計劃，並更努力。不要在工作時瀏覽網頁或使用社群網站，如果這不是工作之一。

2-4

How to Deal with a Difficult Boss?

如何應付難搞的老闆

情 境對話

Sarah is exhausted recently because since her coworker, Lisa, left the department, she has always been assigned to do all Lisa's work, as well as her. Sarah has tried to approach her manager, Linda, several times, but Linda is either in meetings or is never there. It seems Linda just has no time for Sarah to talk about her concern. Until one day, Sarah finally bumped into Linda in the common room during the coffee break.

　　Sarah 最近累壞了，因為自從她的同事 Lisa 離職後，所有 Lisa 的工作都轉到 Sarah 身上，她也還得繼續負責自己的工作。Sarah 曾試著找主管 Linda 談論這件事，但 Linda 不是在會議中，就是不在辦公室。Linda 似乎沒有時間與 Sarah 討論她的問題。直到有一天，Sarah 終於在休息時間碰到了 Linda。

Sarah
"Linda, do you have a minute?"
「Linda，你有空嗎？」

Linda
"I am on the way to the meeting, I really don't have time."
「我正要去開會，真的沒空。」

Sarah
"But this is important. I do need to talk to you. Otherwise, I have to talk to the HR for advice."
「這真的很重要，我需要找你談談，不然，我可能需要尋求 HR 的建議。」

Linda
"Are you OK? Anything serious?"
「你還好嗎？什麼是這麼嚴重？」

Sarah
"Well, since Lisa left, you always assign her work to me. I now have to work overtime. There are endless meetings and paperwork for me now, I can't even focus on my own project. I really feel tired and frustrated about this."
「自從 Lisa 離職後，你一直把她的工作轉到我身上。我現在都得加班，總是有開不完的會跟寫不完的報告，我甚至無法做我自己的案子。我真的好累、好挫折。」

Linda
"But you are supposed to do that. This is part of your job."
「你應該做啊，這是你職責的一部分。」

Sarah

"But, this is unfair. Other workers can go home earlier, but I have to work late every single day."

「但這不公平。同事都可以早點回家，但我每一天都必須工作到很晚。」

Linda

"Are you sure? Is it because of extra workload, or is it because of your ability?"

「你確定嗎？這是因為額外的工作量，還是因為你的能力問題？」

Sarah

"Just like yesterday, I had an appointment in the evening, so I have finished my specific work, and ready to get off. But you just came in and expected me to help other colleagues finish their work too."

「就像昨天，我晚上跟人有約，所以我已經完成我的工作且準備下班了，但你就進來要我幫同事完成他們的工作。」

Linda

"Why didn't you say so yesterday?"

「那你昨天為什麼不說？」

Sarah

"I tried, but you just ignored my words."

「我有啊，但你就沒聽到。」

Linda

"I don't think I have been making unrealistic demands on you."

「我不覺得我有給你不合理的要求。」

Sarah

"I do respect your leadership, but I also need to be respected. I do have my personal stuff to deal with. I cannot devote all of my time to the company."

「我尊重你的領導，但我也需要被尊重。我也有我自己的事情要處理。我不可能把所有的時間都奉獻給公司。」

Linda

"That's what I do. I can do that, you should do that too!"

「我就是這樣啊！我可以這麼做，你也應該這麼做。」

Sarah

"If you cannot help me to change the situation, I will try other path to solve it out. Maybe I will talk to the HR for their advice."

「如果你不能幫我改善這個狀況，我就要尋求其他的方法解決。也許我會去找 HR 談談。」

Linda

"I really don't have time for this. I have to go now."

「我現在真的沒空，我要走了。」

達 人剖析

You couldn't wait to get this dream job, but now you can't wait to leave! However, your financial circumstances make it impossible for you to leave your job. While you are dealing a difficult boss, you can certainly do something! Let Maria Wofford, the author of *Make Difficult People Disappear*, and Aaron Gouveia, the, award-winning journalist, teach you how to deal with difficult boss while you confront the following situations.

你等不及要得到這份夢想中的工作，但你現在等不及要離職！然而，你的經濟狀況卻不允許你離職。當你面對討厭的老闆時，你當然可以有些作為。讓 Maria Wofford（Maria Wofford 是《讓討人厭的人消失》一書作者）及 Aaron Gouveia（他是曾獲獎的新聞記者）來教你，當你處在下列狀況時，如何與討厭的老闆過招。

EX:
Your boss allocates you an unreasonable amount of assignments.

TO DO:
Request for the priority. "Thank you for assigning me these tasks. I am now also working on the X, Y, and Z. I am afraid I cannot get all the tasks done at once, would you prioritize these tasks?"

EX:
你的老闆分配給你不合理的工作量。

你可以這麼做：

　　要求老闆列出優先順序。「謝謝你給我這些任務。我現在同時也在進行 X、Y 和 Z，恐怕沒辦法同時完成這些任務。所以可以請你告訴我這些工作的優先順序嗎？」

EX:

Your boss is disorganized and unclear about your tasks.

TO DO:

Clarify your boss's expectations. "When do you need the proposal? And how many pages are you thinking?"

EX:

　　你的老闆雜亂無章且表達不清你的內務內容。

你可以這麼做：

　　對老闆的期待進行澄清。「你甚麼時候需要企劃書？你希望寫到幾頁？」

EX:

You can't get feedback and feel not be cared.

TO DO:

Ask for feedback. Write your boss an email and ask: "I really need your feedback to improve my performance. How would you rate my performance on this project? How can I get better next time?"

求職面試心理

了解你的老闆

找到職場對的定工位作

你與同事

帶人要帶心

升工作態度遷與

EX:

你得不到老闆的回饋，覺得不被重視。

你可以這麼做：

要求回饋。寫電子郵件給老闆並詢問：「我真的需要你的回饋來讓自己表現得更好。在這個案子上，你會給我幾分？我要怎麼更進步？」

EX:
Your boss is emotionally explosive.

TO DO:

Don't take it personally, and give your boss and yourself some time to cool down. Tell your boss: "Maybe I should come back and talk to you later.".

EX:

你的老闆情緒失控。

你可以這麼做：

不要認為跟你有關，給你老闆與自己一點時間冷靜下來。跟老闆說：「也許我等一下再來找你談。」

EX:
Micromanagement. Your boss always corrects you. S/he checks your progress often. Your boss doesn't trust you.

TO DO:

Push back to limit the interruptions, but suggest regular meetings. "I love you stop by and check in, but is it OK if I finish this and we meet at 2pm?" or "Can we have a regular weekly meeting, so I can report the updated progress to you."

EX:

事事監督。你的老闆總是在糾正你。他／她一直在檢視你的進度而不信任你。

你可以這麼做：

將干擾降低，但建議定期的會議：「我可以接受你過來並檢視，但可不可以先讓我完成這部分，然後我們兩點開個會？」或「我們可不可以每週開會，這樣我就可以向你報告最新進度。」

EX:

You are excluded for the project meetings.

TO DO:

Avoid being confrontational and emotional immediately. It might just be an honest mistake. Talk to your boss: "I have been working on this project for one month, but I am not on the list of the project meeting today. Could you please let me know if you feel any problem about me? So I could get better to benefit the team.".

求職面試心理

了解你的老闆

找到對的工作 職場定位

你與同事

帶人要帶心

升工作態度遷與

EX:

你被排除在專案會議之外。

你可以這麼做：

避免面質與立即的情緒反應。這也許只是個無心之過。與老闆談一下：「過去一個月我一直在做這個專案，但今天的專案會議我並沒有在名單上。可以請你讓我知道是不是你認為我有甚麼問題，這樣我可以改進，讓團隊變得更好。」

EX:

You cannot access your boss. S/he has no time for you.

TO DO:

Let your boss know you value his/her opinions. "I know how busy you are. But do you have a few minutes for me? I need to talk to you because I really value your opinions and guidance."

EX:

你找不到老闆，他／她總時沒有時間見你。

你可以這麼做：

讓老闆知道你很重視他的意見：「我知道你非常忙。但你可不可以給我幾分鐘，我需要跟你談談，因為我真的非常重視你的意見與指導。」

EX:

You are ignored or insulted during the meeting.

TO DO:

Ask for your boss's feedback with a humble attitude. Tell you boss: "I might not express myself very effectively in the meeting, but I do have some good ideas to communicate. Do you have any tip to help me make more contribution for the team?"

EX:

在會議中你被忽視或攻擊。

你可以這麼做：

以謙虛的態度請求老闆給予你回饋：「在會議中我可能沒有表達得很好，但我的確有一些想法想討論。你有沒有一些方法可以幫我，讓我對團隊更有貢獻？」

職 場小故事

Peter has been a brilliant worker since he joined the company from day one. He is hardworking. He also is a quick learner. He always knows what his boss needs, and finishes every assignment perfectly and before the deadline. His boss, John, has started to rely on him more and more. Sooner than he could ever realize, his outgrown confidence starts to affect the chemistry between him and John. Peter sometimes interrupts and corrects John during the team meetings, just like what he does during his casual conversations with John. Peter thinks

求職面試心理

了解你的老闆

找到對的工作　職場定位

你與同事

帶人要帶心

升工作態度遷與

he is just giving a genuine opinion as if John needed the advice. However, John feels rather uncomfortable about Peter's "opinions" during the meetings. John is also worried about the possible damage to his authoritative role as a boss. John starts to exclude John from some meetings. He either holds the meetings while Peter is away from the office or tells him that the agenda is irrelevant to his job duties. To reassure his role as the boss of the company, John assigns more tedious work to Peter, who obviously can handle much more important tasks. To keep him busy, John asks Peter to report his work progress on a regular basis. Peter soon feels trapped by the mundane tasks.

Peter 自第一天進入公司起就一直是個很傑出的員工。他很認真，也學得很快。他總是知道老闆需要甚麼，也能完美且快速地完成每個任務。他的老闆 John 也越來越依賴他。很快的，他也不斷的自我膨脹，也影響到他與 John 之間的關係。Peter 有時會在團隊會議中打斷並糾正 John，就像在平常與 John 對話時一般。Peter 認為他只是給個真心的意見，因為他覺得 John 需要他人的建議。然而，John 對 Peter 在會議中的意見感到不舒服。John 也開始擔心會影響到他身為老闆的權威角色。John 開始將 Peter 排除在會議外，常在 Peter 不在公司時開會，或是告訴他會議內容與他的職務無關。John 為了要確保自己老闆的地位，他交辦更多乏味的工作給 Peter，事實上 Peter 可以處理更多更重要的工作。為了讓 Peter 更忙，John 也要求 Peter 定期報告他的進度。Peter 開始覺得被這些乏味的工作困住了。

求職面試心理

了解你的老闆

找到職場對的工作定位

你與同事

帶人要帶心

升工作態度遷與

達 人提點

⦿ Strengthen your mind too! 你也該增強你的心智！

You do need some action plans while dealing with your difficult boss. But most importantly, you need to strengthen your mind. See some tips suggested by the American Psychological Association and other professional psychologists to help you have a stronger mind to deal with your boss and colleagues in your workplace.

在應付難搞的老闆時，你的確需要一些行動計畫。最重要的是，你需要加強你的心智。以下是美國心理協會及其他專業心理之的建議，幫助你有更強韌的心智來應付職場中難搞的老闆與同事。

1. Manage your own negative emotion and thinking
管理你的負向情緒與想法

No matter what your boss's behavior is, focus on the bright side rather than complaining. Other people can only affect you if you allow them to do so. You should 'filter' other negative things and your negative thoughts.

不論你老闆的行為如何，專注在正向面而非抱怨。其他的人會影響你，因為你讓他們能夠影響你。你應該過濾掉其他負面的事情及你負面的想法。

2. Communicate your concerns 談論你的擔心

Talk to your boss about your concerns with a helpful, positive manner and problem-solving atmosphere.

跟老闆討論你的擔心，並以一種幫忙的、正向的態度及解決問題的氛圍進行討論。

3. Empower yourself 讓自己增權

Tell yourself you have the right and power to control the situation. Remember you have values. Find your identity which should not be tied to your job.

告訴自己你有權利與能力去控制這個狀況。記得你是有價值的人。找到你的自我認同，且這樣的認同不應該與工作牽綁。

4. View things from a different perspective
從另一個角度看事情

Try to see the criticism from your boss as valuable information which helps you to do better, rather than a personal attack. Try hard to control your impulses to react emotionally or defensively.

試著將老闆的批評視為有用的資訊，來幫助你做得更好，而非人身攻擊。試著克制自己的衝動，避免情緒化的反應，或是急于替自己辯解。

5. Keep calm and confident 保持冷靜與信心

If you feel you have been unfairly criticized by your boss, discuss your concerns calmly without confrontation or further damaging your relationship with your boss. Remember you deserve to be treated with respect. Respond unfair behaviors with dignity and confidence.

　　如果你覺得被老闆不公平的批判，冷靜的與老闆談談你的想法，而非去面質，或用其他會傷害你們關係的方式。記得你值得被尊重。保持尊嚴與自信地回應這些不公平的行為。

6. Be proactive 主動

Have an action plan ready. If your boss behaves negatively, put your plan into action. If your boss behaves positively, reinforce the good behaviors by saying "Nice meeting!", "Good!" or "Thank you!"

　　把你的行動計劃準備好。如果老闆開始有負面行為，就進行該計畫。如果老闆的行為表現是正向的，就以「會議很棒！」、「謝謝」等字眼稱讚他以給予增強。

7. Be prepared 做好準備

You already know the pattern of your boss's bad behaviors. You have to ask yourself: What are you willing to do? Do you have options? Can you deal with the

求職面試心理

了解你的老闆

找到對的工作　職場定位

你與同事

帶人要帶心

升工作態度　遷與

worst outcomes? Try to write down all the possible responses and action plans, and practice how to deliver them.

你已經知道老闆壞行為的模式了。你要問自己：「你願意做甚麼？你有選擇嗎？你可以接受最壞的結果嗎？」把所有可能的答案與行動計畫寫下來，並練習如何進行這些計畫。

8. Be persistent 堅持下去

It is a long run because your boss won't change overnight. Be persistent into putting your plans into action while bad behaviors turn up.

這是一場長期抗戰，因為老闆的行為不會一夜變好。當老闆又出現壞行為時，要堅持地進行你的行動計劃。

9. Move forward 向前走

You need to mentally and emotionally accept your boss, and then move forward. Stop seeing your boss as good or bad. Even the worst persons have good qualities. So allow yourself to appreciate this person for what s/he does well, and block out the things which drive you crazy, you are on your own way. Just focus on what you could control.

心理上與情緒上去接受你的老闆，並向前走。不要一直去看你老闆是好是壞。即使最壞的人也有好的一面。所以讓自己可以去欣賞好的一面,並讓自己不要看那些讓你抓狂的部分。你是自己的主人,專注在你能控制的事情上。

Vocabulary 字彙

- ★ Journalist 新聞記者
- ★ Interruption 干擾
- ★ Insult 攻擊
- ★ Brilliant 傑出的
- ★ Genuine 真心的
- ★ Agenda 議程
- ★ Mundane 平凡的
- ★ Empower 增權
- ★ Dignity 尊嚴
- ★ Reinforce 增強

- ★ Micromanagement 微觀管理
- ★ Confrontation 面質
- ★ Humble 謙遜的
- ★ Rely 依賴
- ★ Authoritative 權威的
- ★ Tedious 枯燥乏味的
- ★ Filter 過濾
- ★ Identity 自我認同
- ★ Proactive 主動積極
- ★ Persistent 堅持的

MEMO

求職面試心理

了解你的老闆

找到對的工作 職場定位

你與同事

帶人要帶心

升遷與工作態度

Chapter **3**

Finding the Right Job for You

職場定位

找到對的工作

3-1

How To Find a Right Job
如何找到對的工作

情 境對話

Lauren, an undergraduate student in her sophomore year, had been wondering what she would do after college. There were so many career paths that she had considered taking, and Lauren didn't know which direction she should go.

Lauren 大學二年級，一直思考畢業後該做些甚麼。她考慮過很多不同的職業方向，但她仍不知道該往哪個方向。

After having decided that she needed help, Lauren made an appointment with her college counselor, Mr. Bernard, to discuss her career. When the day of the appointment arrived, Lauren was excited, but also a bit nervous.

她決定尋求幫助。Lauren 與大學輔導老師 Mr. Bernard 約了時間，討論她的職涯。這一天到了，Lauren 有點興奮也有點緊張。

Mr. Bernard

"Good morning, Lauren. Please have a seat, and let me know what you want to talk about."

「早安，Lauren。請坐，告訴我你今天想要談些甚麼？」

Lauren

"Well, Mr. Bernard, I just don't know what to do when I get out of school. I'm a sophomore now, and I am confused about my future. There are two things I've considered doing for a living, but choosing what to do is the hardest part. I bet I'm the only sophomore who has no clue what field to enter, and what if I choose wrong and end up hating my job? Then I'll have to go get another degree, and get more student loans, and more debt, and..."

「Mr. Bernard，我只是不知道畢業後我要做甚麼。我現在已經二年級了，但對未來感到困惑。我有想到可以做兩件事，但要選擇哪一個真的很困難。我猜我一定是二年級中唯一對未來沒有概念的人，而且如果我選錯了，最後恨這份工作怎麼辦？然後我就必須再進修，然後借更多學貸，然後就會負債更多，然後…」

Mr. Bernard

"Lauren, calm down. I promise you that you're not the first sophomore without clear future direction to come into my office."

「Lauren，冷靜一下。我向你保證你不是二年級中第一個對未來沒有目標而來找我的人。」

求職面試心理

了解你的老闆

找到對的工作 職場定位

你與同事

帶人要帶心

升工作態度遷與

Lauren

"Really?"

「真的嗎？」

Mr. Bernard

"Of course not. It's only Wednesday, and you're the fifth sophomore with this dilemma that I've seen this week! It's a common thing. Tell me, what careers are you considering?"

「當然不是，今天星期三，而你已經是這週第五個有困擾而來找我的大二學生。這是很平常的事。告訴我，你有考慮過哪些工作？」

Lauren

"I love art and drawing, so I thought I might like being an artist. But I also enjoy tutoring and helping others, so I figured maybe being a teacher is better for me."

「我喜歡藝術和畫畫，所以我在想可以當藝術家。但是我也喜歡教人和幫助人，所以也許當個老師更適合我。」

Mr. Bernard

"What about a combination of the two?"

「那如果結合這兩者呢？」

Lauren

"What do you mean, Mr. Bernard?"

「甚麼意思？」

Mr. Bernard

"I mean you can both enjoy making art and teaching at the same time by becoming an art teacher. You don't necessarily have to teach in a school, either. You could open your own art studio, give private lessons, or even become an art professor."

「我的意思是，你可以同時享受藝術跟教學，也就是成為美術老師。你也不一定要在學校教書。你可以自己開個工作室教學，甚至以後成為藝術教授。」

Lauren

"Wow! I haven't thought about this possibility before. It's such a great idea to combine my interests. You are right, maybe I could have my own studio some day!"

「哇！我以前都沒有想過這種可能！能結合我的興趣真是個好點子。也許你是對的，有一天我可以有自己的工作室。」

After hearing this, Lauren knew that being an art teacher would be the ideal career for her. She thanked Mr. Bernard and headed off to make her plan more specific.

經過討論，Lauren 覺得成為美術老師是個很理想的職業。她向 Mr. Bernard 道謝，回去將她的計畫想得更具體。

達 人剖析

Finding a perfect job is easier said than done. You have to be serious about having a career that you truly are passionate about, and just can't wait to get to work each day. You really don't want a job you dread.

　　找到完美的工作，説得比做得簡單。你必須認真思考你會有熱情的工作，而且每天都會等不及去上班。你真的不希望對工作心生恐懼。

Roman Krznaric, author of *How to Find Fulfilling Work (2013),* illustrates five dimensions of meaning in a career in his book:

1. Earning money.
2. Achieving status.
3. Making a difference.
4. Following your passions (interests).
5. Using your talents (skills).

　　Roman Krznaric，如何《找到能實現抱負的工作》(2013)一書作者，在書中提到五個面向讓工作充滿意義：

1. 賺錢
2. 達到社會地位
3. 與眾不同
4. 符合熱情（興趣）
5. 運用天分（技術）

You can use these dimensions while you are looking for a job, or assess your current job. Here are some tips which help you to find a meaningful job.

你可以利用這些面向來找工作，或檢視你目前的工作。以下是一些幫助你找到有意義工作的技巧。

1. Don't trap yourself 不要困住自己

It is extremely normal to feel confused about career choice. So accept your confusion. Think thoroughly before making decision; once you make a decision, accept the consequences. Even the wrong choice is better than no choice because you can learn something from the previous mistakes. And remember, it's not the end of the world.

對職業的選擇感到困惑是非常正常的。所以接受你的困惑。在做決定前仔細思考，一旦做了決定，接受任何結果。即便是最壞的選擇都比沒有選擇好，因為你可以從過去的錯誤中學到經驗。記住，這不是世界末日。

2. Take care of yourself 照顧好自己

Before you worry about meaningful work, you need to be able to support yourself, at least have the basic covered.

在擔心工作的意義前，你需要能夠養活自己，至少能應付基本開銷。

3. Understand your personality 了解你的個性

Do you know yourself well enough? Make a list of all

求職面試心理

了解你的老闆

找到對的工作　職場定位

你與同事

帶人要帶心

升工作態度遷與

your main personality traits before you start thinking about jobs. You personality is the key to finding the right job.

你有足夠認識自己嗎？在開始想工作的事情前，先列出你的主要人格特質。你的人格特質是讓你找到對的工作的主要元素。

4. Find your value and talents 找到你的價值與天分
Find a career that matters to you, and allows you to do what you are really good at.

找到可以符合你的工作，也可以讓你發揮所長。

5. Don't get too specific 不要太過侷限
Do not pinpoint the exact job. You can explore what fields would be a potentially good fit for you, and head in the right general direction. Moreover, you can change your direction many times!

不要僅考慮單一工作。你應該探索你擅長的領域，並往對的方向去。此外，你也隨時可以變換方向。

6. Get the right information 取得正確資訊
Research before you look for a job. Don't rely on second-hand information, find out for yourself. You can talk to someone who actually does the role, so you can learn what the job is like.

在找工作前要先做功課。不要依賴第二首資訊，要自己找資訊。你可以與真正從事該行業的人聊聊，這樣可以對這份工作有更多了解。

7. Act and reflect 行動並反思

No matter how long the lists you draw up, you still won't get the job. You still have to think about the meanings about the job, but most importantly, you have to act. Submit your CV, prepare your interview, try to volunteer or do an internship in the similar field, and learn and reflect from the experience. All these actions can help you be closer to your right job.

不論你列了多長的清單，你還是不會得到工作。雖然你還是要思考工作的意義，但最重要的是，你必須有所行動。寄履歷、準備面試、在相關行業中當志工或實習生都可以，然後從中學習經驗並反思。這些行動都可以幫助你更靠近適合你的工作。

職 場小故事

Annie loved reading since she was still a child. After she graduated, she got the seemingly dream job. She worked in a bookstore. She thought she could spend most of her time on reading all kinds of books. At first this was true, Annie got this privilege to read newly published books and meet the authors when they did the signings in the store.

求職面試心理

了解你的老闆

找到對的工作 職場定位

你與同事

帶人要帶心

升工作態度遷與

Annie 自小便愛閱讀。畢業後，她找到了夢想中的工作——在書店工作。她覺得可以在書店中閱讀各式各樣的書。剛開始是如此，她可以看盡所有新出版的書，也可以在作者來店辦簽書會時親眼見到作者。

She did not have a second thought about this job until recently. The store manager was overtly keen on elevating the sale numbers. She then assigned Annie tasks that were not so relevant to reading. She asked Annie to plan and run lots of activities that could help promote the business. For example, the store started to host a series of story-telling events, in which Annie had to organize the event schedule, make sure there would be a substantial number of people participating, prepare little gifts for children, and clean the place after each event. Annie was more of an introvert, quiet person. Spending time alone on the reading was fine for her. But to mingle with people and build social connections with potential customers? Annie could live with doing them occasionally but not becoming her main responsibility of the work. She soon felt tired and frustrated at her job. It was very different from what she had expected. She finally had it enough and went to the manager for getting out of the situation, under which she had to act like an outgoing, talkative person. The manager could not get what Annie was trying to tell her. She told Annie that she was in the real world now. And real world changed constantly. She needed to be adaptive in order to survive.

她一直很滿意這份工作。直到最近，經理非常希望可以提升銷售量。Annie 於是被指派了一些與閱讀無關的任務。經理要求 Annie 計畫並執行許多活動以刺激銷售量。例如，書店開始舉辦一系列的說故事活動，Annie 就必須安排流程、確保有許多人參加、準備小禮物給小朋友、及會後清理工作等。Annie 是一個害羞安靜的人。獨自安靜的閱讀對 Annie 來說很棒；但與人交際並與潛在客群建立社交關係？對 Annie 而言，偶爾做這些事無妨，但無法接受這些成為她的主要任務。她開始覺得好累也好挫折。這些與她原先預期的工作內容非常不同。她受夠了，於是去找經理討論如何避免假裝很外向多話的狀況。經理並不了解 Annie 的意思。她告訴 Annie，現實世界就是這樣，因為會一直改變，所以為了生存必需要去適應它。

Annie felt confused and frustrated. She went to see a career advisor for the situation. The advisor encouraged her to focus on the good parts. Annie recalled that she actually liked to see the children having good times during those storytelling events. They reminded how Annie herself was fascinated by stories when she was a little child. That was exactly how she fell into reading from the start. The advisor also asked her to think about what she would do otherwise if she was the owner of the bookstore. Strangely, Annie felt a lot more relieved when she looked at things from her manager's perspective. She then decided to give herself a chance to experience and learn more about the job.

　　Annie 覺得很困惑也很挫折。她尋求就業輔導員的意見。就業輔導員鼓勵她看到工作上好的一面。Annie 想到她的確喜歡看到小朋友們在說故事時間中開心的模樣，這也讓她回想起她小時候對故事也非常著迷，這也正是她愛上閱讀的開始。就業輔導員也問她，如果她是書店老闆，她會怎麼做？特別的是，Annie 從經理的角度看事情時，突然感覺放鬆了不少。於是她決定再給自己一個機會去體驗與學習這份工作。

達人提點

What if you can't change your job?
如果你不能換工作該怎麼做？

If you have to consider the practical realities and can't afford to leave it, you still have to do some changes of you current job. Otherwise it keeps damaging you physically and mentally. Here are some suggestions.

如果你考慮現實狀況，而無法離職的話，你仍然必須為現在這份工作做些改變。否則，這樣的狀況只會一直傷害你的身體與心理。以下是一些建議。

1. Figure out what you don't like and what you do
思考甚麼事是你不喜歡的，以及甚麼事是你喜歡的

Make a list of the things you don't like your job. You may hate something about your job which makes you miserable, and it seems as if you hate it all. Take some time to think thoroughly and specifically. Don't just say "I hate everything." And make another list about what makes you happy about your job. This exercise can help you clarify your thoughts about your job, good and bad.

　　條列式寫下你不喜歡這份工作的事情。你可能討厭讓你痛苦的那些事情，但這會讓你以為你討厭這份工作的全部。花一點時間仔細且具體的思考。不要只是說「我全部都討厭」。之後，在條列式寫下這份工作中令你快樂的部分。這樣的練習可以讓你釐清你對這份工作的想法，好的及壞的。

2. **Find some values in your current job** 找到這份工作的價值

If you cannot change this boring job, change your attitude and focus on what you can enjoy. This give you the strength to tackle the tough parts. Value your colleagues' professional abilities; your ability to solve the problems of your clients; your coworkers' humor and kindness, etc. Viewing things from other aspects will help you get some control of your job.

　　如果你不能換掉這份無聊的工作，就改變你的態度並專注在你享受的部分吧。這可以帶給你力量去應付工作中困難的部分。賞識同事的專業能力、你能幫客戶解決困難的能力、享受同事的幽默與好心等。從這些角度看事情可以幫助你為這份工作找到一些控制權。

3. **Let go of anger and blame** 放掉憤怒與抱怨

These negative emotions are normal but make you feel less energetic and productive at work. Focus on the positive side, and what you can control. By letting go of the negative thoughts, you will feel better, make progress and move past it.

求職面試心理

了解你的老闆

找到對的工作 職場定位

你與同事

帶人要帶心

升工作態度遷與

會有這些負面情緒是正常的，但會讓你降低工作上的活力及生產力。著重在正向部分以及你能控制的部分。放掉負面的想法，你會感覺更好、更進步並向前看。

4. Looking for more 尋求更多

Find out what educational benefits you can get from your company, so you can develop your professional abilities.

看看公司中有那些職能教育上的好處，這樣你可以精進你的專業能力。

5. Balance your work and life 平衡工作與生活

Make your life more meaningful and satisfying. Your family, relationships, hobbits, and interests can bring you a lot of joy. Try to appreciate that you are having a job to pay the bills and support you to do other meaningful things in your life.

讓生活更有意義及滿足。你的家人、朋友、嗜好與興趣都可以為你帶來許多樂趣。試著去感謝這份工作讓你可以有錢付帳單，並支持你做這些生活中有意義的事情。

6. Make friends at work 在公司中交到朋友

Having one or couple friends at work to chat with can help you to relieve the stress from the job. However, you have to find someone positive rather than negative.

When you are with positive people, your positive views will increase.

在公司中交到一兩個可以聊天的朋友可以幫助你釋放工作上的壓力。但是，你要找到樂觀而非負面的朋友。當與樂觀的人在一起，你的正向想法才會增加。

7. Having a plan for the future 規劃未來

Even you are unable to have any change currently, you can still plan for someday in the future. Keep looking for something you are passionate about, and keep learning new skills and knowledge for new possibilities in the future.

即使你目前無法換工作，你仍然要為未來計畫。繼續找到你有熱情的事物，並為了未來換工作的可能性繼續學習新的技術與知識。

Vocabulary 字彙

★ Sophomore 二年級
★ Dread 懼怕
★ Substantial 大量的
★ Introvert 內向的人
★ Fascinate 著迷
★ Tackle 著手應付

★ Studio 工作室
★ Fulfilling 實現抱負
★ Participating 參加
★ Mingle 往來
★ Miserable 悲慘的

求職面試心理

了解你的老闆

找到對的工作 職場定位

你與同事

帶人要帶心

升工作態度與遷

Section 3-2

Job Satisfaction
工作滿意度

情 境對話 **1**

You probably have heard about the story of the three bricklayers:

你可能聽過三個泥水匠的故事：

While walking down the street, a man saw three bricklayers at work. He walked up to the first bricklayer and asked, "What are you doing?" The first bricklayer replied, "I am laying bricks."

一位男子走在路上看到了三個泥水匠正在工作。他走近第一個泥水匠，問他："你在做甚麼？"泥水匠回答："我在砌磚。"

The man walked up to the second bricklayer and asked, "What are you doing?" The second bricklayer replied, "I am building a wall."

130

男子走向第二個泥水匠，問他：＂你在做甚麼？＂泥水匠回答：＂我在蓋一面牆。＂

The man walked up to the third bricklayer and asked, "What are you doing?" The third bricklayer replied, "I am helping to build the most beautiful museum the world has ever seen, and people will come for miles just to gaze upon its beauty."

男子走向第三個泥水匠，問他：＂你在做甚麼？＂泥水匠回答：＂我在建造世界上最美的博物館，人們會不遠千里而來只為看看它的壯麗。＂

All three bricklayers were doing the exact same thing, working on the exact same project. But which of those bricklayers you think had the greatest satisfaction with his work?

三位泥水匠都是做相同的事，進行相同的工作。但你覺得哪一個泥水匠對他的工作最滿意？

情 境對話 II

Rita and Jack been together for five years since they were undergraduate. After they left the university, Rita had a decent job at a famous international bank. Jack always likes cooking, so he worked at the section of ready-to-eat food of one local supermarket. In the first three months, Rita was extremely excited. She said, "I can't believe they give me the offer! My dream finally came true. I must do my best to prove that they do pick the right person!" So she did work very hard to fit in and be familiar with everything about the bank.

Rita 和 Jack 從大學就在一起了，至今已經五年。他們大學畢業後，Rita 找到一份很好的工作，在一家知名國際性銀行。Jack 一直對烹飪很感興趣，所以他在一家地區超市的熟食部門工作。在最初三個月，Rita 非常興奮。她說：「我不敢相信他們雇用我！我的夢想終於成真了！我一定要盡力來證明他們沒有選錯人。」所以她非常努力去打入並熟悉該銀行的一切事務。

Jack was happy for his girlfriend. However, he had a hard time in the first three months. One of his coworkers who had been working there for six years, so he thought he knew everything, and asked Jack to exactly follow his command. Jack told Rita, "My coworker is so annoying! I really don't know how to get along with him."

Jack 很為他的女友感到高興。但是，在最初三個月他卻不太順利。他的一位同事已經在那工作六年了，所以認為自己甚麼都懂，要求 Jack 一切都要聽他的指令。Jack 告訴 Rita：「我的同事真討厭！我真的不知道該怎麼跟他相處。」

However, one year later, things had changed. Rita always went home from work exhausted and frustrated. She constantly complained about her work to Jack, "You know what? My manager is so unreasonable. How can he ask me to have a business trip next month? And one of my clients had a lot of requests. I spend whole afternoon to deal with her problems!"

然而，一年後事情不一樣了。Rita 回到家總是又累又挫折。她常常向 Jack 抱怨：「你知道嗎？我的經理真的很沒道理。他怎麼可以要求我下個月出差？還有，我有一個客戶要求好多，我花了一整個下午在處理她的問題。」

On the contrary, Jack now enjoyed his work very much. He was happy to prepare all kinds of ready-to-go meals. He was proud of himself that those busy families could also eat healthy because of these prepared meals he made.

相反的，Jack 現在非常享受他的工作。他非常開心可以準備各式各樣的熟食。他很驕傲自己可以讓忙碌的家庭也吃得很健康。

達人剖析

Do you look forward to going to work every morning when you wake up?
Do you have good relationships with your colleagues in the workplace?
Do you think you have been paid fairly?
Do you feel you have been appreciated by your coworkers or manager?

Do you feel your job matches your personality and expertise?
Are you looking for progress in the field you work?

你每天早上醒來後，是否等不及想上班？

你與同事的關係是否良好？

你覺得薪水是否合理？

你覺得同事或老闆是否看重你？

你覺得你的工作與你的人格及專長相符嗎？

你希望自己在這個領域有所進步嗎？

The more you answer positively for these questions, the more satisfaction you get from your job. But what is job satisfaction? Job satisfaction is defined by Locke (1976) as "a pleasurable or positive emotional state resulting from the appraisal of one's job or job experiences".

針對這些問題，你的「是」的答案越多，你對目前的工作滿意度就越高。但，甚麼是工作滿意度？Locke（1976）將其定義為:「你對工作經驗的評價是愉悅或有著正向感受的。」

How can the employees create job satisfaction?
員工如何創造工作滿意度？

Even if you feel dissatisfied about your job currently, it is important to know that it is possible to get job satisfaction!

即便你對現在的工作不滿意，工作滿意度仍然可以獲得！

1. Increasing self-awareness 增加自我覺察

You have to understand yourself, including your personality, your talents, your skills, strengths and weaknesses. The more you know about yourself, the better chances you can maximum your strengths and minimize your weaknesses. By increasing your self-awareness, you will be more realistic, and set appropriate goals and expectations. Then you will have greater chances to achieve job satisfaction.

你要了解自己，包括自己的人格特質、天分、技術、優勢與缺點。你越了解自己，就越有機會將優勢最大化並將缺點最小化。藉由增加自我覺察，你可以更符合現實，設定合理的目標與期待。然後你就越有可能獲得工作滿意度。

2. Looking for more challenges 尋求更多挑戰

Even your job is not at the top of the field, you can still make it challenging by setting the performance standards for yourself; teaching others your skills; asking for new responsibilities; committing your professional development.

即便你的工作不是該領域的佼佼者，你仍然可以讓其充滿挑戰，藉由為自己設定表現目標、教其他人你會的技術、要求新的任務，及致力於專業發展。

求職面試心理

了解你的老闆

找到對的工作 職場定位

你與同事

帶人要帶心

工作態度與升遷

3. Avoiding boredom 避免厭倦

If you feel bored, you lack of interest and enthusiasm, and gradually feel dissatisfied with your job. There are some ways to avoid feeling bored: learning new skills, asking to work a different shift, taking on new tasks, or having a holiday.

當你開始厭倦，你就會興趣缺缺也沒有熱情，漸漸地，就會對工作感到不滿意。有一些方法可以避免厭倦：學習新技術、要求工作輪調、接受新任務、或去度個假。

4. Having positive attitude 有正向的態度

Negative attitude makes you feel unhappy about everything; even a tiny little thing may upset you. Although you can't change your way to view this world or your job overnight, you should have a strong commitment and keep practice.

負向的態度會讓你對每件事情都不滿意，即便是很小的事也會讓你生氣。雖然你無法一夜之間轉變你對這世界與工作的看法，但你應該要堅定改變的信念並持續練習。

5. Telling yourself you have more control and options 告訴自己有更多的控制與選擇

You can only be trapped by yourself. You may tell yourself you can only work this boring job until retired; there is no other company will hire you. But it's not exactly the truth. You need to keep your faith and tell yourself you definitely have choices.

你只會被自己困住，因為你告訴自己你必須做這無聊的工作直到退休，或沒有其他人會僱用你。但這不全是事實。你應該保持信念，並告訴自己你絕對有選擇。

6. Maintaining balanced lifestyle 維持平衡的生活

You need other non-work-related activities to let you get away from work from time to time. You also need support system to share your feeling, good or bad. So having balanced lifestyle helps you work more efficiently.

你三不五時需要其他非工作相關的活動來讓你遠離工作。你也需要支持系統來分享你好的或壞的心情。所以平衡的生活可以幫助你工作更有效率。

7. Finding the benefits of your work
找到這份工作的好處

Focus on what the benefits the job, e.g. paying bills, supporting your hobbies, providing good health insurance, helping you to become an expert, etc.

專注在工作帶來的好處，如支付帳單、讓你可以進行嗜好、提供健康保險、或幫你成為這個領域的專家等。

求職面試心理

了解你的老闆

找到對的工作
職場定位

你與同事

帶人要帶心

工作態度與升遷

Dustin woke up on Monday morning excited about getting to his job. He was the top sales manager in his district, and he really enjoyed making deals and helping the customers who came into the store. Years before rising in the retail ranks and becoming a manager, Dustin worked as a legal assistant. Though he made a decent living in his former field, it was a job that wasn't well-suited for his personality. He also detested having to write and do data entry each day. After experiencing deep disappointment in being a legal assistant, Dustin made the choice to pursue a career in retail sales; it was an excellent decision.

Dustin 週一早上睜開眼，就開始對工作充滿期待。他是該區的最高銷售經理，他非常享受完成交易與幫助來到店裡的顧客。數年前在還沒在零售產業擔任經理時，他是個法務助理。雖然當時他的生活過得很好，但法務助理工作並不適合他的人格特質。他也厭惡每天得文書工作及資料輸入。在對法務助理這份工作感到深深失望後，Dustin 選擇轉換跑道進入零售產業。這是個非常棒的決定。

Working in retail was a much better match for Dustin's gregarious and outgoing personality. He got to be around and meet many different people each day, and he was a very charismatic and effective salesperson. Once he became a manager, Dustin also discovered that his great people-skills made him a good leader. He successfully maintained a balance between meeting the store's sales goals, and ensuring his employees felt valued and knew what was expected from them.

零售業的工作更為適合 Dustin 喜歡人群及外向的個性。他每天都會遇到許多不同的人，他是一個非常有魅力也有效率的銷售員。當上經理後，Dustin 發現他的社交技巧讓他成為一個很棒的領導者。他成功地讓店內銷售成績達到目標，同時也確保員工感受到價值，並知道 Dustin 對他們的期望。

All of this was in the stark opposition to how Dustin felt working as a legal assistant. He often thought that his creativity was stifled, and he would sit bored with the tasks before him day in and day out. As a sales manager, Dustin had plenty of opportunity to flex his creative mind to solve problems and come up with ways to bring in new customers.

這一切都與 Dustin 過去在擔任法務助理的感受完全相反。他一直覺得自己的創造力被扼殺了，而且對每天在辦公桌前面對這些工作相當厭煩。當銷售經理讓 Dustin 有許多機會展現創造力去解決問題及尋找新客源。

Another aspect of his sales management job that contributed to Dustin's satisfaction was the pay and benefits. He earned an average salary as a sales manager, but he also earned large bonuses and commissions. In addition, Dustin's employer offered a great health insurance package that was very

求職面試心理

了解你的老闆

找到對的工作 職場定位

你與同事

帶人要帶心

升工作態度遷與

affordable, which put his mind at ease.

另一個讓 Dustin 對擔任銷售經理一職相當滿意的原因是薪資與福利。擔任銷售經理的薪水一般，但他可以獲得大筆獎金與佣金。此外，Dustin 的老闆也提供很棒且負擔的起的健康保險，讓他放心。

He has enough time and energy to help out more at home and be a better husband and father. He was so thankful that he had made the choice to change careers.

他有時間與精力陪伴家人，扮演好先生與父親的角色。他非常感謝自己做了轉職的決定。

How can the employer increase satisfaction of the staff? 老闆如何幫助員工更具工作滿意度？

1. **Positive work environment 正向的工作環境**

   Good working atmosphere is important. Even the workers have much workload, a pleasant working environment without hassles and disturbance is helpful to reduce stress for the employees.

   好的工作氣氛很重要。即便員工的工作量很大，好的工作環境、沒有爭執與麻煩都可以幫助員工減低壓力。

2. **Big picture 願景**

   Employees want to feel that they are contributing and

making a difference. Help your employees to see the big picture and how they contribute to a functioning whole. This will also empower employees to make decisions and improve employee satisfaction.

員工想要感受到自己可以有所貢獻並帶來改變。讓員工看到公司的願景，且員工可以如何協助。讓員工參與決策也可以讓他們更為增權並更感滿意。

3. Communication constantly 時常溝通

Through communication, the boss or managers can share and explain important information, and the workers can share their thoughts, too. There is then less misunderstanding between top-down.

經由溝通，老闆可以分享與解釋重要的資訊；員工也可以分享他們的想法。上層與基層間的誤會可以大為降低。

4. Fair pay 合理的薪資

Reward is a very vital factor that has a contribution to increasing the employee job satisfaction. The company should reduce the difference between what the employees should earn and what they do earn. If the employees are paid at the market rate, or slightly above, it shows that their skills and hard work are valued.

報酬是增進員工滿意度的重要因素。公司要降低員工所得

求職面試心理

了解你的老闆

找到對的工作 職場定位

你與同事

帶人要帶心

升工作態度遷與

與員工應得之間的落差。若員工的薪資與市場行情差不多甚至更高，這代表他們的技術與辛苦工作有被認可。

5. Feedback 回饋

Telling the workers that they are doing a good job. If they do something wrong, providing some feedback as well to let them know where improvements can be made. Don't just ignore the staff.

告訴員工他們做得很好。若他們有哪裡出錯，也告訴他們，才可以讓員工更為進步。不要忽略員工。

6. Complexity and variety 複雜性與多元性

People feel bored if their job are too easy and become routine. Providing some challenges and variety, the employees will feel more a sense of achievement.

太過簡單與一成不變的工作讓人感到無趣。讓工作多些挑戰與多樣化才可以讓員工感到成就感。

7. Work together 共同合作

Treat the staff as partners rather than slaves. Collaborate with the staff can create more profits for the company. In addition, the staff feels valued and respected.

視員工為夥伴而非奴隸。與員工合作為公司創造更多利潤。如此員工也可以感受到被重視與尊重。

8. Support 支持

The employees want to know their company cares about them. If the company can provide appropriate material support as well as emotional support, their workers experience higher job satisfaction.

員工希望公司是關心他們得。若公司可以提供物質上與精神上的支持，他們也會有較高的工作滿意度。

9. Opportunities for development 成長的機會

Professional trainings help the employees to have the opportunity to learn new skills and develop new capabilities, so they feel they are improving, which increases their professional confidence and fulfillment.

專業訓練可以讓員工有機會學到新的技術及發展專業能力，這樣才會感覺到自己在進步，專業信心與成就感也就增加。

10. Flexibility 彈性

According to a study by Kelliher and Adnerson (2009), employees with flexible hours work harder, and are more satisfied. So providing flexible hours for the employees to do their job is a win-win solution.

根據 Kelliher and Adnerson（2009），能有彈性工時的員工其工作更認真，且對工作滿意度更高。所以提供彈性工時對員工和對老闆而言是雙贏的局面。

求職面試心理

了解你的老闆

找到對的工作 職場定位

你與同事

帶人要帶心

升工作態度遷與

3-3

Job Burnout
工作倦怠

情 境對話

Mrs. Reed finally got off work at 7:15pm; she was supposed to leave the office at 5:00pm, but she had a ton of case files to sort through before morning. As a defense attorney, it was quite common for Mrs. Reed to get home late.

Mrs. Reed 終於在 7:15pm 下班了。她其實五點就應該離開了,但她還要處理一堆明天早上需要的檔案。Mrs. Reed 身為辯護律師,加班已成為常態。

After walking into her house, Mrs. Reed saw her children's shoes spreading over the floor, her husband's papers on the coffee table, and muddy paw prints from the family's dog leading from the front door to the kitchen.

Mrs. Reed 走進家門,看到小孩的鞋到處亂放,先生的報紙放在桌上,從門口到廚房的地上也滿是小狗的泥濘腳印。

"Where is everyone, and what is this mess?", Mrs. Reed called out.

「大家都跑哪裡去了？怎麼會這麼亂？」Mrs. Reed 大叫著。

"I'm on the computer", responded her husband, James. "I think the boys are in the backyard. Or they might be in their room, I'm not sure."

「我在用電腦。」先生 James 回應著。「我想兒子們大概在院子玩。或是在他們的房間，我不確定。」

"Not sure? James, you only have to watch them for an hour before I get home, and you can't even keep track of what they're doing? It's bad enough that you don't help with the cooking, cleaning, or shopping, but you can at least know where your kids are."

「你不確定？James，你只需要在我回來前看住他們一小時，你卻連這都做不到？你沒幫忙煮飯、清理和採買已經夠糟了，你至少可以幫忙看著小孩吧！」

"What's with you, Helen?", asked James.

「Helen 你怎麼了？」James 問道。

"What's with me? It's almost 7:45pm. I've still got to make

求職面試心理

了解你的老闆

找到對的工作
職場定位

你與同事

帶人要帶心

升工作態度遷與

dinner, do laundry, check the boys' homework, and, apparently, mop up these paw prints. Yet you're sitting here checking sports scores on your laptop: that's what's wrong with me."

「我怎麼了？現在快 7:45pm，我還要煮晚餐、洗衣服、看小孩的作業，還有，很明顯的，還要擦掉地上的爪印。你只是坐在那裏上網看著運動比賽的分數。這就是我的問題。」

"You make it sound like I do nothing at all."

「你説得好像我什麼都沒做。」

"You don't do anything. You go teach for a few hours at the university, have coffee with your colleagues, half-watch the kids for an hour, and that's it. I do everything and I'm sick of it!"

「你是什麼都沒做。你每天就在大學教幾小時的書，然後跟同事喝咖啡，愛看不看地照顧孩子一小時，就這樣！我卻要做每件事，我受夠了！」

James was offended, but he saw just how tired and upset his wife looked. As a psychology professor, he was well aware of what was happening.

James 覺得被攻擊了。但他看到太太這麼得疲憊和生氣，身為大學心理系教授，他覺察到有些不對勁。

"You're burnt out, Helen. Run ragged from working all day, then coming home to work all night. I'm so sorry, I haven't been doing my share. Sit down, and I'll go check the boys' homework and make dinner. On second thought, I'll order a pizza."

「Helen，你應該是工作倦怠。整天工作都累壞了，回家還要工作整晚。很抱歉，我沒有分擔我得部分。坐下來，我會檢查兒子們得作業並準備晚餐。不如我們訂披薩吃好了。」

達 人剖析

Mrs. Reed apologized for her outburst. She then sat down to relax, something she hadn't done for quite a long time.

Mrs. Reed 向先生道歉。然後坐下來休息，其實她已經好久沒這麼坐著休息了。

The term burnout was firstly defined by Herbert Freudenberger (1974) as: "the extinction of motivation or incentive, especially where one's devotion to a cause or relationship fails to produce the desired results." Although burnout is not a recognized clinical psychiatric or psychological disorder, it is becoming a common problem in the workplace which causes physical and psychological damage.

工作倦怠這個詞是由 Herbert Freudenberger（1974）首次定義：

「過度使用精力，導致動機或動力上的耗竭而無法在工作上達到理想的結果。這種現象在以創造性或關係性為主的專業中更為明顯。」雖然工作倦怠在臨床上並未被視為精神疾病或心理疾病，但是職場中很常見的問題，傷害著我們的身心。

⠿ Sources of burn out 工作倦怠的來源

1. Work overload 過多的工作量

Having a heavy workload at work is really common, and can be tiring. Workers have to work long hours, and have no time to take a break.

職場上，有沉重的工作量很常見，且這很累人，員工因此得長時間工作無法休息。

2. Value conflict 價值觀衝突

The workers' core personal values are inconsistent with the organizational or boss's values and goals.

員工個人的核心價值與機構或老闆的價值及目標互為衝突。

3. Lack of personal control 缺少掌控感

Workers feel restricted and have limited control about their work.

員工感覺受限，且對自己的工作掌控有限。

4. Lack of recognition 缺少認可

Workers put most of their efforts but get insufficient feedback, awards, or other recognition of accomplishment.

　　員工花了很大的努力卻得到有限的回饋、獎勵或其他形式的認可。

5. Unclear requirement 不清楚的要求

If the job description or requirements are unclear or constantly changing, workers will not be confident and feel it hard to enjoy their work.

　　若對職務上的描述或要求不清楚或一直在變，員工無法有信心，且無法享受工作。

6. Poor job fit 工作屬性不合

Workers' interests and skills do not match the job itself.

　　員工的興趣與技術與工作本身不合。

7. Work without other lives 只有工作沒有別的生活

Workers devote all their time to work and other work-related activities, but lack of activities, like hobbies, exercises or relationships, to relieve stress. Work and life is out of balance.

求職面試心理

了解你的老闆

找到對的工作 職場定位

你與同事

帶人要帶心

升工作態度與

員工奉獻了所有的時間在工作或工作相關的活動上，卻缺少其他活動來減壓，如嗜好、運動或人際關係。工作與生活失去平衡。

8. Lack of supportive resources 缺少支持系統

If there is lack of support from work, backup, and social support, workers could not temporarily offload responsibilities or emotional burdens to others when necessary.

如果缺少工作上的支持、後盾及社會支持，員工在需要的時候無法暫卸責任或宣洩情緒。

Symptoms of burnout 工作倦怠的症狀

If you have one or few of these following symptoms, you may be experiencing job burnout.

如果你有以下一種或數種症狀，你可能有工作倦怠了。

1. Lack of physical energy 缺少活力

You feel tired easily. You just want to take more rest and lack of energy to do anything else. You have constant headache, backache, or other physical complaints.

你容易疲累，只想多休息而沒有活力做任何事。你經常頭痛、背痛或其他身體不適。

2. Emotional breakdown 情緒崩潰

You are moody or have negative feelings most of the time. You become irritable or impatient with others.

你很情緒化且常有負面感受。你對別人變的易怒不耐煩。

3. Poor performance 表現不好

You are less effective and productive at work. And you feel unsatisfied with your achievement.

你工作上較無效率及產出，且對自己的成果不滿意。

4. Criticizing others 批評他人

You become more cynical or critical at work then before. You don't feel satisfied with your boss or your colleagues.

你在工作上變得憤世嫉俗或常予以批評。你對老闆或同事都不滿意。

5. Social withdrawal 社會退縮

You are less interested in interpersonal relationships.

你對人與人的關係變得較不感興趣。

求職面試心理

了解你的老闆

找到對的工作 職場定位

你與同事

帶人要帶心

升工作態度遷與

6. Absence from work more frequently 常請假

You don't want to stay in the work place because it makes you feel uncomfortable. Or you call in sick to work constantly.

你不想待在公司，因為它讓你感到不舒服。或你經常告病請假。

7. Change of sleeping or eating habits 改變睡眠或飲食習慣

You become sleepy or eat too much or too little. You even try to use drugs or alcohol to make you feel better.

你變得睡得多或吃得太多或太少。你甚至嘗試吃藥或喝酒來讓自己感覺好些。

職 場小故事

Upon realizing that she had been doing far too much at work and home for too many years, and almost breaking down because of it, Helen Reed found the courage to do two things: change her routine, and take a much-needed retreat. She left her office an hour early on Friday, and checked into a charming local bed and breakfast. Though she looked forward to spending time alone, catching up on reading mystery novels, and giving herself a pedicure, Helen couldn't help but worry about all of the things she wasn't doing at home. She'd even turned off her cell phone so that clients couldn't interrupt her alone time, which made her a bit anxious. Even so, Helen resisted the urge to turn on her phone or go home early to check on her family; if she was going to avoid getting burned out again, she had to make some changes.

在發現到自己多年來在工作上或家庭上付出太多，幾乎快崩潰後，Helen Reed 找到了力量做兩個改變：改變作息，及讓自己退後些。她週五早一小時離開公司，並住進附近一家很棒的民宿。雖然她對於可以獨處、讀讀懸疑小說及做做足部治療感到興奮，但她忍不住會擔心家裡沒有做的事情。她甚至關掉手機，這樣客戶才不會打斷她的獨處時間，但她還是有些擔心。即便如此，Helen 堅持不打開手機或提早回家。她知道如果她想要避免再次有工作倦怠，她一定要做些改變。

The weekend away did Helen a world of good, and after returning home on Sunday afternoon, she called her family in for a talk. She let them know that she simply couldn't carry the load by herself at home anymore. Helen's husband and two sons would have to do their share; after all, they were a family, and it wasn't fair or healthy for all of the cleaning, shopping, cooking, and maintenance to fall on her. Going forward, she and her husband would alternate weeks when it came to shopping, her 14 year old son would take out the trash and clean the floors twice per week, and her 11 year old son would wash dishes every other day and do a better job of putting his toys away.

求職面試心理

了解你的老闆

找到職場對的工作定位

你與同事

帶人要帶心

升工作態度遷與

153

週末過去了，她感覺很棒。週日下午回到家，她與家人們一同討論。她告訴大家她無法獨自承受這麼多的家事，丈夫和兩個孩子必須共同分擔家事；且他們畢竟是一家人，僅由她一人承擔所有的打掃、採買、煮飯等工作並不公平也不健康。所以她與丈夫輪流負責採買，14歲的兒子負責倒垃圾及一週清潔地板兩次，11歲的兒子則負責每隔一天洗碗及收好自己的玩具。

After returning to work Monday morning, Helen also had a meeting with her staff. She decided to limit the number of clients that her law office would handle in order to prevent working so late into the evening and on weekends. Helen also made the decision to hire a personal assistant and outsource the firm's marketing to a consultant. It was no wonder that Helen had burnt out after handling marketing, administrative tasks, and organizing her case loads on her own. Hiring people to help her would definitely keep the office from getting so hectic.

　　週一早上回到公司，Helen 與員工開會，決定減少個案量，以避免晚上及週末需要加班。Helen 也決定雇用個人助理，並將市場行銷工作外包給專業顧問。之前 Helen 需要負責行銷、行政業務及自己的個案，也難怪會產生工作倦怠。雇用一些人來幫她一定可以讓公司較不那麼忙碌。

Several months after following her new plans, Helen found herself with a sense of calm that she had never experienced before: she had finally achieved balance between work and home.

在 Helen 實行新計畫後的幾個月，她回復冷靜，且終於讓工作與家庭達到平衡了。

達 人提點

Personality traits and burnout 人格特質與工作倦怠

You may feel curious sometimes: why your coworkers are doing fine, but only you feel stressful? E. Scott (2014), the stress management expert, has identified several personality traits which increase the risk for burnout.

有時你也許會好奇，為什麼有些同事沒事，但卻只有你覺得壓力很大？E. Scott（2014），壓力管理專家，找出了幾個容易有工作倦怠風險的人格特質。

1. Perfectionist tendencies 完美主義

Perfectionism can cause excessive stress. People who are perfectionists always beat themselves up if everything is not perfect.

完美主義會帶來極大的壓力。完美主義的人通常會打敗自己，如果事情沒有那麼完美。

求職面試心理

了解你的老闆

找到對的工作 職場定位

你與同事

帶人要帶心

升工作態度與遷

2. Pessimism 悲觀主義

Pessimists tend to see everything negatively. They expect bad things happen and worry all the time, so they cause themselves unnecessary stress in their daily life.

悲觀主義的人會負面解讀每件事情。他們預期不好的事情會發生，且總是在擔心，所以讓自己處在不必要的壓力中。

3. Type A personality A 型人格

In Friedman's book *Type A Behavior (1996),* people with Type A personalities have three major symptoms: (1) free-floating hostility, which can be triggered by even minor incidents; (2) time impatience, which causes irritation and exasperation; and (3) a competitive drive, which causes stress and an achievement-driven mentality. All these three characteristics are risk factors for stress and burnout.

在 Friedman（1996）《A 型人格的行為》一書中，A 型人格主要有三種症狀：(1)處處感到敵意，即便很小的事情也敵意歸因；(2)沒耐心，因此容易生氣；(3)具競爭性，會造成壓力及業績導向的心理狀態。這三種特質都是壓力與工作倦怠的危險因子。

求職面試心理

了解你的老闆

找職場定到對位的工作

你與同事

帶人要帶心

升工作態度遷與

How can you prevent burnout? 要如何預防工作倦怠
Change your work style 改變你的工作模式

1. Make a priority list 列出優先順序

Schedule and prioritize your tasks, so you will be clear about how to do your work.

規劃手邊任務並規劃優先順序，才會對如何進行工作更為清楚。

2. Set boundaries 劃出界線

You have to set boundaries and say no earlier. Don't wait until you are overloaded and cannot take it anymore.

你必須劃出界線並早點說不。不要等到工作量過大無法負荷時。

3. Slow down your pace 減慢步調

Work is not a race. Set your own speed and take your own time.

工作不是比賽。順著自己的步調與時間。

4. Aware your stress 察覺你的壓力

You have to self-aware and recognize that you are in stress situations, then start your coping strategies before it gets worse.

你必須覺察到你處在壓力中，然後再變得更糟前予以因應。

5. **Take breaks during the working day** 在工作中休息一下

Stepping away from your desk for few minutes. Taking a walk, going for a run, or having lunch away from your office would all do you good.

離開你的桌子幾分鐘，去散步、跑步或到辦公室遠一點的地方午餐都不錯。

6. **Let it go** 放手

No matter who gives you a hard time, try to be less angry and let it go.

不論處境多困難，試著少些生氣並放手。

Change your life style 改變你的生活模式

7. **Balance your life and work** 平衡生活與工作

Keep your hobbies and relationships in your life.

保有自己的生活。讓生活中有些嗜好與人際相處。

8. **Do something pleasurable** 做些愉悅的事

Try to do something challenging but interesting. It will give you more energy.

做一些具挑戰性但有趣的事，這會帶給你更多能量。

9. **Go outside and get moving** 走到戶外動一動

Even 5 or 10 minutes of exercise can enhance your mood.

即便五分鐘或十分鐘的運動都可以增進你的心情。

10. **Take short time off** 請假一小段時間

You don't need a long vacation. A short weekend will benefit and refresh you.

不需要很長時間的度假，一小段假期就對你有益。

11. **Away from your digital devices** 遠離電子產品

While you are taking a break, don't check your email or answer phone call from the office. Give yourself a total peace and quiet.

當你休息時，不要檢視電子郵件或接公司電話。給自己全然的平靜。

求職面試心理

了解你的老闆

找到對的工作　職場定位

你與同事

帶人要帶心

升工作態度遷與

3-4

Personality Dimensions and Your Job
人格與工作

情 境對話

As Sam stood in front of the room to make his presentation, he was very nervous. Even though he did the same thing each and every Wednesday afternoon, exactly at 1:30pm, he was still anxious and dreaded the task. However, it was a key part of his job. Sam worked as a publicist for a large, well-known financial firm, and he often had to make presentations, speak to crowds, and even conduct press conferences.

Sam 在台前做著簡報,非常緊張。雖然他每週三下午 1:30pm 都做著同樣的事,他對簡報還是相當焦慮擔心。然而,這就是他主要的工作內容。他是一家知名財務公司的公關人員,所以常常需要做簡報、對很多人演說、甚至舉行記者會。

Sam also didn't enjoy having to call and talk to so many people each day, but it was another duty essential to being a successful publicist. Even worse was the fact that he had to be available after office hours, even on holidays. Whenever the firm had a PR crisis or an important issue made its way to the media, Sam had to be ready to handle it.

他每次都很不喜歡在這麼多人面前說話，但這是成功的公關人員重要的工作之一。更糟的是，他在非上班時間也要能工作，甚至在假日。只要公司有公關上的危機或向透過媒體宣示某些重要事項，Sam 都必須處理。

When he could find a few moments of peace away from the firm's staff, various media directors, and a seemingly endless stream of telephone calls, Sam wondered what it would be like to have a job where he could be more to himself. He was always a bit introverted. Though he was able to adapt and work with and around people constantly, he much preferred to work alone. Sam certainly wished he didn't have to make so many presentations; public speaking wasn't his favorite thing to do, and he never got used to it. The only thing about being a publicist that Sam enjoyed was all of the writing he had to do.

當他離開公司、遠離媒體及無盡的電話，有片刻喘息的時候，他不禁想著有甚麼樣的工作可以更做自己。他其實是個內向的人。雖然他可以適應這份工作並處在人群中，他其實更希望可以獨自工作。Sam 當然希望可以不需要做這麼多簡報；公開演說不是他喜歡的事情，他也一

求職面試心理

了解你的老闆

找到對的工作｜職場定位

你與同事

帶人要帶心

升遷與工作態度

直無法適應這個部分。擔任公關人員唯一讓他喜歡的事是他可以做些文字的工作。

After finishing his presentation and allowing his nerves to settle, Sam got back to his office and found an email from the firm's director. Apparently, Sam would need to prepare for a televised press conference on Friday. Once again, Sam had a knot in his stomach and he was getting anxious.

做完簡報稍微緩和情緒後，Sam 回到公司看到了總監寫來的信。顯然地，他要準備週五電視直播的記者會。Sam 的胃又開始痛了，也開始緊張了。

While he made it through the press conference without making any embarrassing mistakes, Sam had enough of his job. Though he had been a publicist for four years, he had to face the fact that it wasn't a good fit for him; a career change was in order. That weekend, Sam made plans to find a different job that was better suited for his personality.

記者會結束且沒有出甚麼錯，Sam 覺得受夠了。雖然他擔任公關人員已經四年了，他必須要面對一個事實，即他不適合做這份工作，勢必該換工作了。那個週末，Sam 開始找其他適合他個性的工作。

求職面試心理

了解你的老闆

找到對的工作　職場定位

你與同事

帶人要帶心

升工作態度與遷

達 人剖析

Big five personality dimensions 五大人格特質

Psychologists are interested in what differentiates one person from another. Many contemporary psychologists believe that there are five basic dimensions of personality. Each dimension of personality has its specific tendency. They also have different strengths and weakness in the workplace. It is believed that the Big Five traits are predictors of the performance outcomes. Some businesses, organizations, and interviewers assess individuals based on the Big Five personality traits. These five categories are usually described as follows.

心理學家一直對人與人之間的差異感到興趣。許多當代心理學家相信有五大人格特質。每一種人格特質有其獨特的特徵。他們在工作上也各有優缺點。一般相信五大人格特質可以預測工作表現。有一些公司行號或面試官會以五大人格測驗來篩選員工。以下是五大人格特質介紹。

1. Neuroticism 神經質

The neuroticism is not a positive character trait. It relates to one's emotional stability and degree of negative emotions.

神經質並不是正向的人格特質。它與個人的情緒穩定性及負面情緒程度有關。

High score:
People often experience negative emotions like depression, anger, fear, sadness, embarrassment, guilt and disgust. It also indicates that a person is prone to having irrational ideas, being less able to control impulses, and coping poorly with stress.

高分：
在此項得分高者會有負面情緒，如憂鬱、憤怒、害怕、傷心、尷尬、罪惡及厭惡。這種人也會有不理智的想法、較難控制衝動、及對壓力因應能力較差。

Strengths:
Sometimes their critical feedback could be helpful for the team which provides opportunity for improvement.

優勢：
有時他們的批判可以為團隊提供改進的空間。

Weaknesses:
It's difficult to work with them. They cope poorly with stress, and are less creative at work.

缺點：
難以與他們合作。他們因應壓力能力較差，工作上也較缺乏創造力。

Low score:

People with low Neuroticism is indicative of emotional stability, calm, even-tempered, relaxed and able to face stressful situations without becoming upset.

低分：

在神經質一項得分較低者表示情緒穩定、冷靜、較少發脾氣、放鬆及能夠面對壓力情境且不會感到沮喪。

Strengths:

They have more inner strength to face the stressful situations more soundly. They seem to be mature, cool and not likely to overreact in stressful environments.

優勢：

他們有更多內在能量好好面對壓力情境。他們較為成熟、冷靜且對壓力情境不會過度反應。

Weaknesses:

Although they are low in negative emotion, they are not necessarily high on positive emotion.

缺點：

雖然他們的負面情緒較少，不代表他們會有較多的正向情緒。

求職面試心理

了解你的老闆

找到對的工作 職場定位

你與同事

帶人要帶心

升工作態度與遷

2. Extraversion 外向性

It indicates the person's level of sociability and enthusiasm.

這表示個人社交及熱情的程度。

High score:

The traits include sociability, assertiveness, activity and talkativeness. Extraverts are energetic, optimistic and characterized by positive feelings and experiences.

高分：

高分的人很會社交、有魄力、主動及能言善道。他們充滿精力、樂觀及充滿正面感受與經驗。

Strengths:

The extroverts are excellent motivators and work well in teams. They are good at networking events such as seminars and trade shows. Since they are very sociable, they can bring a lot of unexpected opportunities for the company.

優勢：

外向的人很會激勵他人，在團隊中也能合作的很好。他們善於在社交場合交際，如研討會或展示會。他們很會社交，因此常會為公司帶來意想不到的機會。

Weaknesses:

Sometimes extraverts are insensitive about others feelings. And they feel bored easily.

缺點：

　　有是外向的人對他人的感受較為遲鈍，且容易感到無聊。

Low score:

Introverts have lower energy level and are quiet, low-key, deliberate, and less involved in the social world.

低分：

　　內向者精力較低，安靜、低調、謹慎、且較少參與社交場合。

Strengths:

They are not sociable, but they will be quite pleasant when approached. They can choose the jobs that they work alone, such as analysts or engineers.

優勢：

　　他們雖然不善社交，但與他們相處通常是令人舒服的。他們會選擇獨立工作，如分析師或工程師。

Weaknesses:

They are withdrawn, and they usually shy away from conflict. It is hard for others to get to know them.

求職面試心理

了解你的老闆

找到對的工作　職場定位

你與同事

帶人要帶心

升工作態度遷與

缺點：

　　他們較退縮，且會避開衝突。他人較難進入他們的心。

3. **Openness to experience** 經驗開放性

Openness is a general appreciation for art, emotion, adventure, unusual ideas, imagination, curiosity, and variety of experience.

　　指對藝術、情緒、冒險、新奇的點子、想像、好奇與各種經驗感興趣的程度。

High score:

Open individuals are curious about both inner and outer worlds, and their lives are experientially richer. They tend to be unconventional and willing to question authority.

高分：

　　開放的人對內在與外在世界都很好奇。他們的生命經驗豐富，不想依循慣例，也質疑權力。

Strengths:

They have capability to analyze matters differently. They are usually rated higher on their performance and creativity at work.

優勢：

　　他們有能力以不同角度分析事情，他們的工作表現與創造力也都比較好。

Weaknesses:

They easily feel bored about routine.

缺點：

　　他們很容易對一成不變的事感到無聊。

Low score:

Closed people prefer the plain, straightforward, and obvious. They prefer familiarity over novelty; they are conservative and resistant to change.

低分：

　　保守的人較喜歡樸實、直接且清楚的事物。他們喜歡熟悉的事物而非新奇的事物。他們較為保守且不願改變。

Strengths:

Closedly stick to the routine; complete mono tasks really well. They are down-to-earth and practical.

優勢：

　　保守的人可以堅守常規，並對單一任務表現得很好。他們也很務實。

求職面試心理

了解你的老闆

找到對的工作　職場定位

你與同事

帶人要帶心

升工作態度與遷與

Weaknesses:

They do not like change, and don't try to be explorative in finding new ways to solve a particular problem.

缺點：

他們不喜歡改變，且不願對某一問題探索新的解決方法。

4. Agreeableness 友善性

It relates to the level of friendliness and kindness.

與友善及仁慈程度有關。

High score:

An agreeable person is fundamentally altruistic, sympathetic to others and eager to help them, and in return believes that others will be equally helpful.

高分：

友善的人是利他、同情他人、並喜歡幫助人，他們也相信別人同樣是樂善好施。

Strengths:

They are quite adaptable and can work together with others. They resolve issues by creating win-win situation by their flexible attitude. So agreeable individuals may lead to success in occupations where teamwork and customer service are relevant.

優勢：

他們很能適應並與他人合作。他們解決問題時會因為他們的彈性而達到雙贏局面。所以友善的人在團隊工作或幫助客戶等相關工作上容易成功。

Weakness:

They try to please everyone and tend to take criticism personally. They are less able to make tough or absolute objective decisions.

缺點：

他們一直試著討好他人，並容易將批評放在心上。他們較無法做出困難或全然客觀的決定。

Low score:

They are detached, suspicious, unfriendly, uncooperative and very analytical. They place self-interest above getting along with others.

低分：

他們離群索居、多疑、不友善、不擅合作且善分析。他們最重視自己的利益。

Strengths:

The low scorer can be hard headed and practical. They do well in careers where they have to treat people like objects, for example, prosecution lawyers.

求職面試心理

了解你的老闆

找到對的工作 職場定位

你與同事

帶人要帶心

升工作態度與

優勢：

他們理性務實。他們在把人單純視為物體的工作上表現得很好，如訴訟律師等。

Weaknesses:

They are less likely to help others sacrificing their personal interests.

缺點：

他們不會為了幫助他人而犧牲自己的權益。

5. Conscientiousness 謹慎性

Conscientiousness refers to the level of organization and self control.

謹慎性是指組織事物與自我控制的能力。

High score:

The conscientious person is purposeful, organized, hardworking, persistent, dependability and determined.

高分：

謹慎的人較有目的性、善組織、努力、堅持、可信賴及有決心。

Strengths:

People can rely on them. When solving problem, they

try to be risk-free.

優點：

　　他們值得信賴。當處理問題時，會試著做到零風險。

Weaknesses:

They have workaholic behavior. Chaos can give them mental stress.

缺點：

　　他們通常是工作狂。混亂的狀況會帶給他們心理壓力。

Low score:

Low scorers are sometimes careless, unreliable, lack of ambition, and failure to stay within the lines.

低分：

　　低分者通常漫不經心、不可靠、沒有野心、且不依循規則。

Strengths:

They focus on the present, and learn things by doing.

優勢：

　　他們重視當下，且從經驗中學習。

求職面試心理

了解你的老闆

找到對的工作　職場定位

你與同事

帶人要帶心

升工作態度與遷與

Weaknesses:

They lack of long-term planning, and are less likely to work in a mannered way, which could be leading to stressful chaos.

缺點：

　　缺少長期計畫，且做事毫無章法，常會造成一團混亂與壓力。

Vocabulary 字彙

★ Publicist 公關人員
★ Press Conferences 記者會
★ Neuroticism 神經質
★ Extraversion 外向性
★ Introversion 內向性
★ Deliberate 謹慎的
★ Openness to experience 經驗開放性
★ Unconventional 不依慣例的
★ Conservative 保守的
★ Agreeableness 友善性
★ Altruistic 利他的
★ Hard headed 理性
★ Prosecution 訴訟
★ Conscientiousness 謹慎性

Chapter 4

You and Your Co-Workers

你與同事

Get Along with Your Co-Workers
與同事好好相處

Janice was a librarian who was well-liked by everyone at the university. She was not only a smart worker who did her job well, but also very friendly and helpful. Unlike her co-worker, Mrs. Davis, the head librarian, Janice had an approachable demeanor, and students won't feel awkward whenever they are in need of assistance.

　　Janice 是個大學圖書館員，大家都很喜歡她。她不只是一個聰明的員工，總是把工作做得很好；她還很友善且樂於助人。她的同事，也是圖書館主任 Davis 女士卻非如此。Janice 讓人容易親近，且當學生有問題需要協助時，她不會讓對方感到尷尬。

Because she was so personable, Janice's boss let her be in charge of planning the library's student events and annual Book Fairs. He knew that Janice is capable of planning fun, enjoyable, and educational events that will be beneficial for the library.

因為她有這麼的好風度，Janice 的老闆讓她負責規劃學生活動及年度書展。他知道 Janice 可以規劃出有趣、好玩、具教育性且對圖書館有利的活動。

During one of the the most recent events, a lecture series held at the library, Janice not only impressed the library's dean, but also the university's president and many educational leaders in the community. They all felt that her warmth and kindness would help to make the event be conducted very pleasant.

在最近一次的活動中，圖書館舉辦一系列的演講活動，Janice 的策畫讓大家驚豔，包括了圖書館館長、大學校長及其他社區中的教育單位主管。他們都覺得 Janice 的溫暖與友善讓活動進行地非常愉快。

One morning, a new librarian named Kathy started to work at the university. While Mrs. Davis was a bit cold and unwelcomed to Kathy, and expected her to immediately know all of the library's procedures and rules, Janice was much more friendly. Janice showed Kathy the ins and outs of the library, told her all about the university's library rules, and she even gave her suggestions on good places to eat lunch around the campus. Just like the way she treated with others, Janice approached Kathy actively, and Kathy started to feel more at ease with Janice. Janice and Kathy quickly developed a friendship.

求職面試心理

了解你的老闆

找到對的工作 職場定位

你與同事

帶人要帶心

升工作態度遷與

一天早上，圖書館的新館員 Kathy 開始上班。Davis 女士對她有點冷漠且不歡迎，且希望她馬上可以了解圖書館所有的流程與規則。Janice 卻很友善，帶著 Kathy 參觀圖書館，告訴她大學圖書館的規則，甚至告訴她在校園中有那些地方可以吃午餐。跟對其他新人一樣，Janice 主動接近 Kathy，Kathy 感到放鬆也開始喜歡 Janice。她們兩個很快成為朋友。

Shortly after, the dean in charge of the library, Mr. Bond, noticed attributes Janice possesses, kind and friendly, which are favorable for her, which not only had more students began to visit the library since Janice started working there four years ago, but had also secured a great amount of book and donations fund for the events she planned. He was also very impressed with how Janice immediately helped Kathy get acquainted with her new job. Mr. Bond felt that Janice would make an excellent leader, and so he decided to promote her to the assistant head librarian.

不久後，圖書館館長 Mr. Bond 先生注意到 Janice 的正向態度及友善的特質都是她所具備的有利條件。自她開始在這裡工作的四年來，有更多學生會來圖書館；且由於她規劃的這些活動，讓圖書館的贈書與捐款都有著落。Janice 對 Kathy 即時的幫助，讓 Kathy 能盡快熟悉新工作，這點也讓館長印象深刻。館長認為 Janice 會是一位很棒的領導者，所以他決定讓 Janice 升職成為圖書館助理主任。

After being promoted to her new position, Janice felt even more satisfied from her job, and she made sure that she will keep the same friendly demeanor that will help her earn her promotion.

被升職後，Janice 對自己的工作更感滿意，且她保證一定會保持友善的態度，就是因為這樣的態度讓她在工作發展上更為順利。

達 人剖析

Why getting along with your co-workers is important?
為什麼與同事好好相處很重要？

You spend at least 8 hours at your workplace with your co-workers every day. Sometimes you spend more time with the people at work than you do with those you live. If you cannot get along with them, how can you survive during this long period?

你每天至少花八小時在公司與同事在一起。有時候你甚至花比家人更多的時間在工作上。如果你不能與同事好好相處，要如何度過這麼長的時間？

Here are some benefits if you want to get along well with your co-workers.

以下是與同事好好相處的好處。

求職面試心理

了解你的老闆

找到職場對的定工作位

你與同事

帶人要帶心

升工作態度遷與

1. Job satisfaction 工作滿意度

According to the American Psychological Association, social factors play a stronger role in job satisfaction than the nature of the work. Even you have a dream job, your co-workers constantly drive you crazy, you may not feel happy at the workplace. On the contrary, if you have several good team members, you may feel excited and expect to go to the office every morning to work together with your team.

　　根據美國心理協會的解釋，社交因素比工作本身更會影響對工作的滿意度。即使你有一份夢想中的工作，但若你的同事常讓你抓狂，你也不會感到快樂的。相反的，如果你有一些很好的夥伴，你每天早上都會很興奮地期待去上班與他們一起打拼。

2. Productivity 生產力

You cannot work independently. You need others to work together to achieve your goals and objectives. You and your co-workers can work as a team to share workload and responsibility, and to make tough decisions together. With the assistance of your co-workers, you will be more productive and efficient.

　　你不可能獨自工作。你需要和其他人一起工作以達成你的目標。你及同事可以是個團隊，一起分擔工作量與責任，並一起做一些艱難的決策。有了同事的幫忙，你會更有生產力與效率。

3. Social support 社會支持

Your investment in others will likely pay off down the road with a network of people who want to support and develop your career. You may never know when you'll need an extra dose of support from the people you see the most. If you have closer relationships with colleagues you spend all day, they are drawn closer to you and care about you. Your friends at work can give you emotional support, while you are under pressure. They will cover your work if you are away for some reasons. Even if you eventually leave the job, good relationships there will ensure that you have solid references and a strong professional network in the future.

你對他人的付出，總有一天會回饋到你自己身上，他們會支持你。並協助你職涯上的發展。你永遠不知道何時會需要同事的支持；若能與你每天相處的同事有較緊密的關係，他們也會與你較為親近並關心你。你工作上的朋友可以在你面臨壓力時給你情緒上的支持；在你需要離開崗位時代理你的工作。就算你最後離職了，與同事間好的關係會確保你能要到一封不錯的推薦信，以未來工作路上的專業連結。

4. Less stress 壓力較小

Multiple studies find that interpersonal relationships play

求職面試心理

了解你的老闆

找到對的工作　職場定位

你與同事

帶人要帶心

升工作態度遷與

a big role in overall stress levels. Getting along well with your fellow workers means there are less conflicts between you and your co-workers. Consequently, you experience less stress from your relationships with the peers.

　　許多研究都發現，人際關係對整體壓力程度有很深的影響。與同事相處融洽意味著你們之間的衝突較低，因此，你就較不會有與同事相處上的壓力。

5. Health benefits 健康助益

According to the research published by the American Psychological Association (2011), people who have a good peer support system at work may live longer than people who don't have such a support system, especially when the co-workers were helpful in solving problems and that they were friendly. On the contrary, if you have a bad relationship with your co-workers, it may increase your stress level which may damage your physical and mental health. So, if you want to live longer and healthier, get along with your co-workers!

　　根據美國心理協會的研究（2011），在職場上有好的同儕支持可以比沒有支持系統的人活得更久，尤其是同事樂意協助解決問題及很友善。相反的，如果與同事的關係不好，會增加壓力程度進而影響生理與心理健康。所以如果你想活得久一點、健康一點，就與同事好好相處吧！

求職面試心理

了解你的老闆

找到對的工作 職場定位

你與同事

帶人要帶心

升工作態度遷與

職 場小故事

Since Kathy started working at the university library and got acquaintance with Janice they soon became good friends. After enjoying lunch together many times while at work, Janice and Kathy started going on outings and doing activities together outside of work as well. Janice had invited Kathy and her husband over to her house for dinner several times, while Kathy invited Janice to her book club and out for Sunday brunch. They even made play dates with each other's children, and liked taking them to the park together.

Kathy 自從來大學圖書館工作遇見 Janice 後，很快地就成為好朋友。他們經常一起午餐，Janice 與 Kathy 也開始在工作之餘一起出遊或參與活動。Janice 邀請 Kathy 及她的先生到家中一起吃飯幾次了，Kathy 也邀請 Janice 參加她的閱讀俱樂部活動及一起在週日享用早午餐。他們也訂了雙方小孩的共同遊戲日，也喜歡一起帶小孩一起到公園玩。

Not only did they do things together, Kathy and Janice confided in each other. Whenever either of them was having problems, an issue, or simply wanted to talk about personal matters or work, they felt comfortable directly calling on each other. They would also share advice, wisdom, recipes, and stories from their lives. On one occasion, Kathy was having problems with a task she was given at work, and so she asked Janice for her advice. Kathy admitted that if it hadn't for their friendship, she probably would not have asked for any help. She was a bit embarrassed for her inability of completing the task, but Kathy knew Janice won't criticize her since they were true friends.

她們不僅常再一起，Kathy 和 Janice 也會向彼此吐露秘密。當其中以一方遇到困難、有困擾、或只是想要聊聊人際問題或工作，她們會直接打電話給對方。她們會分享建議、智慧、食譜、及人生故事。有一次，Kathy 在工作上遇到問題，她就詢問 Janice 的意見。Kathy 承認如果不是她們的友誼，她可能就不會尋求幫助。因為她對於自己無法完成任務有些不好意思，但她知道 Janice 不會因此批評她，因為她們的好交情。

At work, Janice started calling upon Kathy's assistance with planning the library's events, something that she has never done before. Janice's never encountered any colleague who would be so kind and wholehearted to make activities successful. However, Janice knew that Kathy had a personality very similar to her own, and she felt confident that Kathy would be able to help her hold bigger, better events than she had ever organized during her time at the library. She was right. Not only were Janice's events even more successful, planning the affairs were much less stressful with Kathy helping things around.

在工作上，Janice 開始會請 Kathy 協助規劃圖書館活動，Janice 也從未請求別人協助過。Janice 從來沒有碰過哪個同事也可以這麼親切與全心投入讓活動完美成功。但是，Janice 知道 Kathy 有著與自己類似的特質，所以她相信 Kathy 願意協助她，讓活動比以前自己辦理時更盛大更好。她是對的。有了 Kathy 的協助，Janice 的活動不但更為成功，規劃過程的壓力也減輕許多。

One afternoon, Janice and Kathy's boss, Mr. Bond, found Kathy discussing a ceremony being held in Janice's honor. Since they seemed to be such good friends, and since they were co-workers, Mr. Bond thought it was appropriate that Kathy be the one to present Janice with her award. Kathy was happy to do so. When the day of the ceremony came, Janice was overwhelmed to with joy after hearing Kathy's speech in her honor.

　　一天下午，Janice 與 Kathy 的老闆 Mr. Bond 找 Kathy 商量為 Janice 舉辦的授予典禮。由於她們是好朋友好同事，Mr. Bond 覺得找 Kathy 出席這個授予典禮很適合。Kathy 很高興地接受了。典禮當天，當 Janice 聽到 Kathy 對自己光榮事蹟的演說感到相當欣喜。

達 人提點

How to be a good co-worker yourself
如何讓自己成為好同事

An individual cannot work alone. Everyone needs people around. It is wise to share a warm relation with your co-workers because you will never know when you need

求職面試心理

了解你的老闆

找到職場對的定工位作

你與同事

帶人要帶心

升工作態度遷與

them. You may need them any time, but they would come to your help only when you are nice to them. Below is a list of suggestions to help you become a better co-worker.

每個人不能獨自工作，需要有人共同打拼。與同事建立溫暖的關係是明智之舉，因為你不會知道何時會需要旁人的協助。你可能隨時需要他人，但也只有你對他們好，他們才會幫助你。以下是一些讓你成為更好的同事之建議。

1. Listen 傾聽

Sometimes just being a good listener can go a long way. Listen to your co-workers' suggestions or thoughts and value their opinions. Even you don't agree with them, keep it to yourself.

有時候，單純做一個傾聽者就足以維持長久的關係。聽聽他們的建議或想法，並重視他們的意見。就算你不同意，也不需要說出口。

2. Respect 尊重

According to Maslow's Hierarchy of Needs, the fourth level is the need for appreciation and respect. Every individual needs to feel respected. So do not make racial, ethnic and sexist statements or jokes. And never talk or joke about sexual orientation, religion, or politics. Respect your co-worker's personal choices or values.

求職面試心理

了解你的老闆

找到對的工作 職場定位

你與同事

帶人要帶心

升工作態度遷與

根據馬斯洛的需求理論，第四層需求就是得到肯定與尊重。每個人都需要被尊重。所以不要針對種族、族群或性偏見發表高論或嘲笑。也不要談論性取向、宗教或政治立場。尊重你同事個人的選擇與價值觀。

3. Be aware 覺察

Your need to be aware of personal and professional boundaries. Do not do things that may annoy your co-workers. Respect others' privacy and personal boundaries. Stay professional and behave appropriately during working hours.

你要能覺察到個人或專業上的界線。不要做一些蠢事惹惱同事。尊重他們的隱私與個人界線。也保持專業，並在工作時有適宜的行為。

4. Help out 助人

Lend a hand whenever you can. Bring a sandwich for someone who cannot leave the office, or take over responsibilities if someone is sick or goes on vacation. Remember you are doing so because you want to, not because you want other's appreciation.

若可以，就幫人一把吧！幫留守公司的同事帶個三明治；同事生病或休假時分擔一些責任。記住，你會這麼做是因為你想要這麼做，而不是期待他人的感謝。

5. Avoid the blame game 避免怪罪他人

Everyone makes mistakes. If you have made a mistake, admit it and correct it as soon as possible because honesty is always the best policy. Don't blame others.

每個人都會犯錯。若犯了錯，就盡快承認並改正，因為誠實是最好的政策。不要怪罪他人。

6. Don't be the gossip 不要八卦

Gossip can damage your relationship with your peers. The best rule is to keep anything you heard to yourself and walk away. Do not spread any untrue information.

八卦會傷害你與同事間的關係。最好的原則是把所有聽說的事留在心裡並走開，不要傳播不實的消息。

7. Communicate effectively 有效的溝通

Don't hide behind the computer and use email as the only tool for communication. Have face-to-face communications can avoid misunderstandings and improve relationships.

不要只是藏在電腦後面，並只用電子郵件作為溝通的工具。面對面的溝通可以避免誤會並增進感情。

8. Hedgehog's dilemma 刺蝟效應

A group of hedgehogs all seek to become close to one another in order to share heat during cold winter. They must remain apart; however, as they cannot avoid hurting one another with their sharp spines. At last, after many turns of huddling and dispersing, they discovered that they would be best off by remaining at a little distance from one another. So keep a safe distance from your co-workers will help you have better relationships with them.

一群刺蝟在寒冷的冬天想要互相取暖而彼此靠近，但他們必須遠離彼此以避免被對方刺傷。經過幾次的嘗試，分分合合，牠們終於找到可以彼此取暖卻又不會互相傷害的方式，即保持一點距離。所以與同事保持安全距離可以讓你們有更好的關係。

ocabulary 字彙

★ Demeanor 舉止行為

★ Asset 資產、有價值的物品

★ Recipe 食譜

★ Reference 推薦信

★ Personable 風度好的、優雅的

★ Confide 吐露秘密

★ Ceremony 儀式

★ Hedgehog's dilemma 刺蝟效應

求職面試心理

了解你的老闆

找到對的工作 職場定位

你與同事

帶人要帶心

升工作態度遷與

Section 4-2

Deal with Difficult Co-workers
應付難搞的同事

情 境對話

Thomas was on his lunch break at work when he saw Lisa approaching the employee break room. Lisa was known at work for being overly talkative, gossiping, and prying into her co-workers' personal business.

Thomas 正在員工休息室午餐，Lisa 走進來。Lisa 是大家公認的大嘴巴，很愛八卦及打探同事的私事。

Lisa
"Thomas, have you heard that Benjamin and his wife was getting divorced? The whole office is talking about it, especially because she works in human resources."

「Thomas，你有聽說 Benjamin 要跟太太離婚的事嗎？整個辦公室都在討論這件事，尤其是因為他太太在人事部門工作。」

Thomas

"No, I haven't heard about that, Lisa. But it's really not any of my concern, or anyone else's."

「沒有，沒聽說。但這不關我的事，也不關任何人的事。」

Lisa

"Oh it is. They work here! But that's not all", gasped Lisa. "There's also the rumor about the new guy they're hiring to replace Mr. Stewart after he retires. But the truth about that is, Mr. Stewart's wife is making him retire, and I guess she got tired of him constantly being away from the house all these years. Anyhow, word is this new guy got fired from his old job for stealing! And now he's supposed to come here, and I hope he doesn't take anything from me."

「當然有關係啊！因為他們也在這裡工作。」Lisa 繼續八卦著。「有一個傳言，公司聘的新人來取代退休的 Mr. Stewart。但事實上是Mr. Stewart 的太太要求他退休的，我猜因為她覺得這些年來先生投入工作而沒有顧家。無論如何，聽說新來的人前一份工作被老闆炒魷魚，因為他偷竊。現在他要來這裡工作，我希望他不會拿走我任何東西。」

Thomas

"I see."

「這樣喔。」

求職面試心理

了解你的老闆

找到職場定位對的工作

你與同事

帶人要帶心

升工作態度遷與

Lisa "There was a guy that used to steal at my old job, but he never got fired. Actually, it wasn't company money he stole, he took people's lunches and snacks from the fridge. It was horrible! I went in to get my yogurt one day, and sure enough, it was gone. You just can't trust anyone these days, you know what I mean?"

「我之前的公司,有一個人也是常偷東西,卻沒有被炒魷魚。事實上,他偷的不是公司的錢,而是偷冰箱中的午餐跟點心。這好可怕!有一天我要吃優格時,卻發現優格不見了。這年頭你不能相信任何人,你明白我的意思嗎?」

Thomas "I've got to get back to work, Lisa. Enjoy your lunch." Thomas was eagerly leaving the break room.

「Lisa,我要回去工作了,好好享用你的午餐。」Thomas 急忙地離開休息室。

Lisa "Bye, Thomas. See you later."

「Thomas 待會見。」

Thomas didn't enjoy listening to Lisa's gossiping and constant talking, but he didn't want to be rude. He wondered if she knew how annoying her talkative habits and gossiping were, yet he didn't want to hurt her feelings by confronting her. Thomas decided that he would continue to avoid Lisa when he could and ignore much of what she said, and if it ever got to be too uncomfortable for him to handle on his own, he would then have a talk with their boss.

Thomas 並不喜歡聽 Lisa 到處八卦及說個不停，但他也不想太沒禮貌。他在想，她是否知道自己多話及八卦有多討人厭，但卻又不想直接跟她說，這樣會讓她難過。Thomas 決定他要繼續避開 Lisa，不要聽她說甚麼；如果事情太超過而無法應付時，這時 Thomas 就會告訴老闆。

達 人剖析

The most annoying co-workers 最討人厭的同事

In the book *Reply All...And Other Ways to Tank Your Career*, Richie Frieman illustrates the most annoying types of co-workers who will make you feel terrible at the workplace.

在《全部回覆…及其他增進工作的方法》一書中，作者 Richie Frieman 提到了最討人厭的同事類型，會讓你在公司上感到深惡痛絕！

1. Mr. / Ms. Know-It-All.

This type of co-workers will tell you how right and knowledgeable they are, or they can do things much better than you.

Strategy:

If you are communicating something with this co-worker, prepare your supporting documents to defend your viewpoints. If you know you are right, and everyone else does too, don't argue with them. You just nod and smile at the boasts.

萬事通先生／小姐

這種同事總是告訴你他們總是對的,他們知識淵博,且他們可以比你做得更好。

策略:

如果你需要與萬事通先生／小姐討論事情,先準備好能支持你觀點的文件資料。如果你知道自己是對的,且每個人也都知道你是對的,那麼就不要與對方爭論;你只需要在一旁對他們的自吹自擂微笑點頭即可。

2. The Cubicle Invader.

The invaders just pop into your personal space and start chatting. They interrupt your routine and work all the time.

Strategy:

Make your area unwelcoming by putting stuff on the available space or on the extra chair, so they can't stay long. Or, pretend you are making an important phone call and are unavailable. Finally, just escape away by going to the toilet or heading for a meeting.

入侵者

入侵者常闖入你的私領域然後開始大聊特聊。他們總是打斷了你的程序與工作。

策略：

讓你的領域看起來不歡迎他人進來，放一些東西在一些空間或空椅子上，這樣他們就無法久待。或假裝你在打個重要電話而無法聊天。最後，你可以假裝上廁所或趕著去開會而逃跑。

3. The Office Bully.

They mistreat you by annoying language or bad behaviors.

Strategy:

Do not show you are offended. Just walk away unaffected, or hit back with a smart remark.

辦公室霸凌

他們以不堪的語言或不當的行為對你。

策略：

不要表現出你被羞辱到了。要看起來毫無受影響地走開，或聰明的回擊。

求職面試心理

了解你的老闆

找到對的工作 職場定位

你與同事

帶人要帶心

升工作態度遷與

4. The Gossip.

The gossips know everyone' business in the office, and they like to share all the information with others.

Strategy:

Avoid to be together with them. If you sense a wave of gossip is coming on, step away by using work-related excuses.

八卦者

八卦的人知道辦公室每個人的事情,且他們喜歡把這些事情與他人分享。

策略:

避免與他們走在一起。如果他們要開始說八卦,用一些工作上的藉口走開。

5. The Loud Talker.

They talk loudly that makes you hard to concentrate on your work.

Strategy:

Explain to them that they are speaking way too loud and becoming an embarrassment.

大聲公

他們總是說話大聲,讓你無法專心工作。

策略：

告訴他們說話太大聲了，這樣會影響他人。

6. The Stud.

They think they are charming. Their behaviors or jokes sometimes lead to sexual harassment.

Strategy:

Don't laugh along with everyone toward their jokes or behaviors. This will encourage their behaviors. Ignore their inappropriate behaviors or statements. If they keep doing so, tell them seriously that you don't feel comfortable.

萬人迷

他們認為自己很有魅力。他們的行為或玩笑常常已經造成性騷擾。

策略：

當他們有一些笑話或行為時，不要跟著別人一起笑，這會助長他們這些行為。忽略這些不適當的行為或言論。若他們繼續這麼做，嚴肅地告訴他們你感到不舒服。

7. The Best Friend.

He or she will follow you to anyway, and ask you if you need anything. S/he invites you to have lunch or even dinner together.

求職面試心理

了解你的老闆

找到對的工作 職場定位

你與同事

帶人要帶心

升工作態度與遷

Strategy:

Reject him/her in a good manner. If s/he keeps doing so and starts to affect you, alert the boss.

最好的朋友

他／她總是跟著你，並問你需要甚麼。他們也會邀請你一起午餐或晚餐。

策略：

有禮貌地拒絕他們。若他們繼續纏著你也影響到你，就告訴老闆。

8. Mr. / Ms. Do-You-Know-Who-I-Am?

They have the genetic luck to fall into the company because their parents or grandparents did something cool. They think they have a certain level of authority and are so arrogant.

Strategy:

You don't have to be the best friend of this type of coworkers, but you can find a common interest and form a connection with them. This may loosen them up to become somewhat tolerable.

你知道我是誰嗎？

他們只是基因上比較幸運，因為他們的父母或祖父母做了些好事，所以他們才能進來這家公司。他們覺得自己屬於某種權力階層，所以也顯得傲慢。

策略：

　　你不需要與這類型的同事成為最好的朋友，但你可以找到一些相同的話題來拉近距離。這樣可以讓他們較為放鬆神經而讓人較可以忍受。

職 場小故事

Wilbert enjoyed working at the architecture firm, as he felt he was a very talented designer. However, Wilbert did not enjoy being around two of his co-workers, Daniel and Steve. Both were very brash, aggressive, and a bit too competitive. Wilbert usually tried to stay out of their way, but eventually, he had to learn how to be assertive with them.

　　Wilbert 很喜歡在建築事務所工作，因為他覺得自己是個有天分的設計師。但 Wilbert 不喜歡兩位同事，Daniel 和 Steve。他們兩人無禮又具攻擊性，且過於愛競爭。Wilbert 通常會試著離他們遠一點，但他終究還是必須學習如何在他們面前表現得更為自信。

Daniel "Every single one of these designs is basic, boring, and just not up to par for this firm, Wilbert."
「Wilbert，所有你的設計都太過基本、無趣且達不到事務所的基本水準。」

求職面試心理

了解你的老闆

找到職場對的定工位作

你與同事

帶人要帶心

升工作態度遷與

Steve

"I agree. Although, it's not that you can produce much better, Daniel. Still, this is terrible work and you really ought to do it again, Wilbert."

「我也這麼覺得。雖然 Daniel 你的作品也好不到哪裡去。不過，Wilbert 你的作品太糟糕，應該要重做一次。」

Wilbert

"What's wrong with it?"

「哪裡有問題啊？」

Daniel

"Aside from being too much like the house series that we planned two years ago, you haven't added any flair to it. Where's the creativity, the ingenuity?"

「你的設計與兩年前我們設計一系列的建案太相似，你也沒有加上任何的新元素。你的創造力與獨創性呢？」

Steve

"Actually, my problem with it is it's just a bad work. I haven't seen a design this terrible since I finished my freshman year of college. Get it together, Wilbert, or you'll find yourself out of here just like the guy who was fired before you."

「我覺得這根本就是個爛作品。我自從大一起就沒有看過這麼爛的設計。Wilbert 你振作一點，不然你的下場就會跟之前被解聘的人一樣！」

Steve and Daniel then laughed, and Wilbert stood there wondering whether he is a good architect. Just then, Wilbert's boss, the owner of the architecture firm, Mr. Easton, walked into his office and complimented his design work. Wilbert realized that he shouldn't let others second guess his abilities, much less be so disrespectful towards him. Wilbert then walked back into Steve's office.

Steve 和 Daniel 笑著走開，留下 Wilbert 站在那思考自己到底是不是個好建築師。就在此時，Wilbert 的老闆及這間事務所的負責人 Easton 先生走進他的辦公室，並稱讚 Wilbert 的設計很好。 Wilbert 這才了解到，他不應該讓別人質疑自己的能力並這麼不尊重他。Wilbert 走回 Steve 的辦公室。

Steve
"You haven't thrown those designs away yet, Wilbert? I guess you'll have to learn the hard way, once Easton sees this mess you've made."
「Wilbert 你還沒把設計案交出去吧？一旦 Easton 先生看到你的爛東西，你就慘了！」

Wilbert
"Actually, he has seen it, and he thinks it's great. In fact, he said my designs will be the featured plans in the firm's newest house series. I don't mind constructive criticism, but please keep your taunts and disrespect out of it. We're not in competition. We're supposed to be working together."

求職面試心理

了解你的老闆

找到對的工作 職場定位

你與同事

帶人要帶心

升工作態度遷與

「事實上，他看過了，且覺得不錯。而且他還說我的設計可以成為本事務所最新建案系列的特色設計。我不介意具有建設性的批評，但請不要嘲笑不屑。我們不是競爭者，我們應該要一起合作。」

Steve reluctantly apologized. Wilbert then felt a surge of confidence and knew he'd made the right decision by being assertive.

Steve 不情願地道歉。Wilbert 更加有信心，且知道他決定要自我肯定是對的。

達 人提點

🐾 Deal with conflict 處理衝突

Conflict is inevitable in the office. You and your co-worker do not actually share the same thoughts, feelings, interests, or values. Conflict always increases negative emotions like anger, frustration, and worry. If you just ignore or avoid conflict and leave it unsolved, it will damage your mental health. In addition, unsolved conflicts can lead to serious problems for the company because individuals just engage in internal conflict and has less time and energy to spend on working. Eventually, it can cause expensive mistakes and business failures. So try the following tips to resolve the conflicts in your workplace.

在公司，衝突的發生是無可避免的。你和同事不可能有同樣的想法、感受、興趣或價值。衝突會讓負面情緒升高，如生氣、挫折與擔心。如果你只是忽略或避免衝突，讓衝突懸而未決，就會對心理健康造成影響。此外，未解決的衝突會對公司造成更嚴重的問題，因為員工都忙於處理內部衝突，而花在工作上的時間與精力就減少了。最後可能需要為這個錯誤付出昂貴的代價，甚至導致公司的失敗。所以試著下面的技巧來解決職場上的衝突。

1. Communication 溝通

The best way to identify the nature of conflict is to communicate with your co-worker to clarify his or her motivation which leads to conflicts. Get correct and first-hand information about their opinions and thoughts by. Do not assume anything in advance. Additionally, when you communication are communicating with each other, use true language rather than emotion. Avoid using the words "I feel…", because that is an emotional statement with less proof and facts. Only discuss about the issues that really matter.

找出衝突原因最好的方式就是與同事溝通以澄清造成衝突的動機。藉由溝通獲得第一手且最正確的資訊，才能了解同事的看法與想法。不要事先假設任何事。此外，當你們彼此溝通時，使用真正的語言而非情緒性發言。避免使用「我覺得…」的語句，因為這是情緒性的言論，缺乏證據與事實。只需要針對真正相關的議題進行討論。

2. Stay calm 保持冷靜

Do not communicate with emotions. Using aggressive, non-stop verbal attacks is not an efficient way to communicate. You are doing so because you want to silence the opponents. However, you miss the chance to understand the situation and opinion on the issue from your co-worker's perspective.

不要帶著情緒溝通。使用具攻擊性、連珠炮式的方式打擊對方並非有效的溝通方式。你會這麼做是因為你要對方閉嘴。但是，你會因此錯失了了解狀況與同事對問題想法的機會。

3. Do not expect conflict 不要期待衝突

Don't raise your anger and build your hostility every time you pass or talk to this person. Just interact with him/her objectively.

不要每一次看到對方就讓自己的憤怒與敵意飆升。只需要客觀地對方互動即可。

4. Do not take it personally 不要覺得是針對自己

Your co-worker may have different feelings about the project, but don't personalize or internalize these disagreement.

針對這個專案，你的同事可能與你有不一樣的看法，但不要覺得對方是在針對自己，或是將這樣的不同意見放在心上。

5. **Compromise** 妥協

Compromise can keep things going smoothly to a win-win situation. Both parties know there is no perfect solution, but by using the strategy of compromise, the result cannot be optimal but acceptable.

妥協可以讓事情更為順利，達到雙贏的局面。其實雙方都知道沒有最完美的解決方法，但透過妥協，結果雖不完美但能接受。

6. **Respond unreasonable attacks smartly** 聰明回應不合理的攻擊

If your co-worker does make personal attacks on you, the best solution is to walk away from the situation. Although you can fight back, there is a highly possibility that this will result in a long-term negative consequence. Documenting the facts and reporting to the manager or HR are a better option of response. If the conflict continues or gets worse, both of you can find a third party to intervene and mediate the conflict. To do so can bring the conflict to an objective level which is fairer for everyone.

如果同事真的有針對性的攻擊，最好的方式是離開現場。雖然你也可以反擊，但很有可能會拉長戰線而有負面的結果。記錄下這些狀況然後向主管或人資處報告是更好的回應方式。如果衝突更加惡化，你們雙方可以找第三者來介入與協調，如此可以讓衝突較為客觀且較為公平。

Office Politics
辦公室政治

情 境對話

Teddy worked at a call center and had formed a friendship with some of his co-workers who were also in their mid-20s. Teddy's clique wasn't the only one at his job; there was also a group of female workers in their early 20s. Most of the young, female workers were a part of this clique, except for one woman named Ginny. She preferred to stay to herself, and eventually Teddy noticed she became a target for the clique as he overheard the other young women talking.

Teddy 在客服中心工作。在公司裡,他有幾個也是二十來歲的朋友。Teddy 所屬的小團體並不是公司中的唯一一個團體;另外還有一個二十出頭女性所屬的小團體。幾乎所有的年輕女性都加入那個團體,除了一個女生 Ginny。Ginny 喜歡獨來獨往,但最後 Teddy 發現她成了其他女生攻擊的目標,因為他聽到了其他女生在談論她。

"She can work as hard as she wants to, it's not like she's ever going to be the boss of anyone", said Tiffany, a member of the clique.

「她可以盡情的工作，反正她不可能會成為我們的主管。」小團體成員 Tiffany 說著。

"I know. She comes in here, acting high and mighty, always trying to show off. We don't have an employee of the month award here. I don't get what she's trying to do", said Eva, another member of the group.

「對阿。她來到這裡，姿態總是很高，也好像甚麼都會，只想炫耀。我們這裡又沒有每月最佳員工制度，我真不懂她想幹麻。」另一位成員 Eva 說著。

"I asked her yesterday if she wanted to come to lunch with us, and you know what she said? She said she was going to do some reading instead! The nerve. I don't even want to sit next to her anymore", said Tiffany.

「昨天我問她要不要跟我們一起吃午餐，你知道她說甚麼嗎？她竟然說她要去看一些書！天啊！我再也不想坐在她旁邊了。」Tiffany 說著。

Teddy usually didn't like to intervene in other people's business, but he felt like it was unreasonable and unfair for the members of the clique to take such a stance against Ginny.

求職面試心理

了解你的老闆

找到職場定對的工作位

你與同事

帶人要帶心

升工作態度遷與

Teddy 通常不會管別人的閒事，但這次他覺得這群小團體成員對 Ginny 的攻擊不合理也不公平。

"I overheard, since you're so loud, and it doesn't seem like you really have a good reason to be rude to her", said Teddy.

「我不小心聽到了，因為妳們説得太大聲。但我覺得你們真的不能這樣對 Ginny。」Teddy 説。

"She doesn't want to be around us, she shows off around here, that's a problem. She really needs to go. We should run her off", said Eva, to the agreement of the other women in the clique.

「她又不想跟我們在一起，但卻又一直在我們前面炫耀，這就是問題所在。她應該離開，我們要讓她離開。」Eva 説著，其他成員也贊成。

"That's ridiculous. She doesn't have to hang around with you. And since when she shous off the work? You don't have to like her or even hang around with her, but it'd be wrong to try and get her to leave her job."

「這太可笑了！她不需要跟你們混在一起。且她甚麼時候真的有炫耀工作了？妳不需要喜歡她或跟她混再一起，但要她離職太過分了！」

"Teddy is right", said Patty, the manager of the call center who had also overheard the women's conversation. "It would be against company's, policy to do so, and I would never allow an employee of mine to be bullied."

「Teddy 說得對。」Patty 說著。Patty 是公司的經理，也側耳聽到這群女生的對話。「妳們這麼做違反了公司政策，我絕對不允許我的員工被霸凌。」

達人剖析

❀ Cliques at the workplace 職場中的小團體

In Maslow's hierarchy of needs, belongingness is part of one of his major needs that motivates human behavior. The need for love and belonging lies at the center of the pyramid as part of the social needs. Maslow believed that the need for belonging, including such things as love, acceptance, and belonging helped people experience companionship.

在馬斯洛的需求理論中，歸屬感是其中一項影響人類行為的主要需求之一。愛與歸屬是社會需求金字塔的中間層。馬斯洛相信歸屬感的需求，包括愛、接受與歸屬都可以讓人們感受到他人的陪伴。

Our need to belong is what drives us to seek out stable, long-lasting relationships with other people. It also

求職面試心理

了解你的老闆

找到對的工作 職場定位

你與同事

帶人要帶心

升工作態度遷與

motivates us to participate in social activities, such as clubs, sports teams, or religious groups. This can explain why there are small groups or cliques in the workplace. Cliques usually are small and closed groups. People join a clique to feel a sense of security, identity, and belonging.

對歸屬感的需求讓我們尋求與他人穩定、長期的關係；也讓我們參加一些社交活動，如社團、運動團體或宗教團體。這說明了為什麼公司也會有小團體的存在。小團體通常規模不大且是不開放的。人們加入小團體可以感受到安全感、認同與歸屬。

Facts about cliques 一些關於小團體的事實

However, joining a clique is not as wonderful as you imagine. Although there are healthy cliques at the workplace, toxic cliques commonly exist. According to a CareerBuilder (careerbuilder.com) survey, there are some negative facts about the cliques at the workplace:

然而，加入小團體並不如你想像中的美好。雖然職場中也會有好的小團體，但不好的小團體也時有所見。根據 CareerBuilder（careerbuilder.com）所做的調查，發現一些小團體不好的面向：

△ *43% of respondents said their office is populated by cliques.*

43%受訪者表示公司中小團體是很盛行的。

△ *17% of respondents who considered themselves to be introverts were members of an exclusive clique at work, which was ten percent less compared to 27% of extroverts.*

17%受訪者認為自己是內向的人且有加入排外的小團體；但27%受訪者認為自己是外向的人且有加入小團體。內向者比外向者少了 10 個百分比。

△ *11% of respondents said they feel intimidated by cliques.*

11%的人表示會受到小團體中威脅。

△ *20% said they have done something they are really not interested in, or didn't want to do just to fit in with a clique.*

20%的人表示他們會在小團體中做一些自己不感興趣、或完全不想做的事，只是為了融入團體。

△ *21% watched a certain TV show or movie in order to discuss it with co-workers the next day.*

21%的人會看特定的電視節目或電影，只是為了隔天可以跟同事討論。

求職面試心理

了解你的老闆

找到對的工作 職場定位

你與同事

帶人要帶心

升工作態度遷與

△ **19% made fun of someone else or pretended not to like them.**

19%的人表示會取笑他人或假裝不喜歡某些人。

△ **17% pretended to like certain food.**

17%的受訪者表示會假裝喜歡某些食物。

△ **9% took smoke breaks to fit in with an office clique.**

9%的人會在休息時間抽菸只為了融入辦公室小團體。

△ **15% said they hide their political affiliation.**

15%的受訪者表示他們會隱瞞自己的政治取向。

△ **10% didn't reveal personal hobbies.**

10%的人表示不會表現出個人嗜好。

△ **9% kept their religious affiliations and beliefs a secret to avoid being excluded.**

9%表示會隱藏自己的宗教與信仰以避免被排斥。

△ **13% of workers said the presence of office cliques has**

had a negative impact on their career advancement.

13%的受訪者表示職場中的小團體對工作升遷有負向影響。

Being a member of the 'in group' can provide short-term satisfaction, advantageous connections, and feeling of belongings; however, you're spending so much time with one group that you miss out on what other co-workers have to offer. You also have to hide who you really are or what you really care about in order to fit in the particular group. Eventually, you will feel confused about your actual values, interests, or even your identity, and traits. Cliques can be counterproductive for you and your career.

成為團體中的一員可能可以帶來短暫的滿意、有助益的連結與歸屬的感受；然而，你花太多時間在某一個團體上，卻錯過了其他同事可能可以給予你的東西。為了融入某一團體，你也必須隱藏真正的自己與真正關心的事。最後，你會對自己真正的價值觀、興趣、甚至認同與個性等都感到困惑。小團體會對你及你的職涯都產生不良後果。

職 場小故事

Barbara had managed a group of workers at a company for about four months when she first noticed the cliques her employees had formed. These groups of people who banded together at work were not only noticeable, but at times, they

求職面試心理

了解你的老闆

找到職場對的工作定位

你與同事

帶人要帶心

升工作態度遷與

were also problematic. Thus far, she hadn't noticed the cliques affecting the workplace atmosphere to the point that it was uncomfortable, but she had noticed that gossip was being spread around much faster than before the cliques had started.

Barbara 在一家公司擔任主管，管理一群員工。四個月前，她發現員工形成了小團體。每個團體的成員聚在一起不僅很醒目，有時也帶來一些問題。到目前為止，她還沒有發現小團體有影響到公司氣氛到令人不適的地步，但她也發現自從小團體形成後，八卦傳遞的速度比以前快得多。

She observed what appeared to be four distinct cliques at the company: the young, female workers, who liked to eat lunch together and chat between calls; the young, male workers who would take each other's calls when someone from the group got bored or tired, and who liked to hang out together after work; the experienced workers, both male and female, who looked down on the younger employees and thought they had bad work ethic; and the more timid employees, who kept to themselves and didn't like to shake things up much at all.

她觀察到公司中有四個不同的小團體：年輕女性團體，她們會一起吃午餐，也會用電話聊天；年輕男性團體，若其中有人對工作厭煩或厭倦，他們會幫忙接電話，也喜歡在下班後混在一起；資深員工團體，有男有女，他們對年輕員工很感冒，覺得他們的工作倫理非常差；及一群害羞的員工也會聚在一起，不會掀起甚麼波瀾。

Barbara didn't see much trouble coming from the timid clique, but it was a problem that the young male workers were passing their job duties to each other. Not only did that make it more difficult to track the quality of the tasks, but it was against the company's rules. Barbara was glad that as long as these particular workers felt comfortable, trusted each other enough, and are able to take on each other's work, it was just unacceptable.

這群害羞的員工聚在一起的小團體沒有甚麼大問題，但 Barbara 覺得年輕男性團體常常把工作丟給別人做是個問題。因為這不僅難以追蹤工作的品質，也違反公司規定。雖然 Barbara 覺得只要他們願意且相信彼此，能在工作上互相幫忙是好事，但這樣的做法就是不能接受。

She also ran into a few issues with the young female clique Sometimes they talked too loud on occasion, and since they often came back from lunch late due to all of their gossiping. Surprisingly, Barbara also had issues with the clique of middle aged workers, as they would often disparage the younger employees and shame them about their bad work habits.

年輕女性團體也有一些問題。因為她們有時說話太大聲，以及他們常常出去吃午餐到很晚才回來，因為一直在聊八卦。令人驚訝的是，Barbara 也覺得中年團體有問題，因為他們常常輕視年輕員工，對他們不佳的工作習慣不以為然。

Though Barbara didn't see there is a need to formally make a

求職面試心理

了解你的老闆

找到職場對的定工位作

你與同事

帶人要帶心

升工遷作與態度

rule of disbanding the cliques, she did feel it was a good idea to remind them all that no matter what friendships or associations they had formed, everyone had to work together as a team in order to meet the company's goals.

雖然 Barbara 不覺得有需要正式訂定規則解散這些小團體，但她覺得有需要提醒員工，不論他們的交情如何，或有形成甚麼樣的默契，但每個人都應該要像個團隊般共同合作，以達到公司目標。

達 人提點

How to deal with cliques at work
如何處理職場中的小團體

Whether you're the insider or the outsider of a cliques at the office, they can make your life tough. But there are ways to cope:

無論你是否為辦公室小團體內部一員，小團體都有可能讓你的日子難過。但下面有一些因應之道：

1. Know yourself 了解自己

Ask yourself some self-discovery questions about your values, interests, and beliefs. Also ask yourself that you want to be part of a group because you need to feel accepted or because you actually share similar values? Has the member of the group changed into something you don't like? How does the clique influence the way people think about you? Does this make you feel good or bad?

問自己一些問題，來探索自己的價值觀、興趣與信仰。也問問自己想要成為小團體的一員是為了感受到接納，還是因為你們有同樣的價值觀？小團體成員是否變成你不喜歡的樣子？小團體是否影響他人對你的看法？這些讓你感覺好還是不好？

2. Control your mind 控制你的心

Don't go along with what you don't believe is right, and say no if you know something is going wrong - even if others are doing it. You are the only one responsible for how you act. Good and professional co-workers will respect your mind, your rights, and your independent choices.

連你都不相信是對的事，就不要隨之起舞。若你覺得有事情不對勁，就勇敢的說不，即便他人也這麼做。只有你能對你自己的行為負責。好的且專業的同事會尊重你的想法、你的權利及你個人的選擇。

3. Observe your co-workers 觀察同事

Do not immediately join a single group. Spend some time with every co-worker and get to know different people. Observe how people act, who have a positive attitude toward job, who have a good performance, and

求職面試心理

了解你的老闆

找到對的工作 職場定位

你與同事

帶人要帶心

升工作態度與遷

who you personally can relate to. You can do so by having lunch with different co-workers every day. In the meantime, treat everyone friendly and politely.

不要馬上加入任何一個團體。花一些時間與每個同事相處，了解他們。觀察他們的行為，誰對工作有正向的態度，誰的表現好，誰是你個人想要多接觸的。你可以藉由每天與不同的同事午餐來認識他們，並對每個人友善且有禮。

4. Assess the necessity 評估必須性

You have to determine whether joining a clique will be positive or negative to your career. Do you really need the benefits of this particular clique? Can you still do your job well if you do not join in any group? You can also describe the cliques to your friends or family to ask their opinions. The outsiders may have a clearer view toward the cliques in the office. Moreover, carefully assess every signal sent by the cliques, which can give you some clues about the reality of the cliques.

你要評估加入小團體對你的事業會有正向還是負向的影響。你真的需要加入這個小團體以獲得某些好處？如果你加入任何團體，還可以好好地工作嗎？你也可以跟朋友或家人討論你對這些小團體的看法。局外人可能會有更清楚的看法。此外，也仔細評估小團體中每個成員散發出的訊息，這些可能可以給你一些關於這個小團體真實狀況的線索。

5. Don't gossip 不要八卦

If you decide not to join any clique, keep a safe distance and do not engage in gossip with their members. Because this is their trap and try to get you to join. If you are their target and gossip about you, having no reaction is the best reaction.

　　如果你決定不要加入任何團體，就與他們保持安全距離，不要與任何的成員八卦。因為這可能是他們的伎倆，想要讓你加入。如果你是他們八卦的對象，最好的反應就是不要有反應。

6. Find your own friends 找到自己的朋友

Having friends outside of work allows you to take a breath from office politics. More real friends also release the pressure resulted from the office clique. Taking social activities with your own friends makes you feel less isolated if you are not member of any clique, because you don't solely rely on co-workers for your social life.

　　工作外的朋友可以讓你對公司內的政治喘口氣。有越多真正的朋友可以幫助你減緩辦公室小團體帶來的壓力。與真正的朋友一同活動讓你不會覺得被孤立，因為就算你沒有加入任何小團體，你也不需要單靠同事來做為你社交活動的唯一方式。

求職面試心理

了解你的老闆

找到職場定位對的工作

你與同事

帶人要帶心

升工作態度遷與

4-4

Understand Competitive Co-Workers

了解好競爭的同事

David and Joe are both assistant sales managers at the same company who often compete against each other at their job. They try to see who can get the most work hours, make the most sales, and get the most praise from their boss. While a small amount of friendly competition can be a good thing for work productivity, too much can cause problems in the workplace.

David 和 Joe 都是同一家公司的助理銷售經理，所以經常互相比較。他們比著誰工作時間最長、誰業績最好、及誰得到老闆最多的讚賞。雖然正向的競爭對工作是有建設性的助益，但若競爭太過激烈則會為職場帶來困擾。

"I was the employee of the month two months in a row, and I'm going to make sure that doesn't change", boasted Joe to David.

「我連續兩個月獲得是本月最佳員工，且我保證我不會讓它改變！」Joe 對 David 吹噓著。

"It will change this week, since I made more sales than you, earned more commissions, and I was the one who secured the big new account on Tuesday. Once I'm the new employee of the month. I'll make sure that you will never have the title again!" replied David.

「這個禮拜我就會改變這個局面，因為我業績比你好，比你賺更多的傭金，且本週二是我拉了新的大戶。一旦我成為本月最佳員工，我保證你永遠不會再得到這個頭銜！」David 回應著。

"We've still got one day left before the boss announces the new employee of the month, and I still have some tricks up my sleeve. There are several big accounts that you don't know about yet, and I've already made $12,000 in sales just this morning. On top of that, I've heard that I'm the one Mr. Wilson is going to pick for the new sales manager spot that's open", said Joe.

「離老闆宣布本月最佳員工還有一天的時間，我還有一些絕招。有一些大客戶是你不知道的，且今天早上我剛推銷了$12,000。最重要的是，我聽說 Wilson 先生將選我擔任新的銷售經理。」Joe 說著。

求職面試心理

了解你的老闆

找到對的工作 職場定位

你與同事

帶人要帶心

升遷 工作態度與

"You may have sold $12,000 this morning, but you're wrong about that sales manager position. I'm going into Mr. Wilson's office after lunch to sign my new contract, and tomorrow morning at the sales meeting, he will announce me as the new sales manager. I'm guessing he'll probably announce that I'm the new employee of the month, too", smirked David.

「也許你今天早上賣了$12,000，但你對銷售經理一職的推論錯了。今天下午我會到 Wilson 先生的辦公室簽我新的合約；明天早上的銷售會議，他就會宣布我是新的銷售經理。我想他可能也會順便宣布我是本月的最佳員工。」David 做作的笑著。

"That can't be possible!", Joe exclaimed.

「不可能！」Joe 生氣大叫著！

"It is possible. Come Monday morning. You'll have to answer to me." said David.

「當然可能！禮拜一早上，你就必須對我負責」David 説著。

After being promoted to sales manager, David began to treat Joe unfairly, and Joe became very uncomfortable in the workplace. His productivity declined, as did David's, since he became so focused on finding ways to get at Joe. After they both realized how their too-competitive attitudes affected their job performance, both men decided that working against each other only hurt their company in the long run.

David 於升職為銷售經理後，他開始對 Joe 做出一些不公平的事。Joe 開始對公司感到不舒服。Joe 的生產力降低，但 David 也是，因為 David 一直想著要如何整 Joe。最後，他們倆個終於發現互相競爭的態度影響著他們的表現，也認為互相對付只會對公司帶來長期傷害。

達 人剖析

Why are some people competitive?
為什麼有些同事愛競爭？

A bit of competition can be a good thing. Healthy competition among staff can increase motivation and productivity. However, if the workplace is infused with unhealthy competition, the tension increases, and the situation becomes stressful which can stand in the way of collaboration.

輕微的競爭是好事，同事之間正向的競爭可以更具激勵性與生產力。但是，若職場上充斥著負向的競爭，會增加緊張氣氛，也更具壓力，而影響了同事之間的合作關係。

A competitive individual can provoke feelings of irritation, anxiety, or inadequacy that gradually makes you question yourself about your ability and performance. Have you ever wondered why some people are more competitive than others? *Melanie Greenberg, "a clinical psychologist, suggested several factors that contribute to competitive" individuals.*

　競爭者同事會激起不理性、焦慮或不恰當的情緒感受，漸漸地讓你也開始懷疑自己的能力與表現。你曾經想過為什麼有些人比較具競爭性？臨床心理師 *Melanie Greenberg* 提出了幾個較易造成競爭特質的因素。

1. Fragile self-esteem 脆弱的自尊

Some people have unstable or fragile self-esteem. Their self-esteem is based on their accomplishment or other people's impression about them. They feel great even superior to others when they are doing well. On the contrary, they feel shame and self-doubt if they encounter difficulties. They feel anxious easily, and caution about social status and performance. So they keep comparing themselves to others in order to make sure they catch up with others.

　有些人的自尊不穩定或較為脆弱。他們的自尊來自於他人的讚美或印象。當他們表現得好，他們覺得自己很好，甚至覺得自己優於他人。相反的，若他們遭遇困難，他們覺得羞愧並自我懷疑。他們很容易焦慮，並對社會地位與表現非常敏感。所以他們不斷地比較，以確保自己有趕上他人。

2. Scarce resources model 資源不足

Some competitive individuals may have had critical parents who played favorites or were unavailable to their emotional needs. So they have a survival mentality, try to obtain more attention from the parents, or more resources for themselves. Consequently, they are more controlling, jealous, and competitive. They try every method to obtain attention and recognition from others, especially their superiors.

有些好競爭者可能有個很愛批評的父母，也很偏心，或是無法回應他們的情緒需求。所以他們具有生存的本能，會想要獲取父母的注意，或得到更多的資源。因此，他們更具控制性、善妒也好競爭。他們會不擇手段以獲取他人，尤其是長官的注意與認可。

3. Narcissism and sociopathy 自戀狂與反社會特質

Some people are self-centered, seeing others as a reflection or extension of themselves. They think others admire their accomplishment, or threaten their own success. They use or manipulate other individuals as an object to meet their own needs or increase their resources. If they are also sociopathic, they manipulate, deceive, intimidate or mistreat others in order to neutralize or eliminate, threats and competition. They tend to seek out higher positions to have more power

求職面試心理

了解你的老闆

找到對的工作｜職場定位

你與同事

帶人要帶心

升工作態度與遷與

and control over others. This type of competitor is the most difficult to deal with.

有些人較為自我中心，認為他人是自己的反射或延伸。他們覺得他人欣賞自己的成就，或威脅到自己的成功。他們視其他人為物體，會利用或操弄他人以滿足自己的需求或成為自己的資源。如果他們具有反社會的特質，他們就會以操弄、欺騙、恐嚇或不當對待他人來消除他人的威脅與競爭。他們會尋求更高的職位以獲得更多的權力及控制他人的機會。這類型的競爭者最難以應付。

4. Effects of competitive environments 競爭的環境使然

Every work environment has some degree of competition. Healthy competition can motivate staff to do their best job. However, if the environment is nasty, sneaky, and cruel, there are negative influences on the employees, including health problems and worse performance. Moreover, the current recession has resulted in fewer job opportunities and employment uncertainty that increase competitive pressures. The employees have to try harder to protect their position and territory.

每個職場上都有某些程度的競爭。良性競爭可以激勵員工做得更好。然而，如果職場環境令人難受、不光明正大又殘酷，對員工就會有負面的影響，包括健康問題及更差的表現。此外，當今經濟衰退造成工作機會減少及就業不穩定，這讓競爭的壓力更甚。員工必須更努力以保住飯碗及自己的勢力。

求職面試心理

了解你的老闆

找到對的工作 職場定位

你與同事

帶人要帶心

升工作態度遷與

職 場小故事

Roy and Sean worked in a small design studio. The chief designer, who was also the founder of the studio, assigned a new project to Roy and Sean.

Roy 與 Sean 是一家小型設計工作室的員工。首席設計師，也是這家工作室的創辦者，交給他們共同負責一項新的設計案。

Roy was a firm believer of the "survival of the fittest". He saw competitions everywhere and thought there would be only one winner. Sean, on the contrary, enjoyed collaborative work because he liked the idea of having a partner working towards the same goal. He looks forward to the interactions with Roy.

Roy 堅信著適者生存的法則。他總是想競爭，也認為只會有一位贏家。相反的，Sean 享受合作的感覺，因為他喜歡有人一起為共同目標打拼。所以他很期待著與 Roy 一同工作。

Sean quickly set up a time to meet with Roy to start the project. Roy was also prepared. At the meeting, Sean asked Roy if he had any thought on the project. Roy took the opportunity to lead the discussion. He explained how the project work should be divided between the two of them. Although it didn't seem so obvious to Sean, Roy managed to separate the work into two types, which were those easily recognized by, and, those invisible to their boss. He gave seemingly justifiable reasons of why he should take the noticeable ones, and Sean should be in charge of the invisible parts. He told Sean that he was really good with details. So, Roy himself would construct the initial ideas and start off with a little bit of prototypical designs. And Sean was told to go on executing Roy's ideas and finishing the designs that Roy had started. Without a doubt, Sean just followed along what Roy had planned. Sean also had a little admiration for Roy because he seemed to get it all figured out at such an early stage. He thought Roy was really clever and well-organized.

Sean 很快的訂了與 Roy 討論案子的時間。Roy 也有所準備。在會議中，Sean 問了 Roy 對案子有甚麼想法，Roy 也抓住機會主導討論，說明案子要怎麼分工。雖然 Sean 沒有發覺，但 Roy 想將把工作分成兩部分，一部分是容易受到老闆矚目的部分，另一部分則不容易被人注視。他也給了很好的藉口，說明為什麼他自己做了受矚目的部分，而 Sean 非常擅長細節，所以去處理那些較不易被發覺的部分。Roy 自己開始建構靈感，並著手設計，然後要 Sean 繼續著 Roy 的想法並完成設計。無庸置疑，Sean 便照著 Roy 的設計，Sean 甚至對 Roy 有些欽佩，因為他可以在這麼早的階段就做好全面性的規劃。Sean 認為 Roy 很聰明也很有計畫。

The project was eventually completed. They went with Roy's arrangements, and both of them, in fact, felt happy about the collaboration process. On the day before they could present the finished work to their boss, Sean asked if the presentation

求職面試心理

了解你的老闆

找職場定對的工作到位

你與同事

帶人要帶心

升工作態度遷與

could be postponed for another day because he needed to visit a family member staying in a hospital tomorrow. Roy told him not to worry. He suggested that it might not be a good idea to change the time, since the boss had already squeezed this into his busy schedule.

案子照著 Roy 的規畫完成了，且事實上，兩個人對合作的進度感到滿意。在要向老闆簡報成品的前一天，Sean 在想是否可以改天再做簡報，因為他明天需要去醫院探視家人。Roy 告訴 Sean 不用擔心。Roy 覺得改期不太好，因為老闆已經為了簡報特別抽出時間了。

On the day of the presentation, Roy explained to the boss why Sean couldn't attend and carried on presenting their work on his own. The boss liked what she saw and asked Roy a few times during the presentation about who thought of the ideas on certain parts of the work. Roy assertively answered that he was the key person behind most of the ideas without mentioning Sean.

簡報當天，Roy 向老闆說明 Sean 因故無法參加，所以他要自己做簡報。老闆喜歡他們的作品，並問了 Roy 幾次作品中的某些部份是誰的靈感。Roy 很確定的回答多數是自己的靈感，而沒有提及 Sean 的功勞。

Five Most Competitive Co-workers
五種最愛競爭的同事

Robert Half International, the world's first and largest specialized staffing firm, illustrates five most common workplace competitors in the workplace, and suggestions about how to deal with them when working together:

Robert Half International 是全球第一家也是最大家的人力公司，提出五種職場常見的最愛競爭同事類型，並建議如何與他們共事。

1. The Speeder 搶快者

This type of co-worker wants to win every race at all costs. The speeders are always the first persons who respond any request from the boss. They use all kinds of means to complete the request, including resources of other co-workers. The top priority in their mind is to do as quickly as they can to win the game; however, the quality of their work is not promised.

Strategy:

The tendency of the speeder is to race through projects, which means he or she doesn't pay enough time and effort on the assignments. So when working with a

Speeder, make sure you have a chance to review the work to ensure the tasks you work together are always error-free.

這類型的同事不計代價地想要贏得每場比賽。搶快者總是第一個回應老闆需求的人。他們用盡各種方法來完成任務，包括利用別的同事的資源。在他們心中，最重要的事是做得越快越好，以贏得比賽；但工作的品質則無法保證。

策略：

搶快者的特質是視每個任務為比賽，這表示他們為了搶快而不會花足夠的時間與努力在任務上。所以與搶快者同事共事時，要確定你有看過工作內容，以確保你們一起合作的任務沒有出錯。

2. The Loner 獨行俠

The loner prefers to work alone, he or she does not like to work together with other colleagues. And this type of co-worker is reluctant to share the ideas with others and always guards these treasured ideas as secrets.

Strategy:

Give the loner some space when working with him/her. However, you still have to check the update from time to time and make sure the progress is on schedule.

求職面試心理

了解你的老闆

找到職場對的工作定位

你與同事

帶人要帶心

升工作態度與遷與

獨行俠喜歡獨自工作，他／她不喜歡與同事合作。這類型的人也不願意分享自己的想法，總是對自己的想法視為祕密珍寶。

策略：

與獨行俠合作時，給他們一些空間。但是，你還是要時常確認進度，確保有照著時間表進行。

3. The Superstar 耀眼明星

This type of co-worker is willing to accept any challenge, especially the toughest or highest-profile projects. The boss usually considers the superstar is an efficient assistant, and recognizes this spirit. What the superstar wants is the visibility from others.

Strategy:

You can consider to let the Superstar take the lead when working with him/her. However, you don't want yourself become invisible, and your role disappears. So you may suggest the superstar-leader to mention about other team members' ideas and duties at the staff meeting.

這類型的同事願意接受任何挑戰，尤其是最艱困或最受矚目的任務。老闆常視耀眼明星為得力助手，並認可他們的精神。這些耀眼明星想要的，就是別人看到他們。

求職面試心理

了解你的老闆

找到職對場的定工位作

你與同事

帶人要帶心

升工作態度遷與

策略：

　　當你們一起工作時，讓耀眼明星當領導者。但是，你也不希望自己被隱形，且你的角色被遺忘。所以你要建議這類型的領導者在員工會議中提到其他團隊成員的想法及任務。

4. The Weightlifter 任重道遠者

The weightlifter always offers to take on an extra project. However, he or she has not thoroughly considered the reality or ability; the weightlifter just wants to look good to the boss. Sometimes volunteering for too much extra work can lead to a burden for other team members.

Strategy:

You might be able to learn the spirit from this co-worker. If you follow in the weightlifter's footsteps, just be careful you don't take on more responsibility than you can comfortably shoulder.

　　任重道遠者總是願意接受額外的工作。但是他們沒有仔細思考現實面與自己的能力，他們只想在老闆面前當個好員工。有時自願做太多額外的工作可能造成其他團隊成員的工作負擔。

策略：

　　你可以學習這類同事的精神。如果你要追尋他們的腳步，要小心不要承諾太多你無法負擔的責任。

5. The Saboteur 破壞者

This person will do anything, including the evils, to get ahead. For example, the saboteur takes all the credit for a joint project; he or she spreads incorrect information to others which may undermine your work. The saboteur does not feel confident about his or her own abilities. This co-worker tries hard to make others look bad, so s/he can look better.

Strategy:
Keep your distance from the saboteur. If you think a colleague has deliberately undermined your work or spread untrue information, immediately speak to your boss about the situation.

這類型的同事會做任何事,包括邪惡的壞事,來走在前面。例如,破壞者會搶走所有的功勞,或散發不實訊息來破壞你的工作。他們由於對自己的能力信心不足,所以他們盡量讓別人看起來差些,來凸顯他們的好。

策略:

跟破壞者保持距離。如果你覺得這類同事故意破壞你的工作,或散發不實訊息,立即將狀況報告給老闆。

V ocabulary 字彙

- ★ In a row 連續的
- ★ Exclaim 生氣大叫
- ★ Irritation 非理性
- ★ Narcissism 自戀狂
- ★ Deceive 欺騙
- ★ Neutralize 使無效
- ★ Nasty 令人難受得
- ★ Recession 經濟衰退
- ★ Highest-profile 備受矚目的
- ★ Saboteur 從事破壞活動者

- ★ Smirk 嘻嘻笑
- ★ Provoke 煽動
- ★ Scarce 不足的
- ★ Sociopath 反社會特質
- ★ Intimidate 恐嚇
- ★ Eliminate 消滅
- ★ Sneaky 偷偷摸摸得
- ★ Prototypical 原型的
- ★ Weightlifter 舉重者

MEMO

求職面試心理

了解你的老闆

找到對的工作 職場定位

你與同事

帶人要帶心

升遷與工作態度

Chapter 5

Win Your Employees' Hearts

帶人要帶心

5-1

Understand Difficult Employees
了解你那難搞的員工

情 境對話

Mitchell works at a recycling plant, but he's not that a good employee. He is frequently late to work, often complains about his job duties to his co-workers, and frequently fails to follow the plant's safety procedures. Worst of all, Mitchell often tries to get his co-workers to complete his tasks.

Mitchell 在資源回收工廠工作。但他不是個好員工，他常常遲到，向同事抱怨工作，且常常沒有遵守安全流程。最嚴重的是，他常常要同事幫他完成工作。

"I can't stand compressing the metal recycling. This is such a boring way to spend a Friday. Jason, are you busy right now?", said Mitchell.

「我實在不想去壓回收鐵，星期五做這件事真是無聊。Jason，你現在很忙嗎？」Mitchell 問。

"Yes, I'm trying to move these pallets, and then I have to go clean out the storage area", replied Jason.

「對阿，我正要移開這些拖板，接著我要去清理儲藏區。」Jason 回答著。

"That's too bad. Hey, Gerald, are you busy right now? I'm supposed to compress the metals today, but I can't stand doing it. It's my least favorite thing to do."

「太糟了。嘿，Gerald，你現在忙嗎？我今天應該要壓金屬，但我今天實在不想做這事。這是我最不喜歡做的事。」

"I thought that sorting the paper was your least favorite thing to do. At least that's what you told me on Monday when you asked me to do it for you", retorted Gerald. "Forget about asking me to do your work right now. We've got three trucks of recycling coming in full that I have to direct to the back and get sorted out."

「我以為整理紙張是你最不喜歡做的事。至少你星期一的時候要我幫你整理紙時是這麼告訴我的。」Gerald 回答。「現在不要叫我幫你做事。等一下有三大卡車的回收物要來，我要趕快到後面去處理這些事。」

"Fine. I just can't stand doing this. It's so boring. I'll get it done, but first I've got to take a break", said Mitchell. He then went off

求職面試心理

了解你的老闆

找到對的工作 職場定位

你與同事

帶人要帶心

升工作態度 遷與

to the break room for several hours.

「算了！我真不想做這個，真無聊。反正我一定會把它做完，現在我要先休息一下。」Mitchell 說著，然後就到休息室待了數小時。

While Mitchell sat in the break room playing games on his mobile phone, all of his co-workers were hard at work. When two co-workers sorting the metal recycling went to compress it, they found the machine full of metal which was supposed to be handled by Mitchell at the beginning of his shift. Suddenly, the recycling operation got backed up, and all of the workers at the plant headed off to find Mitchell.

當 Mitchell 坐在休息室玩著手機遊戲時，其他同事都很認真工作。兩位同事正要去處理廢鐵回收時，他們發現機器裡都是 Mitchell 本來應該處理的廢鐵。此時，回收車回來了，工廠所有的人都去找 Mitchell。

When they found him wasting time in the break room, they told him what happened and how everyone was now running behind schedule. The manager of the recycling plant soon got word of what was going on, and called Mitchell into his office.

當他們發現他只是在浪費時間在休息室，他們告訴他狀況，及每個人現在都進度落後了。回收廠經理也聽說了這件事，然後叫 Mitchell 到他的辦公室。

Because he had repeatedly been poorly behaved, Mitchell's

manager decided to give him a final warning and put a negative mark on his employee file. Mitchell only had one last chance to turn himself around; otherwise, he will get fired.

由於 Mitchell 一直表現得很不好，經理決定要給他最後的警告，並在員工檔案中記上一筆。Mitchell 只剩最後一次機會扭轉情況，否則他的經理就要解僱他了。

達 人剖析

As a boss or a manager, some knowledge about personality traits of your employees can help you to have more understandings of your staff, and to manage the staff more efficiently. Individuals with different personality traits tend to have certain behaviors; therefore, they should be treated in different ways. Here are some toughest traits at work, and strategies to manage them. Just try to work with your staff's personality traits, rather than against them.

身為老闆或主管，對員工的人格特質有一些認識可以幫助更了解員工，也更能有效管理。不同人格特質的人會有不同的行為表現，因此要以不同的方式對待他們。以下是一些難搞的特質，以及因應策略。試著跟員工的特質相處，而不是敵對。

1. Laziness.
It's not uncommon to come across a lazy co-worker,

求職面試心理

了解你的老闆

找到對的工作 職場定位

你與同事

帶人要帶心

升工作態度遷與

and they're not always easy to deal with. The lazy employees may not want to do their tasks, and do not complete their work on time, which all lead to poor performance. Their lazy characteristic is not just reducing the workplace morale, but also reducing team's effectiveness. Even worse, when their performance is consistently poor, it will have an influence on the profit of the company.

Strategy:

Theory X is just the matched psychological concept for them. Theory X assumes that the workers dislike working, avoid responsibility and need to be directed and controlled. So the managers should supervise every step to monitor the workers and their outcomes.

懶惰

職場上也很常有懶惰的員工，這些人並不好應付。懶惰的員工不僅不想做他們的工作，也不會準時完成，這些都造成表現很差。他們的懶惰特質不僅降低了辦公室士氣，也會影響團隊效率。更糟的是，若他們的表現持續不良，可能會影響公司利益。

策略：

心理學中的 X 理論正好適用在他們身上。X 理論假設員工不想工作、迴避責任且需要被指導與控制。所以主管應該看管他們的每一步，以監督他們的工作與成果。

2. Narcissists.

Employees with narcissistic traits are self-centered; they don't care of anyone else but themselves. They lack of capacity for empathy. They don't care what other people feel. They are arrogant, and competitive with the peers. They are extremely sensitive to criticism; they react badly to any criticism. So they often have interpersonal conflicts with the co-workers in a workplace. They are defensive and anxious, so they sometimes misjudge others who work with them. Narcissists take the power very seriously and value it highly, so they want to run the world. They sometimes manipulate others in order to get ahead.

Strategy:

You could frame things in terms of how it might serve them to make them be productive. In other words, you might need to engage in a little manipulation yourself to get them do their work. For example, you can say: "I can only trust you with this assignment because I believe you have talent and ability to complete this task pretty well." Or you can say something like: "Show me that you are capable for the higher position." By doing so can make them feel special which will help them have a better performance.

求職面試心理

了解你的老闆

找到對的工作 職場定位

你與同事

帶人要帶心

升工作態度與

自戀狂

有自戀狂特質的員工很自我中心；他們不管別人只管自己。他們缺乏同理心，不管他人的感受。他們自大且好與同事競爭。他們對批評很敏感，無法接受任何批評。所以他們常有在辦公室與同事起衝突。他們防衛心重且焦慮，所以常會誤會一起合作的人。自戀狂對權力很認真看待且推崇，他們想要掌控全世界。他們常常操弄他人以超越他們。

策略：

你可以從他們的角度出發來設計任務，好讓他們具生產性。換句話說，你可能需要小小操弄一下來讓他們做好工作。例如，你可以說：「對這個任務我只能相信你了，因為我相信你有天分與能力來把這個任務完成得很好。」或是說：「表現給我看你有接任高階職務的能力。」這麼做可以讓他們覺得自己很特別，就會表現得更好。

3. Passive-Aggressive Types.

Employees, who are passive-aggressive, don't deal with conflict directly; they deal with it passively to express their feelings indirectly. This is a kind of defense mechanism which operates on a subconscious level. They say one thing, but mean another. For example, if they don't want to attend a meeting, they will show up late, but not so late for you to say anything to them. Or, if they think you give them too much work, they won't say no, but they will not complete the tasks on time, or they will finish the tasks with poor quality. They are doing these to show their anger in an indirect way that you might not even notice.

Strategy:

Unlike narcissists, they do have the capacity for empathy. They also want to advance in your workplace. They just don't want to be controlled; they need independence. So do not micromanage them. If you want them to do their job, you have to set extremely clear expectations for them. Tell them precisely what you want them to do and when, but don't tell them how to do it.

被動攻擊型

　　被動攻擊型員工不想直接面對衝突；他們以被動的方式間接表達自己的情緒。這是一種潛意識的防衛機制。他們說一套，但卻有另一層意義。例如，他們不想去開會，所以就遲到，但又不會遲到太久到讓你責備。或是，如果他們覺得你交辦太多工作，他們不會拒絕，但不回準時完成，或完成了但品質不佳。他們會這麼做是為了間接表現憤怒，有時還不一定會被你察覺。

策略：

　　不像自戀狂般，這類型的員工有同理他人的能力。他們也想在公司上精益求精。他們只是不想被控制，他們需要獨立空間。所以不要掌控他們。如果要他們做事，設定非常清楚的要求，告訴他們你確切的需求及時間，但是不要告訴他們如何做。

求職面試心理

了解你的老闆

找到對的工作　職場定位

你與同事

帶人要帶心

工作態度與　升遷

As a very talented design student, Elaine had troubles on keeping up with the project schedules. Whenever she was given a new assignment, she showed a lot of passion and always quickly envisioned what she would achieve. That's the reason that she had been recognized by her teachers and classmates as one of the most creative students. As the project went on, she kept comparing her intermediate results to what she had pictured at the beginning. She felt frustrated because the reality did not always meet her expectations. And the way she coped with the situation was not very constructive. Instead of identifying and working on the real problems, she would give up on the original idea and come up with another "perfect" one. She believed that there must be something wrong with the previous one. It was simply not "perfect". So, she had this new idea and then. She went into new problems. The consequence was she finally ran out of time. She would either miss the deadlines, or, submit a work that greatly mismatched her talent.

　　身為 Elaine 是個非常有天分的設計系學生，但她一直有個問題，就是無法準時交出作品。每次有新的作業，她都展現出很大的熱情，也想像了自己的作品要如何呈現。這也是為什麼她的老師與同學都認為她是很有創意的學生。當作業進行到中程，她仍不斷地把作品與自己原先的構想相較。她覺得很挫折，因為現實總是無法如她原本的預期。她對這狀況的因應方式非常不具建設性。她沒有找出真正的問題並解決它；她的方式是放棄原本的想法，而尋求另一個完美的靈感。她認為原本的想法一定有問題，因為不夠完美。所以她想了另一個靈感，然後又經歷了新的問題。結果，她時間不夠了，她不是無法準時交作品，就是作品品質不佳、非常不符合她天份的作品。

4. Perfectionists.

Perfectionists set very high standards for themselves and don't accept errors. They may miss deadlines because nothing seems good enough based on their high standards. They have difficulty hearing criticism because any negative feedback reminds them there is something wrong with them which is the last thing to be accepted. However, there are some advantages of the perfectionistic employees. They can self-control, and they are reliable, and they can deliver high-quality work which sometimes exceeds your expectations.

Strategy:

You can tell them you appreciate their eyes for details which increase the quality of the work. When giving them feedback, you have to carefully choose the words you say. You can say something good of their work first. Then tell them there is a tiny thing which can be improved next time. If they have a hard time meeting the deadline, you have to understand that it is not because they are lazy, but because they set overly high

求職面試心理

了解你的老闆

找到對的工作｜職場定位

你與同事

帶人要帶心

升工作態度遷與

standards. However, you can set clear guidelines about your expectations, so they don't waste time doing extra things which are less important.

完美主義者

完美主義者設定很高的標準且不接受錯誤。他們可能會因為在自己的高標準下覺得不夠好而無法準時完成工作。他們也難以接受批評，因為任何負面評價都在提醒他們犯了錯誤，這是他們最無法接受的事。然而，完美主義的員工也有優勢。他們會自我控制且值得信任，他們的工作成果品質很高，有時甚至超出你的期待。

策略：

你可以告訴他們，由於他們對細節的重視，讓工作品質提升。要給他們回饋時，也要小心遣詞用字。你可以先說他們工作上好的部分，然後才告訴他們下一次可以改善小小的錯誤。如果他們無法準時完成工作，你必須了解到他們不是因為懶惰，而是因為標準過高。然而，你可以藉由設定清楚的期望值來讓他們無須浪費時間多做一些較不重要的事情。

5. Socially anxious type.

These types of employees usually avoid any social activities or interactions. They may be too shy to interact with others; they may feel fearful of doing the wrong thing while interacting with others; or they may prefer to be alone rather than interact with people. No matter which reasons result in social anxiety, they just don't interact much with other employees.

Strategy:

They have no problem to do the job, as long as they can work alone. Do not force them to attend social events. If not necessary, don't make them come to the meetings. Just leave them alone and avoid interrupting them. Give them notice in advance if you need to talk to them, or need them to attend a meeting or an event where they have to interact with others, so they can have enough time to prepare mentally.

社交焦慮型員工

這類型的員工通常會避免社交活動或與人互動。他們太害羞而無法與他人互動；或他們可能害怕在互動時做錯事；或是單純地只想自己一個人。不論甚麼原因造成社交焦慮，他們就是不想與其他同事互動。

策略：

他們工作能力上沒有問題，只要讓他們自己一人。不要強迫他們參與社交活動。若非必要，也無須強迫他們參加會議。就讓他們自己一人，避免打擾他們。如果你需要與他們談談，或要他們參加會議或有與他人互動的活動，要提前告訴他們，這樣他們才可以有足夠時間做好心理準備。

求職面試心理

了解你的老闆

找到職場對的定工位作

你與同事

帶人要帶心

升工作態遷度與

5-2

Motivate Your Employees
激勵員工

Tanya managed a team of salespersons and customer service representatives at a shoe store. One day, after leading her team's sales meeting, she noticed one of her employees, Anne, looking upset. Anne only started working at the store only three weeks ago, and Tanya had noticed she was having a bit of trouble getting acclimated to her new job.

Tanya 是一家鞋店的管理者，負責銷售與客服人員部門。一天，帶領著團隊開完銷售會議後，她發現一位員工 Ann 不太開心。Ann 三週前才來上班，Tanya 發現 Ann 對新工作有些適應上的問題。

Tanya "Anne, did you have any questions about the sales goals I talked about at the meeting?", asked Tanya.

「Anne，你對我在會議上提到的銷售目標有任何問題嗎？」

Anne

"No. I just don't know if I can do this. I like the store, and everyone is nice, but they're all so much better at selling than I am. I can't even make ten sales a day. For that matter, I can barely sell ten things this week, and it's already Thursday", replied Anne.

「沒有，我只是不知道是否可以做到。我喜歡這家店，每個人也很好，但他們銷售能力都比我好太多了。我一天都賣不到十雙。因為如此，我這週勉強賣到十雙，現在已經星期四了。」

Tanya

"You're new, and this is the largest shoe store in the district. You're working with a team of great salespeople who know their work and are very talented. I only hire people who I feel are skilled and have the ability to ensure we remain the top selling store in the company. I hired you, and that means I'm confident you are cut out for this job", said Tanya.

「你才來這家地區性最大的鞋店不久。你跟一群很棒的銷售團隊一起工作，他們熟悉工作也非常有天分。我只會錄用我覺得有技巧、有能力、且確保我們在公司店面中維持頂尖銷售店。我會僱用你，表示我覺得你能勝任這份工作。」

Anne

"Really? Well, I guess I just need to try a bit harder. But what do I do if I can't meet the sales

求職面試心理

了解你的老闆

找到職場對的定工位作

你與同事

帶人要帶心

升工作態度遷與

goals again? I didn't meet the sales goal last week, and I'm not on target to do it this week, either. I don't want to disappoint you or get fired for not doing well." said Anne.

「真的嗎？我猜我需要更努力些。但如果我又不能達到銷售目標的話應該怎麼做？我上週就沒有達成，且這週恐怕也沒辦法。我不想讓你失望，也不想因為做不好被解雇。」

Tanya

"Firstly, you can meet the sales goal. Maybe not this week, but eventually you will. I don't fire anyone who makes a genuine effort, so just keep at it. I'm going to give you some help by having Tom train you a bit more tomorrow and all next week. He's my top salesperson and assistant, so if anyone can give you tips and techniques, I know he can.", said Tanya.

「首先，妳一定可以達到這樣的銷售目標。也許不是這週，但總有一天妳可以辦到。我不會解雇任何努力的人，所以繼續向前。明天還有下週我請 Tom 給妳一些訓練來幫你。他是我最強的銷售員及助理，所以如果有人可以傳授給妳任何秘訣與技巧，非他莫屬。」

Anne felt better. With Tanya's encouragement, she eventually surpassed the store's sales goals, and she became a more confident, productive employee.

Anne 感覺好些了。有了 Tanya 的鼓勵，她終於超越了公司的銷售目標，且她也更有自信與生產力了。

Motivating people to do their best work is always the challenge for bosses or managers. Let us take a look at how psychological concepts help motivate employees.

激勵員工讓他們表現得更好一直都是老闆或主管的大挑戰。讓我們看看心理學上有那些概念可以協助激勵員工。

達 人剖析

1. Pygmalion Effect and Galatea Effect

These two theories are both based on the power of expectations. The Pygmalion Effect is the phenomenon that the greater the expectation is placed upon the employees, the better they perform. The Galatea Effect is an individuals' expectations about themselves. This is self-driven; if the employee thinks that s/he can perform well, there is a high chance that s/he will do well.

Apply it to the workplace:

When applying the Pygmalion Effect, the superior could set a higher expectation to the employees, to motivate them for a better performance. In the story mentioned earlier, Tanya applied Pygmalion Effect to motivate Anne

求職面試心理

了解你的老闆

找到對的工作 職場定位

你與同事

帶人要帶心

升遷與工作態度

for better achievement. When applying Galatea Effect, the managers could constantly encourage the employees to give them more confidence, which will increase their self-expectations and self-worth, and will positively influence their performance.

畢馬龍效應與加拉蒂效應

這兩個理論都與期待所帶來的力量有關。畢馬龍效應是一種現象，若對員工加諸越大的期待，他們的表現就會越好。加拉蒂效應則是對自己的期待，是一種自我驅力，如果員工認為自己可以表現得很好，就有很高的可能他/她會表現得很好。

職場應用：

運用畢馬龍效應時，主管要對員工設定較高的期待，以激勵他們有更好的表現。在上述的故事中，Tanya 就是運用畢馬龍效應來激勵 Anne 有更好的成就。運用加拉蒂效應時，主管可以不時的鼓勵員工，給他們更多自信，如此可以增加他們的自我期許與自我價值，對他們的表現也因此會有正向的影響。

2. Hartzberg's Two-Factor Theory

Herzberg found there are two factors that influence employee motivation and satisfaction. (a) Motivators: these factors lead to satisfaction of the employees, such as challenging work, recognition, career progression, responsibility, involvement in decision making, achievement; (b) Hygiene factors: The absence of these factors may lead to dissatisfaction and lack of motivation of the employees. Hygiene factors include salary, benefits, company policies, work environment, and relationships with colleagues, etc.

Apply it to the workplace:

Both Motivators and Hygiene factors need to be improved to increase employees' satisfaction and motivation. Make sure your employees are appreciated, valued, and recognized. They can constantly grow and progress in the company. In addition, they need to be paid fairly and received appropriate benefits and reward they deserved. Friendly working environment and supportive relationships between staff are also important factors to prevent employees' dissatisfaction.

赫茲伯格雙因素理論

赫茲伯格發現有兩大因素會影響員工的動機與滿意度

(a)動機因素：

這類因素會影響著員工滿意度，包括工作挑戰性、主管認可、工作升遷、責任、決策參與與成就感等。

(b)保健因素：

缺少這類因素會造成對工作的不滿與失去動力。保健因素包括薪水、福利、公司政策、工作環境、與同事關係等。

求職面試心理

了解你的老闆

找到對的工作　職場定位

你與同事

帶人要帶心

升工作態度與遷與

職場應用：

　　動機因素與保健因素都需要被提升，以增進員工的滿意度與工作動機。確保員工有被感謝、重視與認可。他們在公司裡也可以不斷成長與升遷。此外，他們也需要合理的薪水、獲得適宜的福利與應有的獎勵。友善的工作環境與同事間支持性的關係也是重要的因素以避免員工不滿。

3. Equity Theory

According to the Equity Theory, the motivation of individual is based on what he or she considers to be fair when compared to others. When people feel fairly or advantageously treated, they are more likely to be motivated. On the contrary, if they feel unfairly treated, they feel demotivated and less satisfied. Since people are strongly influenced by their peers, friends, or families to establish their sense of fairness, they evaluate their own input/output ratios based on their comparison with the input/output ratios of other employees. When they feel unfair, they will reduce their contribution to the job.

Apply it to the workplace:

Provide clear rules and conditions about how to gain the rewards, so employees will know everyone is treated fairly, and they can gain a fair return for what they contribute to the jobs.

公平理論

公平理論認為，個人的動機來自於他/她與別人相較之下有獲得公平的對待。若人們覺得有獲得公平或更好的對待，動機就會更為提高。相反的，若人們覺得對不公平的對待，他們的動機與滿意度就會降低。由於人們深受同儕、朋友與家人的影響來建立自己對公平的感受，他們就會評估自己付出／回報比例與其他員工付出／回報比例相較之下的公平性。若他們覺得不公平，就會降低自己對工作上的貢獻。

職場應用：

對於如何獲得獎勵要提供清楚規則與條件，如此員工才能知道每個人都被公平對待；當他們為工作付出努力，也可以獲得公平的回報。

職 場小故事

Green Grocer was one of the most well-known grocery stores in the city, and it had a great reputation. Not only did Green Grocer offer good quality food and products at reasonable prices, it paid the fairest wage out of all of the other grocery stores. While other grocery chains held back on increasing employee wages in order to boost their profits, Green Grocer made it a goal to ensure their employee's salaries kept up with the cost of living.

Green Grocer 是鎮上最知名的雜貨店，名聲很好。店中不僅以合理

求職面試心理

了解你的老闆

找到對的工作

職場的定位

你與同事

帶人要帶心

升遷與工作態度

價格供應品質佳的食物與產品，在雜貨店這行業中，他們的薪資也是最合理的。其他連鎖雜貨店都會停止調薪以增加利潤，但 Green Grocer 卻以希望員工薪資可以負擔生計為宗旨。

In addition to offering its workers a fair wage and benefits, such as health insurance and discounts at local retailers, Green Grocer aimed to provide a comfortable, safe work environment for all employees. Cleanliness was a top priority at the store, which not only impressed its customers, but also made work environments safer, hygienic. The stockers who worked in the store's warehouse received a quality training before using the machines and fork lifts, and Green Grocer's management was sure to replace any old equipment. This also helped keep the works safe.

　　除了薪資、健康保險與員工折扣等福利，Green Grocer 也相當重視提供給員工舒適安全的工作環境。乾淨是店中最高要件，因為會讓顧客有好的印象，也會讓工作環境更安全也更衛生。倉儲人員在使用機器與堆高機前也需要接受訓練。管理者也要確保汰換老舊的設備。這些都可以幫助維持工作安全。

Whenever an employee had an issue, it was a policy for managers to help in any way that they could. Green Grocer allowed employees to request days off ahead of time. The company believed that it was important for employees to have time to rest outside of work and spend time with their families. To that end, it was closed on all major holidays, rather than staying open and forcing employees to miss being with their loved ones.

當員工有困難，主管一定會盡力協助，這是公司政策之一。Green Grocer 允許員工提前請假，公司相信員工能有工作以外的休息時間並與家人共處是很重要的。基於如此，在所有重要的國定假日他們都不營業，而不是繼續營業並勉強員工錯過與所愛的人相處時光來上班。

All managers at Green Grocer were trained quickly not only to motivate their staff to sell, but to understand the people who worked for them and show the workers that they were valued. The managers treated all of the workers fairly, never disrespecting them or mistreating them. When a problem arose, they made sure to handle it as quickly and as smoothly as possible so that workplace disruptions were kept to a minimum. The company's belief was that without its workers, it would be impossible for the store to do as well as it did, which is why most of the employees enjoyed working there. Because of its concern for its workers and its dedication to providing a good work environment, Green Grocer retained its employees much longer than other stores and had one of the lowest turnover rates in the industry.

Green Grocer 所有的經理都會接受訓練，不僅學習關於如何激勵員工的銷售成績，也有了解員工及表現重視員工等訓練。經理都必須對所有員工公平對待，不可以不尊重或不當對待。若有問題，經理也要確保及時處理，且處理得越平順越好，這樣對公司的影響就會降至最低。公

求職面試心理

了解你的老闆

找到職場的對定工位作

你與同事

帶人要帶心

升工作態度遷與

司相信，沒有員工，公司絕對沒辦法做得像現在一樣好。這也正是為什麼員工都很喜歡在這裡工作。因為公司關心員工，也竭盡所能的提供好的工作環境，這裡的員工都比其他公司待得更久，流動率也是業界最低。

4. Maslow's Hierarchy of Needs

Maslow's theory can also be applied to motivate employees. There are five levels of needs; the basic and lower level of needs must be met before achieving higher levels of needs. The hierarchy of needs are: Physiological, Safety, Love and Belongingness, Esteem, and Self-actualization.

Apply it to the workplace:

The company, like the Green Grocer in the story, should provide physical and mental resources for the employees in order to meet their lower needs. While their needs of lower levels are met, they have the motivation to reach to the higher level of needs.

(a) Physiological:

The company should provide fair pay so that the employees can maintain a basic living standard.

(b) Safety:

The company should provide a safe and secure working environment.

(c) Love and Belongingness:

The workplace should be warm, supportive, and friendly, so the employees can feel they belong to the company, and they are cared by others.

(d) Esteem:

The employees should be valued, respected, and appreciated by the co-workers and the superiors.

(f) Self-actualization:

The company should provide growth and development, as well as appropriate career progression, so the employees know that they can keep moving toward the realization of the potential.

馬斯洛需求理論

馬斯洛的理論也可以用來激勵員工。理論中有五個層次的需求,最基本與較低層的需求需要先被滿足,才可以進入較高層的需求。這些需求層次包括:生理需求、安全需求、愛與歸屬感需求、尊嚴需求與自我實現需求。

職場應用:

如同故事中的 Green Grocer 一般,公司應該提供員工生理與心理的資源,以滿足他們較低階的需求。當低階需求被滿足,員工就有動機去追求滿足更高階的需求。

求職面試心理

了解你的老闆

找到對的工作

職場定位

你與同事

帶人要帶心

升工作態度遷與

(a)生理需求：

公司要提供合理報酬，員工才能維持他們的生活開銷。

(b)安全需求：

公司應該要提供安全穩當的工作環境。

(c)愛與歸屬感需求：

工作環境要溫暖、具支持性與友善，如此員工才能覺得公司有歸屬感，且他們得到他人的關心。

(d)尊嚴需求：

員工應該要被同事與主管重視、尊敬與感謝。

(f)自我實現需求：

公司應該要提供成長與發展機會，以及適當的升遷管道，這樣員工才能知道他們可以繼續前進，把自己的潛能發揮到最大。

5. Positive Reinforcement

This technique involves the addition of a reinforcing stimulus following a behavior, so this particular behavior is strengthened and will more likely to occur again in the future.

Apply it to the workplace:

For example, the company can give the employees a bonus if they exceed this month's sales quota. In this case, exceeding monthly sales quota is the particular behavior; giving bonus is the added reinforcing stimulus. By giving praise or reward to refine good behaviors is one effective way to motivate employees' workforce.

正增強

這個技巧是在某一行為出現後外加一項可以增強的刺激，如此一來這個特定的行為被強化了，未來就有可能再次出現。

職場應用：

例如，公司可以在員工達到本月銷售額度時給予紅利，如此達到月銷售額就是特定行為，給予紅利則是增強刺激。藉由讚美或獎賞可以強化好的行為，這是提升員工勞動力的有效方法。

6. Social Facilitation

In the experiment of social psychology Norman Triplett (1898) on the speed records of cyclists, he noticed that racing against each other rather than against the clock alone increased the cyclists' speeds. This is the effect of Social Facilitation. Social Facilitation can have positive or negative impacts on individual's performance. When an individual is good at a task, the performance increased when there is the presence of others; on the contrary, if the individual is doing a difficult task which s/he is not familiar with, the performance decreased with the presence of others. Social facilitation does play an important role in performance.

求職面試心理

了解你的老闆

找到對的工作　職場定位

你與同事

帶人要帶心

升工作態度與遷

Apply it to the workplace:

As a manager, you don't really have to invite audiences to observe your staffs' performance. However, you can constantly announce loudly in relation to staff's good performance, or show it in the bulletin board. So the employees know that others are looking at themselves which may increase their performance. Moreover, if the task is simple or well-learned to the employees, you can assign them to work as a team (but be careful with the negative impact of Social Loafing). If the task is complex or unfamiliar to people, it is better to let them work alone.

社會助長效應

社會心理學家 Norman Triplett (1898)曾做過一個實驗：他分別測量單車選手在有其他選手一起比賽以及單獨比賽時的成績，發現有其他選手一起比賽時的速度更快。這就是社會助長效應。社會助長會對個人的表現有正向或負向的影響。當個人對某項任務擅長，則有他人觀看時其表現會更好；相反的，若該任務過於困難，或個人對該任務不擅長，則旁人的出現反而會讓表現更差。所以，社會助長效應的確會對表現造成影響。

職場應用：

身為主管，你不一定真的找人來觀看員工的表現。但是，你可以定期宣布員工的好表現，或是公布在公告欄。這樣員工們就會知道有別人看得到他們的表現，就會表現得更好。此外，如果任務是簡單或擅長的，可以讓他們以團體工作方式完成（但要小心社會性散漫的負面影響）。如果任務過於複雜或不適員工們擅長的，最好以個人工作方式進行。

7. Psychological contract

After accepting the job offer, new employees come to work with a set of expectations. They have an understanding of their duties and rights. They also learn something about what the company will give them. In other words, they have a *psychological contract* with the company. A psychological contract is an unwritten understanding about what the employee will bring to the work environment and what the company will provide in exchange. When people do not get what they expect, they experience a *psychological contract breach*, which leads to low job satisfaction and commitment, and decreases motivation.

Apply it to the workplace:

For example, if the employee was told before being hired that the company values family, and staffs got along well with each other. However, after working for a while, he or she realizes that they expect employees to work 70 hours a week, and employees are aggressive toward each other. This employee is likely to be dissatisfied and experience a breach in your psychological contract, which also deeply impact the motivation. One way to prevent such problems is for companies to provide the realistic job orientation to their

求職面試心理

了解你的老闆

職場定位
找到對的工作

你與同事

帶人要帶心

工作態度與升遷

employees, so they can have a fully understanding about the company and their own responsibilities.

心理契約

在接受新工作後，新員工帶著期待來到公司。他們了解自己的責任與權益；他們也稍微知道公司可以給他們甚麼。換句話説，這就是與公司的心理契約。心理契約是沒有白紙黑字寫下，指的是員工可以為公司帶來甚麼，公司又可以給員工甚麼的心理上的認知。若沒有達到這些心理上的期待，就會經歷心理契約的毀約，造成低工作滿意度與低工作承諾。

職場上的應用：

例如，員工在被雇用當下，公司説他們是很注重家庭的，同事間也相處融洽。但是工作一段時間後，該員工發現他們期待員工一週工作 70 小時，且同事間彼此競爭。他／她可能感到不滿，心理契約因此被毀約，也深深影響著工作動機。為了避免這樣的問題，公司應該為員工提供符合事實的介紹，這樣員工可以對公司有全面性的了解，也知道他們的責任。

V ocabulary 字彙

* Acclimate 適應
* Turnover 流動率
* Actualization 實現
* Refine 精煉
* Breach 對法律的破壞

* Hygiene 衛生、保健
* Physiological 生理上的
* Reinforcement 增強
* Facilitation 促進
* Relinquish 放棄

5-3

Manage Your Employees
管理員工

Rebecca just accepted a position as the lead manager at her job, and she was excited that the company's director had also secured a spot for her at a local leadership conference. There, she would meet with managers in other industries from companies around the city and learn about how to be an effective manager.

　　Rebecca 剛接受了帶領經理這項新職務，也對於公司執行長要她參加地區領導會議感到興奮。在會議中，她會遇到其他行業、其他公司的主管，並學習如何更有效的管理。

"There are many types of management styles, and it will be up to each of you to choose which route to take", said the conference's keynote speaker. "However, be mindful that there is such a thing as good and bad management. A good management style will help your company accomplish its goals, enforce its policies, and still show your employees that they are a valuable piece of your team."

「管理有很多種模式，由你們自己決定要選擇哪一條路。」特聘主講者説著，「但是，要注意有好的管理方式與不好的管理方式。好的方式會幫助公司達到目標，執行公司政策，且也向員工表達他們是團隊受重視的一員。」

Most of the attendees shook their head in agreement, but Rebecca wondered whether the latter was always so.

多數與會者同意並點頭，但 Rebecca 在想後面那句話是否總是如此。

"Is it always necessary to treat the employees like that? I mean, how are we supposed to make them feel valuable without also giving them permission to run all over us?", asked Rebecca.

「是否一定要這麼樣對待員工？我的意思是説，如果我們沒有賦予權力，他們也會感受到價值嗎？」

"Great question. Actually, showing appreciation has nothing to do with relinquishing your authority, and in fact, those managers who fail to value their employees often don't earn the respect of their workers. There are many ways that managers can show their employees appreciation, while still adhering to the company's rules and achieving its goals. In fact, even the staunchest, most stern managers can do this", said the speaker.

　　「好問題，事實上，表達對員工的感謝並無損妳的的權威；無法對員工表達感謝之意的管理者也無法獲得員工的尊敬。有許多方法可以對員工表達感謝，且無損公司規定同時又可以達到目標。事實上，即便是最鐵石心腸、最嚴苛的管理者都可以做到。」

The conference attendees were now intrigued, and wondered how they could incorporate this advice into their management styles.

　　與會者開始好奇，想著要如何融合這項建議在自己的管理方式中。

"For instance, you can do something as small as sending a congratulatory email at the end of a project to thank your employees, or you can do something as grand as hosting a lunch to thank your workers. It all depends on your responsibility, your company's budget, and just if you have time to do." said the speaker.

　　「例如，簡單的方式像是在完成案子後，妳可以寄一封祝賀郵件，感謝他們的付出；或是較大的感謝包括請他們吃頓午餐。這端視妳的責任、公司預算及妳是否有時間來做考量。」主講者說著。

Rebecca then understood what the speaker meant, and

agreed that showing employees appreciation was important.

Rebecca 了解主講者的意思，也同意向員工表達感謝是很重要的。

"What you cannot do, however, is to disparage your employees in public or in private", said the conference speaker. "Do that, and will you not only lose their respect, but you will surely see their job performance decline. Your job as a manger isn't to be a tyrant, but to be a leader."

「若你無法這麼做，就是對外或私下都貶低妳的員工。」主講者說著，「如此，不只妳會失去他們的尊敬，妳也會發現他們的表現降低。身為主管，妳的任務不是當個暴君，而是當個領導者。」

達 人剖析

How to manage your employees 如何管理員工

Good managers are essential to any organization. They need to make the right decisions and take right actions to ensure the organization is moving toward success. The followings are some ideas about how to manage your employees.

好的管理者對組織相當重要。管理者需要作出正確的決定、採取正確的行動以確保組織朝向成功而去。以下是一些管理員工的概念。

求職面試心理

了解你的老闆

找到對的工作／職場定位

你與同事

帶人要帶心

升工作態度／遷與

1. **Get to know your employees 了解員工**

   You should get to know your employees as soon as you can, and as quickly as you can. You have to know the skills, potentials, abilities, and personality traits of each individual, in order to assign specific tasks accordingly. You can meet them individually in advance, in order to have better understandings of each individual. Make sure that you make the most of your time with your employees to share your vision. Let them know the direction you want to go in. In addition, you also have to listen to your team members and try to understand what they're worried about.

   　　你要越了解員工越好，且越快越好。你要知道每位員工的技巧、潛能、能力與人格特質，這樣才可以根據這些來分派工作。你可以事前個別認識員工以更了解他們。也要確保你花大部分的時間與他們一起打拼，並跟他們分享你的想法。讓他們知道你想要前進的方向。此外，你也要傾聽員工的聲音，試著了解他們的擔心。

2. **Avoid Halo Effect 避免月暈效應**

   Many psychological studies have found that people prefer individuals who are attractive or good-looking over people who are less attractive. This psychological phenomenon called Halo Effect. It is a type of cognitive bias. People are deeply influenced by overall impression of a person, and infer other traits of this person. In other words, we always perceive good-looking people more favorable for their personality traits or characteristics than those who are less attractive; they are smarter, more hardworking, or more honest. In short, Halo Effect can have a huge impact on decision-making. As a manager, you have to be aware of the influence of the halo effect. Do not treat your employees by the impression. You need to thoroughly assess your employees based on their work and abilities, not based on their look. By doing this, you will be able to treat every worker fairly. Another way to overcome this problem is to collect as more data from every facet as possible while making decision, so you don't judge one thing or individual simply by your first impression.

　　許多心理學研究發現，人們會喜歡外表具吸引力或長得好看的人，而不喜歡不具吸引力的人。月暈效應是一種心理現象，屬於認知上的成見。人們通常會以外貌印象來推論他人其他的特質。換句話說，我們會認為長得好看的人比長得不好看的人，其人格也較高尚；他們較聰明、較認真、或較誠實。簡單而言，月暈效應深深影響著人們做決定的過程。身為經理的你應該要覺察到月暈效應帶來的影響。不要以外貌印象來對待員工。你需要深入地了解員工的工作與能力，而不要被長相所影響。這麼做才可以公平地對待員工。另一個克服月暈效應的方式是在做決定前蒐集越多資料與事實狀況越好，才不會以第一印象來評斷一件事或人。

求職面試心理

了解你的老闆

職場定位
找到對的工作

你與同事

帶人要帶心

工作態度
升遷與

3. Give the credit and take the blame 給予讚賞，承擔責備

Even a superstar needs others to work together. So respect your employees and value their efforts. Give the credit to your staff for their contribution and achievement. When something is going wrong, try to find out the solution with them. Do not play the blame games. You can provide performance-based feedback, so every employee can learn from every lesson, good or bad.

即使超級巨星也需要旁人一起合作，所以尊重你的同事並重視他們的努力。對他們的貢獻與成就給予讚賞。當出錯時，試著與他們一起找到解決方法。不要互相怪罪。你可以針對表現給予回饋，這樣每位員工都可以學到經驗，不論好的壞的。

4. Communicate constantly 經常溝通

Communication skills are essential for success. Constant communication can provide a channel for you and your staff to exchange viewpoints, visions, expectations, and concerns. More effective communications can decrease misunderstandings and increase motivation and productivity.

溝通技巧是成功的要素。經常溝通可以提供你與員工暢通的管道，以交換看法、觀點、期望與擔心。有效的溝通可以降低誤會並增進工作動機與生產力。

5. Be cautious of Groupthink and Brainstorming
小心團體迷思與腦力激盪

Psychologists have found that groups suffering all kinds of biases and glitches can lead to poor choices. This is called **groupthink**. People in the group tend to ignore alternatives and take irrational actions. A group is especially vulnerable to groupthink when there is high cohesion within group, or when there is pressure to make a decision. Members are; therefore, less motivated to be realistic and rational. Consequently, decisions shaped by groupthink have low probability of achieving successful outcomes. Groupthink also has influence when brainstorming. Many managers believe that two heads are always better than one. So they gather as many ideas as possible from a group meeting. However, psychologists suggest that brainstorming can only get fewer ideas and less innovation than that produced when working individually. Because in the group, people feel anxious, and their own ideas are soon forgotten while listening to others. They just can't help but respond to others subconsciously. So, when making decision or forming new ideas, the managers can collect relevant information and ideas individually before meetings. You should avoid stating preferences and expectations at the outset. You can also invite one or few experts to the meeting, so outsiders can challenge views of the members.

求職面試心理

了解你的老闆

找到對的工作　職場定位

你與同事

帶人要帶心

升工作態度與

心理學家發現團體會經歷各種的成見與功能不彰而做出不當的抉擇。這稱作團體迷思。在團體中，人們會忽視其他的選擇，並做出非理性的行為。若團體的凝聚力高，或團體處在抉擇的壓力下，就很容易產生團體迷思。團體成員會因此失去尋找事實與理性的動力。團體迷思最後會造成做出失敗抉擇的狀況。團體迷思也會影響著腦力激盪的效果。許多主管相信眾人集思廣益會比單獨思考強，所以他們會開會以獲得更多靈感。但是，心理學家認為，比起獨自工作，腦力激盪得到的靈感更少也更不具創新性。因為在團體裡，人們會感到焦慮，且當聽到別人的想法時，很快就會忘記自己要說些甚麼。因為潛意識中，人們很容易會去附和他人。所以，當作決定或想要有新靈感時，主管可以在會議之前個別蒐集資料或想法，也應該避免在最初表現出自己的喜好或期待。主管也可以在會議中邀請一位或多位專家，外來者可以挑戰成員的看法。

6. Avoid Social Loafing 避免社會性散漫

Individuals tend to put less effort when they are working in a group. This is a psychological phenomenon called Social Loafing. It is because the loafers are not worried about being evaluated. Or, the individuals consider that their efforts are difficult to distinguish from other members. No matter how hard they work, they do not get appropriate recognition as a group member. Therefore, while forming a team, the managers should carefully choose individuals to join a team. Make sure each member has strengths and personalities that will complement other team members. In addition, the managers should encourage team discussion, team loyalty and cohesion constantly during the team work. Finally, make sure there is evaluation based on an individual contribution by the managers, team leader as well as other team members.

人們通常在團體工作中較為不努力，這個現象稱為社會性散漫，這是因為那些懶散的人覺得不會被評估。或者，他們覺得在團體中，自己的努力並不容易被看見，不管他們多認真，都不會獲得適當的讚賞。因此，當成立團隊時，主管要小心的選擇團隊成員，確保每位成員的優點與人格特質可以互補。此外，主管要鼓勵團隊成員在一起工作期間要多討論、有忠誠度及凝聚力。最後，也要確保主管、團隊領導者與成員間有機會對個別的貢獻做出評估。

職 場小故事

Darren liked his job at a local furniture store, but he didn't care much for his manager, Robert. Robert was often rude to the employees, even in front of customers, and he would also demean them whenever anyone had a question or made even a slight error. The employees, however, were at his mercy if they wanted to continue working at the store, since Robert wasn't just the manager, he was the store's owner as well.

Darren 在地方上的家具店工作，他喜歡這份工作，但他不喜歡經理

求職面試心理

了解你的老闆

找到職場對的定位工作

你與同事

帶人要帶心

工作態度遷與升

Robert。Robert 對員工很兇，甚至會在顧客前兇員工。只要員工有問題或犯一點小錯，他會貶低員工。員工若想要留下來工作，就要看他臉色，因為他不僅是經理，也是這家店的老闆。

While Darren was assisting a customer with a purchase at work one day, both he and the customer noticed Robert literally yelling at another employee. The things he said were so rude, and he had made such a point to embarrass her, that the employee began to tear up. Robert made such a scene and was witnessed by a customer Darren serviced, so she decided to buy furniture in other places; she said that she does not want to shop in places where employees are badly treated. That day, seven customers left the store without making a purchase, and the employee he yelled at decided to quit working at the store.

一天 Darren 正在幫顧客採買上的問題，他與顧客都看到 Robert 正在對著另一位員工大吼。他說出口的話都相當無禮，且說了很多令她無地自容的事，所以這位員工哭了。由於 Robert 罵員工這一幕被 Darren 服務的顧客看到了，所以這位顧客決定到其他地方買家具，因為她不想要在不當對待員工的地方消費。那一天，有七位顧客都因此而甚麼都沒買就離開了，那位被吼的員工也決定辭職了。

Over time, Robert's store got a bad reputation for badly treating its employees, and comments on the Internet were mostly about the short-tempered boss. Whenever people around Darren were aware that he worked at that shop, they usually asked him whether the rumor about the boss is true.

不久後，Robert 的店因為不當對待員工而有壞名聲；網路上對這家店的評價也多是「那位暴躁的老闆」。當 Darren 周邊的人得知他在那家店工作，通常會問他關於老闆的謠言是否是真的。

Darren had worked as a retail manager before, and Robert's style of management was unlike anything he had ever seen. It also went against everything that Darren had learned when it came to effective management. He wasn't sure just how long the store could survive its poor reputation, and he wasn't sure whether it was because of Robert being the store's owner that led him be so harsh, or whether it was just because of his personality.

Darren 曾經在零售店擔任經理，Robert 對員工的管理方式是他前所未見的，這也跟他之前所學有效的管理方式相違背。他不確定這家有著壞名聲的店還可以撐多久，他也不知道 Robert 是因為是老闆所以才要這麼嚴厲，還是因為他自己的人格特質所致。

One day at work, Darren witnessed Robert doing something that seemed out of character even for him; he insulted a customer and told him to leave the store and never come back. The only thing the customer had done was to inquire sturdiness of the furniture; Robert's response was absolutely out of line.

一天，Darren 目睹了 Robert 做了一些更誇張的事：他污辱顧客並要顧客離開永遠不要回來。這位顧客做的唯一的事就是詢問某個家具有多堅固，但 Robert 的反應卻太過份了。

求職面試心理

了解你的老闆

找到職場對的定位工作

你與同事

帶人要帶心

升工作態度遷與

It was at that moment point that Darren decided to start looking for another job. He didn't want to be affiliated with a company with such a poor reputation, and such abysmal management, any longer.

就在那個時刻，Darren 決定開始找其他的工作。他不想要跟有著壞名聲的店家及糟透了的管理方式有任何關聯。

達 人提點

How to lose your employees' respect?
要如何失去員工對你的尊敬？

If you don't want to be a good manager, here are some quick ways for you!

如果你不想成為一位好的主管，以下是快速的方式！

1. Overreact 過度反應

When something has gone wrong, you always overreact and blame everyone without clarifying the situation.

當有人做錯事，你就過度反應，並在事情尚未釐清之前責怪每個人。

2. Inconsistently 不一致

You always say one thing but do another, and you never

keep your promise. Eventually, you lose trust from your employees.

　　你說一套做一套，且永遠不遵守諾言。最後，你會失去員工的信任。

3. Claim credit 邀功

No matter how much contribution your team made, you take credit for it. You only care about personal success.

　　不管你的團隊有著多大的貢獻，你把功勞全放在自己身上。你只在意自己的成就。

4. Never admit mistakes 不承認錯誤

You don't want to lose face in front of your employees, so you tell them you are always right, and blame someone else for mistakes.

　　你不想要在員工面前丟臉，所以你告訴他們你一定對，然後將錯誤怪罪到別人頭上。

5. Be closed minded 狹隘

You are unwilling to consider other ideas and viewpoints. You think you are the only one who can see things clearly, and your ideas are always the best ones.

求職面試心理

了解你的老闆

職場定位
找到對的工作

你與同事

帶人要帶心

工作態度與升遷

你不願意聽別人的意見與觀點。你覺得你是唯一看的清楚事情的人，你的想法永遠是對的。

6. Treat others with different standard 用不同的標準對待他人

You expect excellence from your team, however, you treat yourself with different ones.

你期待團隊有傑出的表現，但你對自己卻不是這麼回事。

7. Be defensive 防衛

You become defensive when someone questions your decisions, because you feel insecure about your knowledge, and you are not confident enough.

若有人質疑你的決策，你就會變得防衛，因為你對自己的知識沒有把握，也對自己沒有信心。

8. Never deal with tough issues 從不處理困難的議題

You don't take on the hard parts of your job, for example, you don't give a difficult feedback to your employees; you don't point the right direction; you don't deal with the conflicts between the co-workers, etc. Your employees will see your inability to handle tough challenges.

你不處理職務中比較困難的部分，例如，你不會給予員工比較艱難的回饋；你無法指引正確的方向；你不處理同事間的衝突…等等。你的員工只會認為你沒有能力處理較高的挑戰。

Vocabulary 字彙

★ Adhere 忠於

★ Stern 嚴厲的

★ Incorporate 合併

★ Tyrant 暴君

★ Groupthink 團體迷思

★ Glitch 失靈

★ Loaf 閒晃

★ Mercy 憐憫

★ Reputation 名聲

★ Abysmal 糟透的

★ Staunchest 堅固的

★ Intrigue 激起好奇心

★ Disparage 貶低

★ Halo effect 月暈效應

★ Brainstorm 腦力激盪

★ Subconsciously 潛意識地

★ Demean 貶低

★ Patronize 惠顧

★ Affiliate 緊密聯繫

MEMO

求職面試心理

了解你的老闆

找到對的工作 職場定位

你與同事

帶人要帶心

升工作態度與遷

Chapter *6*

Working Attitude and Promotion

工作態度與升遷

6-1

Positive Working Attitude
正向的工作態度

Tom is an office manager, but he used to feel depressed about his job. His life outside of work was fine, but he didn't care his job much of the time, felt unappreciated by his boss. He hopes he can do the job he likes, and has a higher salary. As he started feeling bored about his job, his performance suffered. However, after Tom decided to change his attitude about work, his job performance improved considerably. This did not go unnoticed by Tom's co-worker, Ben, who felt the same way about work that Tom did previously.

Tom 是辦公室經理,但以前對於工作總是意志消沉。他工作以外的生活還可以,但大多數的時候,他不太關心他的工作,覺得不被老闆重視,也希望可以做他更喜歡的工作且有更高的薪水。當他開始對工作厭煩,他的表現也就很差。但是,當 Tom 決定要改變工作態度時,他的表現進步很多。Tom 的同事 Ben 也注意到了,他對工作的感受跟 Tom 以前一樣。

Ben

"You seem cheerful today, Tom. Quite unusual for a Monday morning."

「你今天看起來很開心，這對星期一早上而言很不尋常。」

Tom

"Yes, but I'm trying to be more optimistic about being here every day. It makes the day go by faster by looking on the bright side, and it helps me feel better in general. You know I used to have the same outlook on this place as you do."

「是啊！我試著每天都樂觀一點。正向態度可以讓一天過得快些，也讓我感覺好一些。你知道我以前對工作的感覺就跟你一樣。」

Ben

"I know, and I was wondering what changed you. I'm happy you're not down about working here anymore, but how did you do it?"

「我知道，而且我在想甚麼改變了你。你對工作不再意志消沉我很為你高興，但你如何辦到的？」

Tom

"First, I had to admit how worse I felt whenever I complained too much or obsessed over what I didn't like about this job. I started to focus on what I did like, and I admit, it wasn't much at first."

「首先，我必須承認，每當我一直抱怨或陷入在我有多麼不喜歡這份工作的情緒中，我會感覺更糟。我開始專

求職面試心理

了解你的老闆

找到對的工作 職場定位

你與同事

帶人要帶心

工作態度與升遷

注在我喜歡的事情上，但我要說，一開始還真找不到多少。」

Ben
"I can relate to that. I just like the fact that I get a paycheck."

「我知道，我只喜歡收到薪水的時候。」

Tom
"And that's enough for a start. You get paid. That's a positive thing. And even though you're not thrilled about this job, you're pretty good at what you do. You're needed around here. That's got to mean something, right?"

「這樣開始就夠了。你可以有薪水，這樣是正向思考。即便你對工作不是太激情，你也很擅長做這份工作。公司需要你，這就有意義了，對吧？」

Ben
"I suppose it does. I guess I can try having a better attitude about work, and see whether it makes a difference."

「恩，我想是這樣沒錯。我可以試著對工作有更好的態度，看看是否會有不同。」

Tom
"I'm sure it will. Pretty soon. You won't see Monday mornings as a horrible thing."

「我相信會有。很快的，你不會覺得星期一早上這麼可怕。」

Tom was right. Very soon after deciding to adopt a good work attitude and focusing on being positive, Ben noticed that his job performance improved.

Tom 是對的，在 Ben 決定要開始有好的態度與正向的心情後，他發現在工作的表現更好了。

達 人剖析

▶ What is attitude? 甚麼是態度？

We all have some ideas about what attitude is, but it is not easy for us to define it without opening the dictionary. According to the Cambridge Dictionaries, attitude is defined as *"a feeling or opinion about something or someone, or a way of behaving that is caused by this."* In a more constructive way, attitude is composed by three elements, the psychologists call it as ***ABC Model of Attitudes***:

我們對態度一詞或多或少有些了解，但若不翻開字典，很難定義態度一詞。劍橋字典中對態度的定義為：「對某事或某人的感受或看法；或由於態度而產生某種行為表現。」更具體來說，態度由三個元素組成，心理學家稱之為**態度三元論**。

A. Affective component:

How an individual feels about the object.

求職面試心理

了解你的老闆

找到對的工作　職場定位

你與同事

帶人要帶心

升工作態度與遷

B. Behavioral component:

How an individual intends to do toward the object.

C. Cognitive component:

An individual's beliefs toward the object

A. 情緒因子：

個人對某件事的感受。

B. 行為因子：

個人對某件事而表現出的行為。

C. 認知因子：

個人對某件事的信念。

If we apply the ABC Model of Attitudes at the workplace, the following two examples illustrate how positive attitude and negative attitude are formed respectively:

如果我們將態度三元論應用在職場上，以下的例子可以説明正向態度與負向態度分別是如何形成的:

(Jade and Vivian both work in the kindergarten, however, they have totally different attitudes toward their jobs.)

（Jade 和 Vivian 在同一家幼兒園工作，但是，她們對工作有完全不同的態度。）

Positive attitude:

A: Jade feels happy when she works with children in the kindergarten.

B: When she is with children, she would like to do anything to make them laugh.

C: She believes every child deserves to grow up happily.

正向態度：

A: Jade 在幼兒園與小孩一起工作時，都會覺得很開心。

B: 每當與小孩在一起時，她會想盡辦法讓小孩開懷大笑。

C: 她認為每個孩子都值得快樂地長大。

Negative attitude:

A: Vivian feels frustrated when she works with children in the kindergarten.

B: She would stay in the office rather than go to the playground with the children.

C: She thinks children are always rude and naughty.

負向態度：

A: Vivian 在幼兒園與小孩一起工作時，她覺得很挫折。

B: 她寧願待在辦公室中也不願到遊戲場與小孩們在一起。

C: 她認為小孩很粗魯又頑皮。

Obviously, individual' feelings, behaviors and beliefs toward the job will seriously influence their attitudes at work.

求職面試心理

了解你的老闆

找到對的工作　職場定位

你與同事

帶人要帶心

升工作態度與遷

很明顯的，個人對工作的感受、行為與信念會嚴重影響對工作的態度。

Why is it important? 為什麼態度很重要

Another example about different working attitudes can clearly be seen from the two main characters in a famous animated television series, SpongeBob SquarePants. SpongeBob and Squidward both work at the Krusty Krab; however, they have different attitudes toward their jobs. SpongeBob is an enthusiastic employee who loves what he does, so he makes the best burgers for his customers. He believes the burgers he made can give his customers an enjoyable time. On the contrary, his co-worker, Squidward, treats his job with a different attitude. He feels his work is boring. He is always reluctant to serve his customers. He believes every customer except himself is uncivilized and lower class.

另一個跟不同工作態度有關的例子，是知名卡通海綿寶寶中的兩位主角- 海綿寶寶與章魚哥。他們都在蟹寶王中工作，但卻對工作有著截然不同的態度。海綿寶寶是個充滿熱情的員工，熱愛他所做的事，所以他做出最棒的漢堡給顧客吃。他相信他做的漢堡可以為顧客帶來愉悦的時光。相反的，他的同事章魚哥對待工作有不同的態度。章魚哥認為工作很無趣，總是很不情願地服務客人。他相信除了他自己以外，每位客人都是不文明且較為低級的。

The employers, of course, like the positive working

attitudes that SpongeBob has because positive attitudes in the workplace have many benefits, including:

老闆當然會喜歡像海綿寶寶一樣有著正向工作態度的員工，因為職場中正向的態度可以帶來許多好處，包括：

- Better communications between colleagues.
- Efficient teamwork
- Higher productivity
- Pleasant working environment and atmosphere
- Better commitment and engagement to the work
- Higher loyalty and low employee turnover

- 員工間的溝通更好。
- 團體工作更有效率。
- 生產力更高。
- 愉悦的工作環境與氣氛。
- 對工作的承諾與付出更好。
- 更高的忠誠度與較低的離職率。

職 場小故事

Tyler is a cashier at a grocery store. He arrives promptly each day, several minutes before his shift is about to start dressing in his store uniform and name badge. On the rare occasion that he is running late due to abnormally dense traffic or a true

求職面試心理

了解你的老闆

找到職場對定位的工作

你與同事

帶人要帶心

升工作態度遷與

emergency, Tyler will make a phone call to his manager beforehand to let the manager know that he'll be a few minutes late. Tyler makes sure that he is well-groomed, cleanly-shaven, and hygienic before going to work. He aims to make a good impression not only on his boss and co-workers, but on the store's customers as well.

Tyler 是一家小超市的收銀員。他每天都準時來,都在他的班開始前幾分鐘就到了,也都會穿上制服和名牌。有些時候因為塞車或真的有急事,Tyler 也會打電話給經理,告知他自己會晚幾分鐘到。Tyler 在上班之前,都會確定他自己有好好梳洗、鬍子刮好、保持乾淨。他希望能給他的老闆、同事,以及顧客一個好印象。

When he arrives at his job, Tyler parks in the employee lot so that he does not occupy the customer parking spaces that are closer to the store's entrance. He follows the store's established clock-in procedures, and counts the money in his cash drawer before heading to his cashier desk. When customers check out, Tyler is very careful to give them the correct amount of change, and he helps them with their electronic payments as needed. He never steals money from his cash drawer, not even to put it back later. He knows that the money belongs to the store, and he knows it is illegal to take any of the store's money with him.

Tyler 來上班的時候,會把車停在員工停車場,不會佔用比較靠近超市入口的顧客停車空間。他相當遵守店裏的打卡規則,在收銀台就定位之前，也會先清點收銀機裡的金錢。在客人結帳的時候，Tyler 對於找零非常地仔細，如果有刷卡支付的需要，他也會幫忙處理。他從來不曾從收銀機裡偷拿錢，連先借用再放回去都不曾做過。他知道錢是屬於這家店的，而且拿了任何店裏的錢，都是不合法的。

On his lunch breaks, Tyler watches the time carefully so that he gets back to his cashier desk on time. After eating, he thoroughly washes his hands so that he can stay hygienic and avoid passing any germs along to the store's customers. He also makes sure that his uniform is clean and straightened before returning from his breaks.

在午休的時候，Tyler 很注意時間，以能準時回到收銀台。午餐吃完後，他會確實地洗手，保持衛生，避免把任何的病菌帶到顧客身上。在午休結束之前，他也會確認自己的制服是乾淨且整理好。

Whenever fellow employees need help, he volunteers to help, and even when Tyler is not assisting a customer, he helps colleagues successfully complete their tasks. When his boss asks him to help gather carts from the parking lot, clean up around the store, or perform tasks other than being a cashier, Tyler does it. He understands that doing other jobs on occasion is part of being a team, and that teamwork helps the store run smoothly.

每當有同事需要幫忙，他自願幫忙。而且當他沒有在協助任何顧客時，他都會幫助同事們完成任務。當他的老闆叫他幫忙把推車從停車場集中推回來、打掃店裏、或是其他不是收銀員的工作，Tyler 都會做。他明白在一個團隊裡面，有時候就是要分擔其他的工作，也是這些團隊合作，才能讓這個超市營運的好。

Working hard, following procedures and directions, and being a dedicated employee made Tyler feel satisfied about the job on what he was going. After many years of being a good employee, Tyler was rewarded with a promotion to assistant manager of the store.

努力工作、遵守步驟及指引、當個投入的員工，讓 Tyler 在這個工作中獲得滿足。幾年下來，這位好員工獲得了升職，成為了助理店長。

達 人提點

Employees with a positive attitude are:

有正向工作態度的員工會：

1. Being responsible 更負責

Individuals with a positive attitude have a strong sense of responsibility for their work. They will show up on time, complete tasks with good quality before the deadline, and try their best to have a good performance. Responsible employees are reliable and trustworthy.

有正向態度的人對工作有強烈的責任感。他們會準時上班；準時完成工作並維持高品質；盡力做到最好的表現。有責任感的員工值得依賴與信任。

2. Motivating themselves 自我激勵

Employees with a positive attitude will look for the positive side, keep their professional confidence, and motivate themselves. They inspire and direct themselves to accomplish better achievement. In addition, they motivate themselves to grow and learn, so they keep learning new things through a professional development.

有正向態度的員工會正向看待事情，保持專業信心並激勵自己。他們鼓勵自己、引導自己以達到更好的成就。此外，他們鼓勵自己成長與學習，所以他們不斷在專業上學習新東西。

3. Learning from experiences 從經驗中學習

When there is an unexpected outcome, individuals with a positive attitude would critically review the process and figure out what can be learn from the experience. They look at these unexpected situations as learning opportunities which help to improve their performance next time.

從經驗中學習。當有任何非預期的結果產生時，有正向態度的員工會批判性地檢討過程並思考可以由經驗中學到些甚麼。他們視這些非預期的狀況為學習的機會，可以幫助他們下

求職面試心理

了解你的老闆

找到對的工作 職場定位

你與同事

帶人要帶心

升工作態度 遷與

次表現得更好。

4. Being passionate 有熱情

Individuals with passion and enthusiasm love what they do. They find meanings and values from their work. They proactively assist others, including their co-workers and customers. They can respond toward criticism maturely, and are willing to improve defects.

有熱情的員工愛他們的工作。他們會在工作中找到意義與價值。他們主動幫助他人，包括他們的同事與客戶。他們對批判會成熟地回應，且願意改正缺點。

5. Being a good team player 是很好的團隊工作者

Employees with a good attitude can get along with others. They are happy to work together with others, respect their peers and help the team to meet the goals. They also recognize others' contribution, rather than take all the credits.

有好態度的員工可以與他人相處愉快，他們樂意與同事合作，尊重同事並幫助團隊達成目標。他們會看到別人得貢獻，而非搶去所有的功勞。

V ocabulary 字彙

- ★ Considerably 相當的
- ★ Respectively 分別地
- ★ Turnover 離職
- ★ Dense 密集的
- ★ Lot 一塊地
- ★ Germ 病菌

- ★ Obsess 迷住
- ★ Uncivilized 不文明的
- ★ Cashier 收銀員
- ★ Groom 使整潔
- ★ Clock-in 打卡
- ★ Cart 推車

MEMO

求職面試心理

了解你的老闆

找到對的工作 職場定位

你與同事

帶人要帶心

升遷與工作態度

Negative Working Attitude
負向工作態度

While Sal was wiping off the counters at the deli one morning, his co-worker Tony. walked in, He was known around the deli for having a poor attitude, which made the other employees, and even the customers, a bit uncomfortable.

Sal 有天早上正在他上班的小吃店裡清理工作台面,他的同事 Tony 剛好走了進來。Tony 在小吃店的態度是出了名的不好,讓他的同事和顧客都不是很舒服。

"You should've had this done by now, Sal. You're wasting my time. I've got to get going before all of these people come in here this morning. It's already bad enough that I have to be here", said Tony.

「Sal,你早就該把這做好了,你在浪費我的時間。我要趕在早上的客人進來之前準備好,我還要來店裏就已經夠糟了。」Tony 說。

"Are you supposed to be off, too? Actually, I'm not supposed to be here, either. It was on my day off, but Barry got sick and called in. I'll be done cleaning in just a minute, though", replied Sal.

「難道你也不應該來嗎？事實上，我才不應該來，今天我放假，只是 Barry 生病了請假不能來。我再一下就清好了。」Sal 回答著。

"I'm not supposed to be off, but I still don't like being here. Whatever, I don't care who got sick or what happened. You're still in my way", said Tony.

「我是沒放假啦，但我還是不想來啊。 隨便啦，我不管誰生病還是幹嘛的，你就是在妨礙我。」Tony 說。

Sal quickly finished cleaning and took his place behind the cashier's desk. He was determined to get through the day without talking to Tony again, until he overheard him rudely addressing a customer. Sal apologized to the customer and gave him a discount on his purchase. Once he left and the deli was empty again, Sal decided to talk to Tony about his bad attitude.

Sal 很快地清理完了，然後就在收銀台後面就定位。他決定今天要再和 Tony 說話了，直到他又聽到他對一個顧客大小聲。Sal 向那位顧客道歉，而且給了他一點折扣。客人離開之後，小吃店裡沒有別人了，Sal 決定和 Tony 談談他的態度。

求職面試心理

了解你的老闆

找到對的工作　職場定位

你與同事

帶人要帶心

升工作態度遷與

"You just cost the store $5.50, but it would have been worse if that customer had decided not to come back again. Who knows, after the way you acted, he just may never come back. It's one thing to be rude to me, and the other people who work here. It's another thing to have a bad attitude with the customers. Maybe you should go talk to the boss if you don't like it here, but no customer deserves to be talked like that for simply asking a question."

「你剛剛讓我們店損失了 5.50 元，但是如果他決定再也不回來消費的話，我們會損失更多。不過誰知道，被你這樣對待，他可能就再也不會來了，你對我或其他同事不禮貌是一回事，但是對客人不禮貌又是另一回事了。也許你應該和老闆談談，如果你是不喜歡這裏的工作，但是沒有客人應該為問了一個簡單的問題，而被你這樣對待。」

"Too late to apologize to him now", said Tony.

「現在和他道歉也太遲了。」Tony 說。

"But it's not too late for you to stop bringing your bad attitude to work", replied Sal. "I used to be somewhat like you, but I found work is a lot easier when you at least try to have a positive outlook."

「但是停止把你那不好的態度帶來上班，還不嫌遲。」Sal 回應說。「我以前也像你一樣，但是我發現，至少表面上試著開心一點，工作會容易很多。」

求職面試心理

了解你的老闆

找到對的工作 職場定位

你與同事

帶人要帶心

工作態度與 升遷

達 人剖析

▶ Negative working attitude 負向工作態度

Work can often be stressful, and it can be difficult to maintain a positive attitude at work if you're feeling frustrated. However, if you choose to have a negative outlook every day, you will feel horrible than before, and have a poorer performance.

工作常常帶來壓力，在感到挫折時難以時常維持正向態度。然而，若你選擇以負向態度來過每一天，你會比以前感覺更糟，且表現也會更差。

People with a bad working attitude usually have the following behaviors:

有負向工作態度的人通常有下列行為：

1. They are disrespectful 他們不尊重他人

They are rude to others, including their co-workers, managers, and boss; sometimes they even insult their clients or customers.

他們對他人無禮，包括對同事、主管、老闆等，有時甚至會侮辱客戶或顧客。

303

2. They don't have good work ethics 他們沒有很好的工作倫理

They are late for work and leave early. They don't follow company's rules and procedures. They never do extra work and think it is not their business. They only do the minimum. Sometimes they don't even finish their own work and leave it to others to complete it. They find various ways to get out of work.

他們會遲到早退。他們不遵守公司規定與流程。他們不願意做額外工作且覺得那些不關他的事。他們只做到最低標準。有時他們甚至沒有完成自己分內的工作，要讓他人幫忙完成。他們找各種理由不去工作。

3. They are not a team player 他們不是團隊合作者

They are arrogant and self-centered; they only care about themselves. They are hostile to others and lack of team spirit. They argue with team members a lot, so it's hard for them to cooperate with others.

他們傲慢且自我中心。他們只關心自己。他們對他人有敵意，且缺乏團隊精神。他們常與團隊成員吵架，所以很難合作。

4. They gossip around 他們散播八卦

They talk lots of gossip behind others' back. And they spread rumors about co-workers which undermine teamwork.

他們會在別人背後説三道四。且他們會傳遞關於同事的謠言而傷害團隊工作。

5. They complain and criticize a lot 他們常常抱怨且批評

They view everything negatively. So they are not happy; they complain and criticize everything and everyone, including their work, workload, their co-workers, managers, boss, working environment, even their clients or customers.

他們負面看待任何事。所以他們不快樂，常常抱怨與批評他人或其他事，包括他們的工作、工作量、同事、主管、老闆、工作環境、甚至他們的客戶或顧客。

The causes of negative working attitude
造成負向工作態度的原因

1. They have wrong beliefs about their work
他們對工作有錯誤的信念

The main cause of bad attitude is wrong beliefs about their work. They believe other people do not treat them well. They believe this job is boring and meaningless. They believe they are smarter than others.

造成負面工作態度的主要原因是對工作的錯誤信念。他們認為其他人不當地對待自己。他們認為工作無聊又沒意義。他們相信自己比他人聰明。

2. They feel unappreciated 他們覺得自己不被重視

Some people used to perform well in the first few months in their work. However, bad attitudes arise when they feel unappreciated or unrecognized by others. Their efforts are ignored, so they no longer want to devote themselves in the work and develop negative attitudes.

有些人在工作的前幾個月表現得不錯。但是，但他們覺得不被重視或認可時，就會開始有負面態度。他們的努力被忽略，所以他們不再投入工作，並開始有負向態度。

3. They are stressful and burnout 他們壓力過大且有工作倦怠

If individuals have increasing workloads and stress which exceed their ability, they gradually have negative attitude in order to express their emotion as well as to avoid further extra work.

若一個人的工作量與壓力持續增加且超過了他們的能力，他們就逐漸會有負向態度以發洩情緒並避免有更多的額外工作。

4. They have psychological problems 他們有心理問題

Some mental problems make people become

求職面試心理

了解你的老闆

找到對的工作 職場定位

你與同事

帶人要帶心

工作態度遷與 升

unpleasant, defensive, aggressive or insensitive. Depression, anxiety, or personality disorders might be the influential factors for presenting bad working attitudes.

　　有心理問題的人可能會不開心、有防衛心、具攻擊性或不敏感。憂鬱症、焦慮症或人格違常等問題可能是造成不好工作態度的影響因子。

職 場小故事

Eric worked at a small local bakery. He enjoyed making the breads and pastries, and even liked helping the customers with their orders, but he despised having to clean the shop's floors and restroom. Eric didn't even clean up the floors and bathroom in his own home because his wife handled that task and he certainly didn't want to do it at work either. At work, he frequently found himself either trying to get out of doing the cleaning or asking a co-worker to do it for him. On one occasion, when he was feeling particularly against cleaning the bakery's restroom, Eric actually paid one of his co-workers a small sum to perform his cleaning duties. A few weeks after, Erica asked this same co-worker to clean the bathroom for him in exchange for payment again.

　　Eric 在一個鎮上的小麵包店工作。他很喜歡做麵包酥點，也很喜歡幫助客人處理他們訂購的東西，但他非常討厭清理店裏的地板及廁所。Eric 連自己家裡的地板和廁所都不會清理，都是他太太負責的，那他當然不會想做店裏的清理工作。在店裡，他常常不是想辦法逃避打掃的工作，就是叫同事幫忙做。有一次，他實在是非常抗拒清掃店裡的廁所，他還付了一點小錢給他的同事，讓他們去做本來是他自己該做的打掃工作。幾個禮拜後，Eric 又找了同一位同事，請她幫忙打掃廁所，他會付她工錢。

The second time when she was asked, Eric's co-worker refused. However, she did ask him just why he didn't like cleaning. Eric couldn't come up with a specific answer, and he said he simply didn't like it. Then, his co-worker listed the many reasons that cleaning up the bakery's restroom and floors were necessary, including maintaining a hygienic environment, making the customers feel good, and helping to keep the bakery looking nice.

但這一次，Eric 的這位同事拒絕了。她問他為什麼這麼不喜歡打掃。Eric 沒辦法很明確的回答，只是說他就是不喜歡。接著，這位同提出了很多原因來說明清理店裏地板及廁所的必要性，包括了維持一個衛生的環境、讓顧客覺得舒服、保持麵包店內的美觀。

Though he agreed with her reasons for cleaning, Eric still protested and made clear his objection to these tasks. He told her that he could tolerate cleaning the dishes and baking equipment, ovens, and even the bakery counters, but he is reluctant to touch the restroom and floors.

　　雖然他也同意這些為何需要打掃的原因，但 Eric 還是不願意做這些工作。他告訴她，他可以接受清洗碗盤、烘培用具、烤箱、甚至工作台，但廁所和地板他就是不想碰。

Suddenly, Eric's co-worker said something which helped him change the way he looks at cleaning. She pointed out that the cleaner the bakery, the more likely they were to keep their loyal customers. And the more loyal customers the bakery had, the better Eric's job security. She told him that he truly should be thankful that he not only had the physical ability to clean, but that he was able to do what he enjoyed for a living.

　　突然，Eric 的同事說了一件事，改變了他對打掃的想法。她點出了如果這個麵包店越乾淨，就越能留住客人。而越多客人給他們支持，Eric 的工作就越有保障。她說他應該對他還有能力打掃覺得感恩，而且也還能以他喜歡的事做為工作。

Eric knew she was right. Though he never did start to like cleaning the bakery's floors and restroom, he definitely stopped complaining about it and never asked a co-worker to complete those tasks again.

　　Eric 知道她說的對，雖然他還是沒辦法喜歡打掃店裏的地板和廁所，但他總還是停止抱怨了，而且再也沒有要求任何同事來幫忙完成打掃的工作。

求職面試心理

了解你的老闆

找到對的工作　職場定位

你與同事

帶人要帶心

工作態度與升遷

Individual with a negative attitude has the same power to influence others as a person with a positive attitude.

有負面態度的人與有正向態度的人一樣都有強大的影響力。

1. Limitation 會受到限制

Individuals with a negative attitude may fear of failure. They do not try new way to solve problems, or propose more creative ideas. The productivity and performance declines because of a poor attitude.

負向的人害怕失敗。他們不願意嘗試新的解決方法,或提出創新的想法。他們的生產力與表現會因為不好的態度而下降。

2. Lower morale 降低士氣

Other co-workers are afraid of talking to the person with a bad attitude to avoid conflicts or pain. Consequently, the morale in the office drops. Other workers may feel unfair if someone with a bad attitude can get away from extra work but the good employees can't. The working atmosphere is also worse because of constant complains and criticism by the co-workers with bad working attitudes. The worst scenario is, it leads to turnover and a loss of experienced staff members, which limits the company's ability to grow.

　　其他的員工會害怕與負向態度的同事交談，以避免衝突或痛苦。這會造成辦公室士氣降低。其他員工會覺得為什麼態度不好的員工可以因此不用做額外的工作，但好員工卻不行。工作氣氛也會因為態度不佳的員工不停地抱怨與批判而降低。最差的情況是會導致離職，公司因此失去有經驗的員工，而讓公司的成長受限。

3. Poor cooperation 無法合作

People with poor attitudes do not communicate with others effectively. They only focus on themselves and don't want to share responsibilities. They lack of can-do attitude so it is difficult for others to cooperate with them.

　　態度不佳的人無法與人有效溝通。他們只重視自己而不想分擔責任。他們缺少願意做事的態度，所以難以與他們合作。

4. Unhappy customers 顧客不高興

Customers who have been treated rudely will never come back again. No customers want to deal with representatives with inappropriate attitudes. This will damage company's reputation and profits.

　　顧客若被無禮地對待一定不會再來。沒有顧客願意被員工以不當態度對待。這會傷害公司的聲譽與利益。

求職面試心理

了解你的老闆

找到對的工作 職場定位

你與同事

帶人要帶心

升工作態度遷與

Section 6-3

Stick to the End
堅持到最後

Paul was very excited that after 6 years working at a local engineering firm and completing his master's degree, he was finally ready to open his own engineering business. He had secured investors for his firm and already had a number of prospective clients. Paul was in his last few days at his job when he was asked to work overtime on a project at a meeting.

經過六年在當地工程事務所工作，也取得了碩士學位，Pauk 終於準備好要自己創立工程事務所。他已經找好投資者，也已經有幾位客戶。Paul 只剩幾天就要離開了，不過在會議中被詢問是否可以加班。

"We need to get this project done quickly, but we need to do it well, as you all know", said Paul's boss, and owner of the firm, Mr. Sutton. "I expect that you will all put in a bit of overtime work until we get this completed, the harder we work, the quicker we will get it done. Except for you, Paul. Everyone else,

I want to see you put in as much effort as you can."

「我們需要盡快把案子做完，但我們也需要做得好，你們知道的。」Paul 的老闆，也是這家店的創立者 Mr. Sutton。「我希望你們大家可以加班，直到完成這個案子。大家越努力，就會越快做完。除了 Paul 以外，我希望看到你們盡全力。」

Paul didn't understand why he was called out, but once the meeting was over he decided to talk with Mr. Sutton.

Paul 不了解為什麼 Mr. Sutton 不把他算在內，所以會議結束後他決定去找老闆。

"Mr. Sutton, I notice you said I didn't have to work overtime this week. Is there a problem?"

「Mr. Sutton，我發現你並沒有要我這週加班，有什麼問題嗎？」

"No, I simply don't expect it. You handed in your resignation weeks ago and are headed out of here at the end of the week."

「沒有，我只是沒有期待你加班。你幾週前就提出離職，且這週結束你就要離開這裏了。」Mr. Sutton 説。

"But I work here now, and I'm still one of the leads on this project. I don't mind putting in some extra time", said Paul.

「但我現在還在這裡啊，而且我是這個案子其中一個帶領者。我不介意加班。」Paul 說。

Mr. Sutton gave Paul a puzzled look. "I'm not certain why you would, but we can definitely use all of the help we can get to meet this deadline."

Mr. Sutton 有點困惑，「我不確定你為什麼要這麼做，不過我們確實需要所有人的幫忙以準時完成。」

"I've spent well over a year preparing to open my own firm, and I've had to learn just how much work goes into not only starting, but growing an engineering business. You've got to do a good job from start to finish. I'm opening my firm because I learned how to keep a good work ethic from being employed here. I wouldn't start slacking off just because I'm leaving at the end of the week", said Paul.

「我已經花了超過一年的時間準備自己開業，我也學到了自己創業有多少工作要完成，不僅是一開始，之後業務的成長也需要。你從一開始到最後都做得很好，我會自己創業是因為我從這裡學到了很好的工作倫理。我不會因為這個禮拜底要離職就變得馬虎。」Paul 說。

Mr. Sutton realized he was wrong for his assumption. With Paul's hard work and expertise, the project was completed before he exited the firm.

Mr. Sutton 發現自己想錯了。有了 Paul 的努力與專業，這個案子在 Paul 離職前就完成了。

達 人剖析

Your last few days 最後的幾天

No matter what is the reason for leaving your current job, you should leave your job gracefully, carefully, and professionally. It is important not to leave a bad impression on your boss and co-workers before your go. Just make your last few days the best for you and everyone.

無論你離職的原因為何，你要優雅、謹慎且專業的離開。不要在離職前讓老闆與同事留下不好的印下。讓你最後的幾天成為你與同事間最棒的幾天。

1. Be professional 要專業

You should remain your productivity even in your last few days. Stay focus on your work until the last minute, because you are still get the paycheck. Do not disappear on the job or distract others. Complete all paperwork and HR procedures before you leave. Being professional will leave your colleagues and boss a good impression about you.

在最後幾天你仍要保持生產力。專注在工作上直到最後一

求職面試心理

了解你的老闆

找到對的工作 職場定位

你與同事

帶人要帶心

升工作態度與

分鐘，因為你還是有領錢。不要消失不見，或影響他人工作。在離開前完成所有文件與人事流程。保持專業可以讓老闆與同事對你留下好印象。

2. Make clear transition 清楚的交接

You should offer your help and transition assistance. Leave detailed information about your daily duties and current projects you are working. The replacement will then have some ideas about how you do your work. However, do not promise anything you cannot do. Your efforts to make the transition smoothly and clearly will be appreciated by people in this company.

　　你可以提供協助與交接工作。對你每日工作與手上的案子留下清楚的說明，這樣接你工作的人會對你如何做你的工作有一些概念。但是，不要答應任何你無法做到的事。你讓交接順利且清楚會讓公司中的人對你感謝。

3. Stay connected 保持聯絡

Do make a plan to keep in touch with your co-workers, friends, and boss. Keep your network strong. They can give you additional resources which may be valuable to you.

　　想一下要怎麼與同事、朋友與老闆保持聯絡。讓你的人際網絡更大，他們可以成為對你有益的資源。

4. **Thank everyone** 感謝每個人

Thank the employer for the opportunity to work here. And thank everyone personally to appreciate their help and working together. Even if you do not get along with some co-workers, do not call names and maintain your manners.

謝謝老闆讓你有機會在這裡工作。也個別謝謝每個人，感謝他們的協助與共事。即使你與某些同事相處不好，也不要口出惡言，而是維持你的禮貌。

5. **Tidy up your workstation** 把工作環境清理好

Clean and organize your desk and office, and leave these space ready for the next person. In addition, you need to remove personal files from the computer, and organize the digital files so your replacement can easily find out. Return company property; do not take away any things that do not belong to you.

將桌面與辦公室清理並歸位，留給下一個人整潔的空間。此外。將電腦中個人的檔案移除，並將電子檔整理好，如此接替的人才可以找到檔案。歸還公司的東西；不要帶走任何不屬於你的東西。

6. **Stay confident** 保持自信

Do not feel guilty about leaving. It may be hard to leave

求職面試心理

了解你的老闆

職場定位
找到對的工作

你與同事

帶人要帶心

工作態度與
升遷

you job, or your boss or co-workers make it hard for you, but focus on the fact that you are leaving to create a better future for yourself. However, do not boast about your new job. You can provide a short statement about your new opportunity, but say no more.

不要對自己的離職感到罪惡。離職也許不容易，或是遭到老闆與同事的刁難，但專注在你將要離開且為自己開創更好未來的事實上。然而，不要吹噓你的新工作。你可以對新的工作做一些簡短的說明，但不要說太多。

7. Do not say anything wrong 不要說錯話

You should maintain good, at least fair relationships with your co-workers and boss, because you may run into them at other social activities. So do not say anything terrible which you will feel regret about it. For example, do not say something like "You are an awful manager."; or "This place is awful, you should look for another job."

你要與同事保持友好、至少平和的關係，因為你以後可能也會在其他社交活動上遇見他們。所以不要說一些連自己都會後悔的壞話。例如，不要說「你是個糟糕的主管！」，或是「這裡太糟了，你應該要趕快找其他的工作！」

求職面試心理

了解你的老闆

找到對的工作 職場定位

你與同事

帶人要帶心

升遷與工作態度

職 場小故事

Mr. Gilbert is a 69-year-old man who has worked for the same auto plant for over 40 years. He started working there at 21 years old, as an assembly worker, and is currently the head of operations. He has seen the auto production industry change numerous times throughout the decades, and he has seen many employees retire instead of continuing to work during their senior years. Mr. Gilbert has the option to retire, as he has earned a healthy pension, but he prefers working. Not only does work satisfy him and keep him active, but he enjoys passing on his knowledge and insight to the younger workers.

　　Mr. Gilbert 69 歲了，他在這家自動化設備工廠工作了超過 40 年。他自 21 歲就開始在這裡工作了，從組裝作業員開始做起，目前擔任營運主任。過去數十年間，他經歷了自動化產業多次的變革，且許多員工在晚年選擇退休而非繼續工作。Mr. Gilbert 也可以選擇退休，因為他已經有退休金，但他比較想要工作。工作讓他開心且可以一直活動，且他還很享受傳遞知識與見解給年輕的員工。

During his tenure at the auto plant, there were many occasions where co-workers, plant management, and even the plant's owner suggested that he consider retirement. Each time, Mr. Gilbert asked them why, and whether his job performance had declined at all in more than 40 years while he had been working there. No one could ever point to even a moment where Mr. Gilbert's work was not as good as it had always been. He promised himself that the day he started to decline or anyone could prove that as long as people have a feeling that his productivity declines or he is not as adept as he used to, he'll retire.

在他工作期間，有幾次同事、經理甚至工廠老闆都建議他考慮退休。每次 Mr. Gilbert 都問他們為什麼？是否因為四十餘年來他的表現下降？但在那個時刻，沒有人會這麼說，因為 Mr. Gilbert 的工作表現一直都很好。他答應只要他們覺得他的表現開始下降，或能證明已經不像過去一般熟捻，他就會退休。

As Mr. Gilbert got older, he was strategic about how he could keep his job and prove himself valuable to the company. Over the years, he had earned several certifications and even a business management degree. He knew that as he aged, he would be unable to do the heavy physical work that he once had, but he also knew that his mind was still sharp and he could contribute his wisdom as long as he kept up with the industry's trends and technology.

當 Mr. Gilbert 年紀更大，他想著要怎麼樣繼續工作且證明他對公司還是有價值的。工作這麼多年，他取得了幾張證書，甚至獲得了商業管理學位。他知道自己年紀大了，無法做如過去般體能負荷過大的工作；但他也知道他的頭腦仍很敏銳，他可以貢獻自己的智慧，只要他能跟上產業的趨勢與科技。

After he stopped doing physical work at the auto plant, Mr. Gilbert started training incoming employees on how to use the equipment and how the company operated. He then moved on to the company's management crew, where he earned a promotion to the plant's head of operations.

當他停止在自動化設備工廠做體能性的工作後，Mr. Gilbert 開始訓練新進員工，教他們如何使用設備及公司如營運等事情。他也進入到管理層級，晉升為營運主任。

The company's other employees and owner all appreciate the input and value that Mr. Gilbert brings to their team. They hope that he will continue working with them for many years.

工廠的其他員工與老闆他很感謝 Mr. Gilbert 的付出與價值。他們希望可以繼續與他一起共事很多年。

達人提點

Value the older employees 老員工是珍寶

Older workers may not be familiar with the updated technology or other fancy skills, but they have years of experience which can hardly be replaced. So respect your older colleagues and value the advantages they have.

老員工可能對最新的科技或花俏的技巧不那麼行，但多年的經驗卻是無法被取代的。所以尊重你的老同事，並重視他們擁有的優勢。

1. They are professional 他們很專業

The older workers have good work ethic; they go to work on time, and they make themselves ready to work every morning. They hardly miss work because of personal matters. They take company policies and procedures seriously. They dedicate their whole life to work and feel satisfied about what they do.

老員工有很好的工作倫理；他們準時工作，每天早上也都讓自己準備好上工。他們很少因為私人事情而請假。他們嚴肅看待公司政策與流程。他們奉獻一生在工作上，且對他們所做的事感到滿意。

2. They are mentally more mature 他們心智更為成熟

They are experienced of work as well as personal interaction. So when there is a problem, they can handle it calmly and confidently. They think thoroughly and critically before making decision or judgement, and they tend to take less risk and are more cautious. So they are more reliable.

他們在工作上與人際關係上都很有經驗，所以當遇到困難，他們可以冷靜有信心地面對。他們在做決定或判斷時會仔細且批判性的思考，且他們不會冒險也比較謹慎。所以他們很受信賴。

3. **They are loyal** 他們很忠誠

They put company missions as the priority, and they are more committed at work. They tend to stay in one company longer and are less likely to frequently change jobs. As long as they know their efforts are appreciated and valued, they would like to devote themselves to the company until their retirement.

他們將公司使命是為優先，且對工作有更多的承諾。他們通常會待在一家公司更久，且很少換工作。只要他們知道自己的努力有被感謝且重視，他們就會對公司賣命直到退休。

Vocabulary 字彙

★ Resignation 辭呈
★ slacking off 鬆懈
★ replacement 代替者
★ tenure 任期
★ dedicate 奉獻

★ Puzzled 困惑的
★ transition 過渡時期、交接
★ assembly 裝配
★ adept 內行
★ Investor 投資者

求職面試心理

了解你的老闆

找到職場定對的工作位

你與同事

帶人要帶心

升工作態度遷與

6-4

Job Promotion
工作升遷

Delia was very into fashion and shopping, so she felt she had landed the job of a lifetime when she was hired as a merchandiser at one of her favorite clothing stores. She had a degree in fashion merchandising and felt she was well-suited for the position. However, after working at her job for a year, she began wanting more. Delia starting eyeing a promotion to the district merchandiser, a position that not only meant a higher pay, but the ability to travel and style each store in the region. The only other merchandiser up for consideration for the promotion was Victoria. Though Victoria didn't have a merchandising degree, she had worked her way up to the position after being employed at the company for five years.

　　Delia 對時尚與購物非常有興趣，所以在她最愛的服飾店裡，當上了採購員的時候，她覺得真是找到一生的志業了。她本身就擁有一個時尚經營的學位，也認為自己很適合這個工作，但是，在工作了一年之後，她終究想得到更多。Delia 開始把眼光放在區域採購員，這個位置不但有更高的薪資、可以到處旅行，並能決定區域內的每家店要走什麼風格。另一個有可能接任這個位置的採購員是 Victoria。雖然 Victoria 沒有經營的學歷，但她在到職後的五年當中，也一步步地爬到她目前的位置。

"I can't wait for the announcement about the promotion tomorrow!", exclaimed Delia during lunch. "I just have a feeling I'll get the position."

「我等不及了，不知道明天會公布誰升職！」Delia 在午餐的時候高呼。「我有種直覺，會是我得到這個工作。」

"You do have the education, and you do a great job styling the displays", said Victoria.

「妳的確是學這個的，而且妳也真的在風格和展示方面做得很好。」Victoria 說。

Just then, Delia and Victoria's boss asked if either of them would clean up the dressing room area since the store was short on staff. While Delia politely declined, Victoria readily went to go help. Later that day, Victoria and Delia talked about the promotion again.

剛好這個時候，Delia 和 Victoria 的老闆，問她們之中有沒有人願意把更衣室附近打掃一下，店裏有點缺人手。Delia 很有禮貌地拒絕

求職面試心理

了解你的老闆

找到對的工作　職場定位

你與同事

帶人要帶心

升工作態度遷與

了，Victoria 就前去幫忙。當天稍晚的時候，Victoria 和 Delia 又聊起了升職的事。

"Can you just imagine me styling all of the stores? You know, it's a very notable position. I'll be called on for interviews. I'll get to speak to the media about our store's events and fashion collections. This is my dream job!", said Delia.

「妳可以想像是我來為每家店塑造風格嗎？你知道的，這可是一個很重要的位置。我還會被訪問，要對媒體說明我們店內的活動及時尚產品。這真是我夢想中的工作！」Delia 說。

"I'm sure you'll be great at it. I'm really happy for you", replied Victoria.

「我確定妳會做得很好，我很為妳高興。」Victoria 回答說。

"Could you please come help at the checkout desk, Victoria and Delia? Today has been so busy, the worst day to be short on staff!", said their boss.

「Victoria 和 Delia，妳們可不可以過來結帳這裏幫忙？今天真的很忙，偏偏又少了一些人力！」她們的老闆說。

"Sure, if you don't mind me working overtime", said Victoria.

「當然可以，如果妳不介意算我加班的話。」Victoria 說。

"Actually, it's time for me to go home", said Delia.

「事實上，我下班回家的時間到了。」Delia 說。

The next day, both Delia and Victoria were shocked when Victoria was announced as the new district merchandiser.

隔天，Delia 和 Victoria 都被嚇到了，因為公布了 Victoria 是新任的區域採購員。

"She's always had a great work ethic, is a leader, very talented, and always goes beyond her duties. Which is why I'm proud to offer you this position, Victoria", said their boss.

「她的工作態度總是非常好，是個領導者，也非常有才華，而且總是願意分擔本來不是她份內的工作。這就是為什麼我可以很驕傲地說，這份工作非妳莫屬，Victoria。」她們的老闆說。

達 人剖析

How to increase your chances 如何增加機會

Most people want to improve their professional position through promotions. A promotion is a form of recognition for employees who make significant and effective work contributions. However, not everyone have the chance to get promoted. If you are expecting a promotion, it is

求職面試心理

了解你的老闆

找到對的工作 職場定位

你與同事

帶人要帶心

工作態度與升遷

important to prepare yourself and upgrade your performance to a better level.

　　許多人希望藉由升遷來提升自己的專業地位。若員工有顯著有利的貢獻，升遷就是對他認可方式之一。然而，不是每個人都有機會獲得升遷。如果你期待可以升職，你要讓自己準備好，並提升自己的表現。

1. Good performance 好的表現

Put more efforts and promote your accomplishments, so you will have more evidence to convince your boss that you are a good employee. In addition, you have to be a team player, who are willing to help other members, work together with others and respect different opinions. You have to demonstrate to your boss that you are a doer with good working attitude.

　　要更努力提升你的成就，這樣就可以向老闆證明並説服他你是個好員工。此外。你也要能團隊合作，願意幫助團隊成員，共同合作並尊重不同的意見。你要向老闆證明你是願意做事的好員工。

2. Prove that you are capable 證明你有能力

People in a higher position must share more responsibilities, have more duties, and make more important decisions. You need to upgrade your knowledge and skills to prove your boss that you are capable and ready for higher position. So you have to go above and beyond what is expected of you.

在更高位的人一定要負更多責任，有更多任務並做更重要的決定。你要提升自己的知識與技巧，來證明你有能力也準備好接更高的位置。這樣你才可以走的更高，符合他人的期待。

3. Speak up 為自己發聲

You can talk to your manager about your interest. If you never say so, no one knows you are interested in the higher position, and they will not recommend you as a candidate.

你可以告訴主管你有意願。如果你從沒説，沒有人知道你對升遷有興趣，他們也就不會推薦你。

4. Be a volunteer 主動協助

There are many other things in the office which need someone to complete them, such as organizing a Christmas party, plan the staff trip, restock the printer, clean the refrigerator, etc. These tasks are not part of your job description; however, asking for more responsibilities shows your interest and desire to help you company to succeed which will also earn you more credits.

求職面試心理

了解你的老闆

找到對的工作 職場定位

你與同事

帶人要帶心

工作態度與升遷

辦公室有許多事情需要有人完成，像是籌辦耶誕派對、舉辦員工旅遊、為印表機放紙、清理冰箱等。這些任務並不屬於你的工作範圍，但主動幫忙顯示你有興趣也想要幫公司更成功，這也會為你加分。

5. Build your network 建立人脈

If you want to be promoted, you cannot just sit in front of your own desk. You need to extend your network. There will therefore be more people know you and your abilities, strengths, and values.

如果你想要升遷，就不行只是坐在你的辦公桌前。你需要拓展人脈，如此才會有更多人認識你、你的能力、你的專長與你的價值。

6. Focus on the most important things 專注在最重要的事

Even being the busiest person in the office doesn't mean you will be promoted. You need to train yourself as a critical player. Put most of your efforts on those tasks which will have a significant impact on your department or your company.

即便是辦公室中最忙碌的人也不代表你會被升職。你要訓練自己成為重要的員工。把較多的心力放在對部門或公司有顯著影響的事情上。

7. Avoid office gossip and clique 避免加入公司的八卦或小團體

Getting involved in office gossip or clique may increase the risk of creating a negative image for yourself. The clever way is stay far away from the office politics, and just focus on your work.

若與公司八卦或小團體有關，可能就會讓別人對你有負面印象。聰明的方法是對公司政治遠離，專注在你的工作上。

職 場小故事

Greg was a diligent worker who had been a pharmacy technician for three years. He was in school to earn a degree to become a full-fledged pharmacist, which is what he ultimately wanted to do for his career. One day, Greg's boss approached him about a promotion to assistant manager at the pharmacy where he worked.

Greg 是一個勤奮的員工，他已經在藥局當助手三年了，也在學校修讀學位，以成為一個合法執業的藥師，這也是他最終想要做下去的工作。有一天，Greg 的老闆找他談，希望升他作藥局的助理店長。

The new position would pay three dollars more per hour, but he would need to dedicate over 20 hours more to working per week. This basically meant that Greg would have to squeeze in his studies between working a much more stressful, strenuous schedule. After learning more about the position, Greg asked his boss for a couple of days to consider the offer. His boss gladly gave him time to make a decision.

這份新工作，時薪可以多三美金，但他每週也要多付出 20 小時來工作。這基本上，是指 Greg 必須在更具壓力、更緊張的時程裡，擠出時間來讀書。在了解到更多新角色的工作內容後，Greg 請老闆給他兩天考慮。老闆也欣然地答應，給他時間作決定。

Greg asked the store's current assistant manager, who was about to retire, what it was like to be in his position. However, Greg never really got a clear answer; Just from his observation, Greg decided that the job was definitely stressful, perhaps more so than the job's pay was worth.

Greg 問了現在即將退休的助理店長，他在這個位置的感想。Greg 終究沒有得到明確的答案。從他觀察中，Greg 覺得這份工作壓力絕對很大，也許都超過了它得到的報酬。

He enjoyed being a pharmacy technician, primarily because he knew it was the good preparation for the job he would eventually do as a licensed pharmacist. What Greg did not enjoy about his job was that he was essentially a customer service representative 70% of the time, and that he did pharmacy duties only about 30% of the time. As assistant manager, Greg knew he had to deal with the pharmacy's customers even more than he already did. He figured that working as an assistant manager wasn't right for him, and Greg decided to turn down the promotion.

他喜歡當藥師助理，主要是他清楚，這對他將來作一個正式的藥師是很好的準備。而 Greg 不喜歡的部份是，他百分之七十的時間，都只是個客服人員，只有百分之三十的時間是在處理藥劑專業的事。而如果當上助理店長，Greg 知道他一定要面對更多的顧客。他覺得助理店長的工作不是很適合他，打算推掉這個升職的機會。

When he went to speak with his boss, Greg first thanked him for his considering Greg for the promotion in the first place. He then explained to his boss that the duties of being an assistant manager would not work well with his school course load, and that he felt it was best for him to concentrate on his classes and working towards being a pharmacist.

在去找老闆談的時候，Greg 首先謝謝他，有讓 Greg 升職的這份考量。然後他向老闆解釋，助理店長的工作和學校的課業，可能無法配合的很好，他覺得最好還是專注於課業，努力成為一個合格的藥師。

Greg's boss was very understanding, He wished him continued luck on his courses, and extended Greg an offer to work at the pharmacy as a pharmacist once he had earned his degree and license.

Greg 的老闆也很體諒。他祝福他課業順利，而且還給 Greg 機會，在他成為完成學位、考到執照之後，讓他可以再回來當正式的藥師。

求職面試心理

了解你的老闆

找到對的工作　職場定位

你與同事

帶人要帶心

工作態度與升遷

達 人提點

░• Turn down the promotion 拒絕升遷

Most people strive to get a raise, receive a better title and advance the career. However, how to say no without hurting your future with the company, if a promotion is not the right career move for you?

多數人積極地想要升遷，獲得更好的職稱與職涯上的更進一步。但若升遷並非對你最好，你要如何拒絕而不傷害你在公司的未來發展呢？

1. Talk to your boss privately 與老闆私下談

Never reject the offer in front of other workers, which makes you look like you don't respect the authority. Talk to your boss face to face, and let your boss know that you are flattered about being offered a promotion.

絕對不要在其他人面前拒絕老闆，這樣會讓你看起來不尊重權威。與老闆面對面談，讓老闆知道你對升遷一事受寵若驚。

2. Share what is holding you back 與他分享讓你牽絆的事

Explain to your boss what are holding you back from accepting it. For example, you have to take care of your older parents and cannot devote extra hours to the new position.

　　向老闆解釋甚麼牽絆住你而無法接受升職。例如，你必須照顧年邁的父母而無法為新工作付出更多時間等。

3. Explain why current job is more suitable for you
解釋目前工作更適合你

Let your boss know that your specific strengths and skills, and if you accept the promotion, your new job would not use these skills.

　　讓老闆知道你的長處與技能。若你接受升遷，你的新職務就用不上這些技巧。

4. Offer to take extra responsibilities
提供你願意負擔額外責任的選項

You can offer to take extra responsibilities until your boss find someone else to take the new job. Your offer will let your boss know you have to reject the promotion for a good reason, and you are still a hard-working employee who put the company as a priority.

　　你可以說你願意負擔額外責任，直到老闆找到別人擔任此職的人選。你的主動性讓老闆知道你拒絕是因為某些好理由，且你仍然是個努力且視公司利益為優先的好員工。

求職面試心理

了解你的老闆

找到對的工作 職場定位

你與同事

帶人要帶心

工作態度與升遷

6-5

Gender and Job Promotion
性別和工作升遷

情 境對話

Marie had worked as a foreman at a logistics and transportation company for eight years, yet she had never been promoted. She had earned several raises throughout the year, but she was still in the same position. Marie felt that she was a great worker with valuable experience, so when an opening for a higher position became available, Marie decided that it was time for her to request a promotion.

Marie 在一家物流通運公司擔任領班八年了，但卻從來沒有被晉升。這幾年她有加過幾次薪，但仍在原職。Marie 認為自己是個很棒的員工，具有很棒的經驗，所以當這次有晉升機會時，她決定該為自己要求升職了。

"Mr. Hobbs, may I speak with you for a moment?", Marie asked her boss.

「Mr. Hobbs，我可以跟你聊一下嗎？」Marie 問她的老闆。

"Sure, I've got some time before my meeting in a half hour."

「當然，半小時候我要開會，但我現在有空。」

"Great. Well, I'm aware that Stanley is retiring, leaving the head foreman position open."

「太好了！我知道 Stanley 要退休了，領班主任這個職務就有空缺了。」

"Yes, that's true", replied Mr. Hobbs.

「沒錯。」Mr. Hobbs 回答。

"I've worked here for eight years, never had any negative disciplinary action taken against me, and I've earned many certifications to do work beyond my current position. In addition, while Stanley had to take leave several months ago, I was the main foreman who helped fulfill his duties. I feel more than suitable for the position of the head foreman, and I would like to be considered for the job."

「我已經在這裡工作八年了，從來沒有不良紀錄過。而且在這期間還取得了許多與工作有關的證照。此外，Stanley 幾個月前就離開了，我也是幫忙完成他的工作的主要領班，所以我覺得我相當有資格來擔任

求職面試心理

了解你的老闆

找到對的工作 職場定位

你與同事

帶人要帶心

升遷與工作態度

領班主任這個職務，希望你可以考慮我。」

"I see. You certainly are good at your position, and I've never had a problem with your work ethic or contributions to this company. However, do you think the others here would see you as a leader? You're a 29-year-old woman-definitely qualified for the job, but how will you handle it?" said Mr. Hobbs.

「我知道了。你在工作上的表現沒話說，我對你在工作倫理與對公司的貢獻上沒話說。但是你覺得其他同事會把你當主管嗎？你是 29 歲的女性，當然是符合這份工作，但你有辦法應對嗎？」Mr. Hobbs 說著。

"I handle it every day that I work here, I lead by example, give the respect to my co-workers, and I demand it in turn. I'm very thick-skinned, or else I would not have made it eight years at this job." responded Marie.

「我每天都在應對這些，舉例來說，我對同事很尊重，也要求他們同樣如此。我的臉皮比較厚，不然也不會在這這份工作做八年。」Marie 回答著。

"Yes, well I'll certainly consider you for the position. Thank you for coming and talking with me", said Mr. Hobbs.

「好，我當然會把你列入考慮。謝謝你來跟我談。」Mr. Hobbs 說

求職面試心理

了解你的老闆

找到對的工作｜職場定位

你與同事

帶人要帶心

升遷｜工作態度與

著。

After giving it much consideration, Mr. Hobbs determined that Marie truly was the best person to fill the position to the head foreman. Marie was beyond thrilled when the announcement was made, and she was also proud of herself for having the confidence to explain to Mr. Hobbs just why she deserved to be promoted.

Mr. Hobbs 經過仔細考慮後，覺得 Marie 的確是擔任領班主任的最佳人選。當這個消息宣布時，Marie 非常興奮，且對自己自信地去找 Mr. Hobbs 討論她為什麼值得被升職這件事感到驕傲。

達 人剖析

Glass Ceiling Effect 玻璃天花板效應

A **glass ceiling** is a term used to describe the barrier for females and minorities.. The Federal Glass Ceiling Commission defined it as "the unseen, yet unbreakable barrier that keeps minorities and women from rising to the upper rungs of the corporate ladder, regardless of their qualifications or achievements." For women, they are deeply influenced by a glass ceiling effect in their workplace. According to the report of the Guardian, the British famous newspaper and the winner of the Pulitzer Prize 2014, women still face a glass ceiling. 73% of females felt berries still existed for women seeking higher level positions, but only 38% of males believed there is a glass ceiling.

玻璃天花板是指女性與少數族群會遇到的阻礙。聯邦玻璃天花板委員會將之定義為「一種看不見但無法破除的藩籬，阻礙他們在組織階層中爬上較高的職位，不論他們的資格或是成就表現皆為如此。」對女性而言，她們在職場上深受玻璃天花板效應的影響。根據英國最有名且獲得 2014 普立茲獎的衛報報導，女性仍受玻璃天花板效應的影響，73% 的女性在尋求更高職位的過程中感受到玻璃天花板的影響，但僅有 38%的男性認為有這個效應的存在。

🔊 But why? 為什麼呢？

There are some possible reasons that, after years of efforts by the government and female groups, a glass ceiling still exists.

經過政府與女性團體多年來的努力，玻璃天花板仍然存在，可能有幾個原因：

1. Family demands 家庭需求

Many women are struggled between work and family. A study of 7000 Harvard Business School graduates, about 80% of men expected their spouses to do most of the child care, and 86% of men, even exceeded their expectation, responded that happened. In contrast, 50% of women expected their spouses share child care equally, however, 75% of women said they ended up doing so themselves. Women are still the ones who interrupt their careers to handle family matters. As a result, women have less energy to put as much efforts as men do for their careers; they also lack of time to engage in the social networking which is also essential to advancement.

　　許多女性仍在工作與家庭之間掙扎。一項針對 7000 名哈佛商學院畢業生的調查顯示，80% 的男性會期待配偶能分擔大部分照顧孩子的責任，結果是有 86%男性的家庭確實如此，甚至比期待值還高。相反的，的 50%的女性期待她們的配偶能共同分擔照顧孩子的責任，但 75%的女性卻是自己承擔照顧孩子的責任。女性確實會需要因為家庭因素而影響到工作，也因如此，她們無法像男性一樣在工作上投注這麼多精力；她們也沒有時間參與對工作升遷很重要的社交活動。

2. Stereotype 刻板印象

Stereotype plays an important role when talking about the glass ceiling effect. For example, people usually consider that effective leaders require masculine traits, such as assertiveness, dominance, or independence. And women, in contrast, are seen as being more submissive, passive, and dependent. These are not considered as positive traits of effective leaders. Even if women have masculine characteristics, they sometimes are viewed as being bossy, pushy, or difficult. These

求職面試心理

了解你的老闆

找到對的工作｜職場定位

你與同事

帶人要帶心

工作態度與升遷

negative stereotypes set barriers for women to advancement.

　　在討論到天花板時，刻板印象扮演了很重要的角色。例如，人們通常會認為好的管理者必備一些男性特質，如魄力、統領或獨立。相反的，女性則被視為較順從、被動與依賴，這些特質都不被認為是有效領導者的正向特質。即便女性具備了男性特質，她們通常會被認為跋扈、野心勃勃或難以相處，這些負向的刻板印象阻礙了女性的升遷。

3. **Gender and Racial Biases** 對性別與族群的偏見

David Hekman, Assistant Professor of Management, University of Colorado, and his colleagues designed an experiment and found out that gender and race both had serious influences on customer satisfaction. The result of the study indicated that white male employee was rated the service provided 19% higher than the woman or the black man. Moreover, white male was considered cleaner. Because white men create higher customer satisfaction, they ;therefore, could get a higher pay, raise or promotion by their companies than their female and minority colleagues.

　　David Hekman，科羅拉多大學管理系助理教授及同事規劃了一個實驗，發現性別與族群會影響顧客的滿意度。實驗結果發現，顧客對白人男性的服務滿意度比女性或黑人男性高出了

19%。此外，白人男性也被認為較乾淨整潔。由於白人男性讓顧客有較高的滿意度，他們可能因此比女性或少數族群的同事獲得較高的薪水、加薪或升遷。

職 場小故事

Marie prepared to start her first day as the head foreman at her job. She had earned a promotion to the position after asking for it, and telling her boss why she felt she was suitable for the job. While Marie had prepared how she would manage being in a position with more responsibility and authority, she was unprepared for the gossip and gender issues which are accompanied by her promotion.

Marie 開始擔任領班主任的第一天。她的升職是因為她自己去要求，告訴老闆她很適合這個職務。她對這個職務的責任與職權已有所準備，但她卻沒有料到八卦與性別問題會隨著升職而出現。

None of her co-workers said anything to her face, with the exception of one named Jason, who had been her friend since high school. When Jason did tell Marie what was being said, she was concerned. From the talk, it seemed that many of her co-workers weren't confident that she was a good choice for the promotion simply because she is a woman.

同事們都沒有在她面前説，但 Jason 卻有告訴 Marie 旁人説了些甚

求職面試心理

了解你的老闆

找到對的工作｜職場定位

你與同事

帶人要帶心

工作態度與升遷

麼。Marie 與 Jason 從高中開始就是好朋友。從旁人的耳語發現，許多同事對於她被升職這件事不看好，因為她是女性。

Some of her co-workers thought she wouldn't be as reliable as a man, since Marie had just gotten married a year before her promotion. They wondered how she would handle the job once she and her husband decided to have children, and also questioned whether it would be safe for her to be about in that state. Marie was shocked that the assumption of her and her husband even wanting to have children would be made, and knew her co-workers wouldn't have brought up that scenario had she been a man.

　　有些同事認為她不似男性值得信賴，因為 Marie 在被升職前一年剛結婚。他們擔心，若她與先生決定生小孩，要如何擔任這個職務，且也擔心她的安全問題。Marie 很驚訝同事們甚至已經假設他們會有小孩，且知道如果她是個男生，同事們絕對不會覺得是個問題。

Other employees at the company felt she didn't deserve the position because she was too young, and not strong enough to handle all of the job duties that many of the men did. Still, there was a small group of employees who were glad that Marie had been promoted, for various reasons. One felt it would be easier for her to get over on and allow him to take more breaks and holidays, while several others had no problem with her promotion since they assumed she still wasn't going to be earning more than they did.

　　公司中另外有一些同事認為她不配擔任這個職務，因為太年輕，且也不像許多男生般夠健壯來處理這個位置需要處理的一些任務。不過，也是有一小群人很高興 Marie 被升職，基於幾點原因。其一是認為如果要放假休假，Marie 比較好說話；另一些人認為她被升職也無所謂，因為她的薪水大概也不會比自己多。

After doing much research and talking to other women in leadership positions, Marie found that these issues were commonly faced by women being promoted to the management position within companies. She knew she couldn't change the minds of many of her co-workers, but Marie decided that as long as she met the company's goals and none of the other employees interfered with her job, she would continue on doing the work that had earned her the promotion in the first place.

　　在自己做了些功課，且與一些女性主管談過後，Marie 發現女性管理者的確常常遇到這些問題。她知道她不可能改變同事們的想法，但 Marie 決定只要她達到公司的要求，且其他同事不會干涉她的工作，她就會繼續下去，畢竟這份職務是她自己爭取來的。

達 人提點

Break through the glass ceiling 打破玻璃天花板
Women should empower themselves to break the invisible barrier for better chances.

求職面試心理

了解你的老闆

找到對的工作　職場定位

你與同事

帶人要帶心

升遷與工作態度

女性應該更自我充權來打破看不見的藩籬以獲得更好的機會。

1. Moving outside a comfort zone 離開舒適圈

According to the Poll by the Financial Women's Association (FWA.org), the key action women should make in 2015 to advance their careers is moving outside a comfort zone (77.86%). It is easy to stay in a comfort zone, because the world outside a comfort zone is full of risk. Do not fear of failure when taking risks. The most important thing is willing to take risk with confidence, and adjust your attitude towards failure.

根據財經女性協會的調查，女性在 2015 年想要在工作上更上層樓的首要行動，就是跨出舒適圈（77.86%）。人很容易待在舒適圈中，因為舒適圈外的世界充滿危機。在冒險時不要怕失敗，最重要的是願意充滿信心地去冒險，並修正態度去接受失敗。

2. See the big picture 看到願景

Be open to any developmental opportunities even if this is not directly related to your current job. You have to train yourself with wider knowledge and insigntful perspectives.

開放自己接受任何成長的機會，即便這些與你目前的工作沒有直接相關。你要訓練自己擁有更廣泛的知識與更具省思的觀點。

3. Take the initiative 主動出擊

The difference between people in the top level and the lower levels is, the former do not sit back and wait for others to tell them what to do. They figure out what needs to be done, willing to take on additional new responsibilities, take the initiative and make it happen.

高階與低階的人最大的差別在於，前者不會坐著等待別人告訴他要做甚麼。他們會自己去想那些需要做的事，也願意負擔額外的責任，並主動出擊讓這些成真。

4. Build the network 建立人際網絡

Women tend to stay in smaller networks with people they like. However, there may be someone you don't know who could provide you with valuable assistance or information. You should build relationships with other people in your office, as well as expend the professional network outside of the office through professional associations or industry conferences.

女性通常會待在小圈圈中，只與她們喜歡的人相處。但是，也許有你不認識的人可以給予你有用的協助或資訊。你要與公司中其他人建立關係，也要藉由專業團體或業界會議來擴展公司以外專業上的人際網絡。

附 錄

Chapter 1

Knudstrup, M., Segrest, S.L. and Hurley, A. E. (2003) The use of mental imagery in the simulated employment interview situation. *Journal of Managerial Psychology*, 18 (6), 573-591.

William Buskist, W. and Bryan K. Saville, B. K. (2001) *Creating Positive Emotional Contexts for Enhancing Teaching and Learning*. Retrieved from http://www.socialpsychology.org/rapport.htm

Tregoning, C. (2013) *5 Tips for Building Rapport in a Job Interview*. Retrieved from https://blogs.jobs.ac.uk/psychology/2013/08/25/5-tips-for-building-rapport-in-a-job-interview/

Tversky, A. and Kahneman, D. (1974) Judgement under uncertainty: Heuristics and biases. *Science*, 185 (4157), 1124-1131. Retrieved from http://people.hss.caltech.edu/~camerer/Ec101/JudgementUncertainty.pdf

Warren, K. (2013) *Take charge of your job interview: 5 classic recruiter personas to know*. Retrieved from https://www.devex.com/news/take-

charge-of-your-job-interview-5-classic-recruiter-personas-to-know-81768

Chapter 2

Wofford, M. (2012) *Make Difficult People Disappear: How to Deal with Stressful Behavior and Eliminate Conflict*. Retrieved from http://www. summary.com/book-reviews/_/Make-Difficult-People-Disappear/

OfficeVibe (2014) *12 Personality Traits of a Great Boss*. Retrieved from https://www.officevibe.com/blog/infographic-great-boss

Marr, B. (2015) *7 Sentences You Shouldn't Say to Your Boss*. Retrieved from http://www.huffingtonpost.com/bernard-marr/7-sentences-you-shouldnt-_b_7187486.html

Broder, L. (2014) *7 Things You Should Never Say to Your Employees*. Retrieved from http://www.entrepreneur.com/article/232657

CareerCast.com (2015) *How to Say No to Your Boss*. Retrieved from http://www.careercast.com/career-news/how-say-no-your-boss

Gouveia, A. (2014) *6 Signs Your Boss Hates You*. http://www.salary.com/6-signs-your-boss-hates-you/slide/2/

Goudreau, J. (2012) *Yes, Your Boss Is Crazy. Here's How to Deal*. Retrieved from http://www.forbes.com/sites/jennagoudreau/2012/04/27/yes-your-boss-is-crazy-heres-how-to-deal/2/

American Psychological Association. *Managing Your Boss*. Retrieved from http://www.apa.org/helpcenter/boss.aspx

Riggio, R.E. (2012) *How to Deal with a Difficult or Bullying Boss*. Retrieved from https://www.psychologytoday.com/blog/cutting-edge-leadership/201201/how-deal-difficult-or-bullying-boss

Chapter 3

Krznaric, R. (2013) *How to Find Fulfilling Work*. N.Y.: Picador.

Locke,E.A. (1976). *The Nature and Causes of Job Satisfaction*. Retrieved from http://en.wikipedia.org/wiki/Job_satisfaction

Kelliher, C. and Anderson, D. (2009) Doing more with less? Flexible working practices and the intensification of work. *Human Relations*, 63 (1), 83-106. Retrieved from http://www.som.cranfield.ac.uk/som/media/images/research/wbl/moreless.pdf

Freudenberger, H. (1974) Staff burn-out. *Journal of Social Issues*, 30

(1), 159-165.

Scott, E. (2014) *Personality Traits and Attitudes that Increase Your Risk for Burnout*. Retrieved from http://stress.about.com/od/burnout/a/mental_burnout.htm

Friedman, M. (1996) *Type A Behavior: Its Diagnosis and Treatment*. . N.Y., Plenum Press.

Chapter 4

Frieman, R. (2013) *Reply All, and Other Ways to Tank Your Career: A Guide to Workplace Etiquette*. St. Martin's Griffin.

CareerBuilder (2013) *Forty-three Percent of Workers Say their Office has Cliques, Finds CareerBuilder Survey*. Retrieved from http://www.careerbuilder.com/share/aboutus/pressreleasesdetail.aspx?sd=7%2F24%2F2013&id=pr773&ed=12%2F31%2F2013

Greenberg, M. (2011) *How to Keep Your Cool with Competitive People*. Retrieved from https://www.psychologytoday.com/blog/the-mindful-self-express/201109/how-keep-your-cool-competitive-people

Robert Half International (2010) *5 Most Competitive Co-workers*.

Retrieved from http://webcache.googleusercontent.com/search?q=cache:
KVehL8MqDtIJ:www.careerbuilder.com/article/cb-1053-the-workplace-5-
most-competitive-co-workers/%3Fpf%3Dtrue+&cd=1&hl=zh-TW&ct=
clnk&gl=tw

Chapter 5

MindTools (2015) *Theory X and Theory Y*. Retrieved from http://www.
mindtools.com/pages/article/newLDR_74.htm

Heathfield, S. M. (2015) *The Pygmalion Effect: The Power of the
Supervisor's Expectations*. Retrieved from http://humanresources.about.
com/od/managementtips/a/mgmtsecret.htm

MindTools (2015) *Herzberg's Motivators and Hygiene Factors*.
Retrieved from http://www.mindtools.com/pages/article/herzberg-
motivators-hygiene-factors.htm

Tanner, R. (2015) *Equity Theory- Why Employee Perceptions about
Fairness Do Matter*. Retrieved from http://managementisajourney.com/
equity-theory-why-employee-perceptions-about-fairness-do-matter/

McLeod, S. (2014) *Maslow's Hierarchy of Needs.* Retrieved from
http://www.simplypsychology.org/maslow.html

Cherry, K. (2015) *What Is Positive Reinforcement?* Retrieved from http://psychology.about.com/od/operantconditioning/f/positive-reinforcement.htm

Long-Crowell, E. (2015) *Social Loafing & Social Facilitation: Definition and Effects of Groups*. Retrieved from http://study.com/academy/lesson/social-loafing-social-facilitation-definition-and-effects-of-groups.html

Businessballs (2015) *Psychological contract*. Retrieved from http://www.businessballs.com/psychological-contracts-theory.htm

Cherry, K. (2015) *What Is the Halo Effect?* Retrieved from http://psychology.about.com/od/socialpsychology/f/halo-effect.htm.

Brown, M. (2012) *Brainstorming Doesn't Work, Groupthink, and the Brainzooming Method*. Retrieved from http://brainzooming.com/brainstorming-doesnt-work-groupthink-and-the-brainzooming-method/11261/

Chapter 6

McLeod, S. (2009) *Attitudes and Behavior*. Retrieved from http://www.simplypsychology.org/attitudes.html

Federal Glass Ceiling Commission. *Solid Investments: Making Full Use of the Nation's Human Capital*. Washington, D.C.: U.S. Department of Labor, November 1995, p. 4.

The Guardian (2011). *Women still face a glass ceiling.* Retrieved from http://www.theguardian.com/society/2011/feb/21/women-glass-ceiling-still-exists-top-jobs

Ely, R., Stone, P., and Ammerman, C. (2014) *Rethink What You "Know" About High-Achieving Women*. Harvard Business Review, December 2014 Issue. Retrieved from https://hbr.org/2014/12/rethink-what-you-know-about-high-achieving-women

Hekman, D.R., Aquino, K.A., Owens, B., Mitchell, T.R., Schilpzand, P., Leavitt, K., (2010) "An Examination of Whether and How Racial and Gender Biases Influence Customer Satisfaction." *Academy of Management Journal*. 53: 238 – 264.

Financial Women's Association (2015) *Women Need to Move Outside Comfort Zones, Financial Women's Association Poll Finds*. Retrieved from http://fwa.org/women-need-to-move-outside-comfort-zones-financial-womens-association-poll-finds/

英語學習—生活・文法・考用—

定價：NT$369元/K$115元
規格：320頁/17＊23cm/MP3

定價：NT$380元/HK$119元
規格：320頁/17＊23cm/MP3

定價：NT$349元/HK$109元
規格：352頁/17＊23cm

定價：NT$380元/HK$119元
規格：288頁/17＊23cm/MP3

定價：NT$329元/HK$103元
規格：352頁/17＊23cm

定價：NT$349元/HK$109元
規格：304頁/17＊23cm

定價：NT$380元/HK$119元
規格：352頁/17＊23cm

定價：NT$369元/HK$115元
規格：304頁/17＊23cm/MP3

定價：NT$380元/HK$119元
規格：304頁/17＊23cm/MP3

英語學習 ─職場系列─

定價：NT$349元/HK$109元
規格：320頁/17＊23cm

定價：NT$360元/HK$113元
規格：328頁/17＊23cm

定價：NT$349元/HK$109元
規格：304頁/17＊23cm

定價：NT$360元/HK$113元
規格：320頁/17＊23cm

定價：NT$369元/HK$115元
規格：312頁/17＊23cm/MP3

定價：NT$369元/HK$115元
規格：320頁/17＊23cm

定價：NT$360元/HK$113元
規格：288頁/17＊23cm/MP3

定價：NT$329元/HK$103元
規格：304頁/17＊23cm

定價：NT$369元/HK$115元
規格：328頁/17＊23cm/MP3

Leader 022

Follow 23 堂心理學英語課成就你的職場巨星之路

作　　者　練家姍
封面構成　高鍾琪
內頁構成　菩薩蠻數位文化有限公司

發 行 人　周瑞德
企劃編輯　陳韋佑
校　　對　陳欣慧、饒美君
印　　製　大亞彩色印刷製版股份有限公司
初　　版　2015 年 7 月
定　　價　新台幣 360 元
出　　版　力得文化
電　　話　(02) 2351-2007
傳　　真　(02) 2351-0887
地　　址　100 台北市中正區福州街 1 號 10 樓之 2
E - m a i l　best.books.service@gmail.com

港澳地區總經銷　泛華發行代理有限公司
地　　　　址　香港新界將軍澳工業邨駿昌街 7 號 2 樓
電　　　　話　(852) 2798-2323
傳　　　　真　(852) 2796-5471

國家圖書館出版品預行編目(CIP)資料

Follow 23 堂心理學英語課成就你的職場巨
星之路 / 練家姍著. -- 初版. -- 臺北市 :
力得文化, 2015.07 面 ; 公分. --
(Leader ; 22)
ISBN 978-986-91914-2-5(平裝)
1. 英語 2. 職場 3. 讀本
805.18　　　　　　　　　104010726